RIVER

ROCKS

STEVE KITTNER

Book Cover Design by: **J. Caroline Ro.**
Graphic Design & Illustration
Book cover copyright 2014 Graphic Design & Illustration

Author photo by Gilberto Salazar / Fotoxpose

For Beverly

RIVER ROCKS

STEVE KITTNER

ACKNOWLEDGMENTS

Growing up in the beautiful hills of West Virginia gives you a vast amount of adventure to write about. When I was a young boy, every time I would step into the woods, I would expect to rediscover something that had not been seen in decades; maybe an old abandoned house, miles away from any road that could get you to it, or a cave or maybe a piece of century-old farm equipment that would become an instant treasure to me. I loved the woods as a boy and was fascinated by the rivers as well—what they held and where they could take you.

There are so many people through the years who have shared these adventures *with* me and have helped influence this book. You know who you are, friends, cousins, aunts and uncles. Thank you all very much! I also thank God and my parents for the good fortune of being raised in West Virginia. There is no better place to be a boy! Thank you, Valentina, my wife, who supported this project and served as my final proofreader free of charge. I want to thank my children who supported me with their enthusiasm and encouragement. I hope you all enjoy it!

CHAPTER ONE

1903

The railroad tracks glistened from the night rain and ran straight as an arrow for about a mile before they made a bend to the south and crossed the newly constructed stone trestle that had just been built by migrant European stone masons. They constructed the limestone structure over a small stream that emptied into the Elk River right at the sandbar.

The two men were hunkered down in a ditch alongside the new C&O Railroad route that ran out of the hills of Kanawha County. Clyde Franklin's eyes widened when he saw the bright headlight of the midnight freighter which originated in Hillsburg and was running right on time out of the hollows of Blue Creek. The train then made the turn towards them and lit up the mile-long stretch of parallel steel.

The night sky illuminated with lightning as rain poured on them as if it were being dumped out of buckets. Water washed off the hills above them and thunder crashed every few seconds. Clyde was worried the matches wouldn't light because of the rain, and they would have no lantern. His partner leered at him, and then slowly nodded his head.

 Clyde reached into an inside pocket of his long overcoat and pulled out a scrap piece of sandpaper. He stayed crouched over it to protect it from the rain and then pulled one of the long matches from the same pocket. With rain running down over his hat and his overcoat and onto the ground, Clyde kept everything dry as he quickly scratched the match across the sandpaper and it instantly fired to life. He kept his coat arched around the flame as Arthur Otis maneuvered the red and green railroad oil lamp into the protected area of his partner's coat. He opened the glass door to the lamp and Clyde touched the match to the wick. The lamp then came to life, and both men grinned.

The scruffy-looking man nodded once again.

They crawled their way up out of the ditch and onto the tracks as the train rounded the curve nearly a mile from them. Arthur, the older of the two, held the lantern high and swung it back and forth to signal the train in an official-looking manner.

Both men were close in age, somewhere in their fifties, Clyde Franklin being the more social of the two. He was clean-shaven, held a regular job and upheld the law most of the time... up until this point in his life, that is. Clyde lived in a modest house along the side of the road that paralleled Blue Creek, a rather large creek really, which poured out into the Elk River. It was at the intersection of these two waterways that earlier pioneers had erected a small store for trading and buying dry goods, and had constructed a few small houses, calling their town; Blue Creek, just like the creek itself.

Clyde's partner Arthur, on the other hand, was a rough-looking mountain man. Sort of wild-eyed and crazy in appearance, he lived in the mountains with very little in the way of extras. His full, un-trimmed beard, long hair and large, bulging eyes gave him a very intimidating demeanor. Most kids were afraid of him and would stay close to their parents in those days, when he would come down from the mountains and mingle among them. He would do so to trade his furs monthly at the little General Store in Blue Creek. He had a real nasty side to him, folks would say, and Arthur Otis was a man whom you didn't want to be on the other side of the gun pointed at you in 1903.

The train flashed its light and Otis stood his ground and waved the lantern back and forth in the stormy night as the train cut its engine with a whoosh of steam and started grinding to a halt on the cold steel tracks.

The engineer certainly didn't want to stop the train, considering the additional high-value cargo they were secretly hauling that evening, but felt safe with the added security men on board. A swinging train lantern sometimes indicated track trouble ahead such as rockslides or mudslides in these hills during a nasty storm, and the veteran engineer would, of course, take no chances. After all, the lantern light and signal style was official-looking, and they were in an area of frequent rockslides.

The train finally came to a halt at the beginning of the turn that would point them east. After a few puffs of steam from various relief valves on the old engine, the white-haired engineer stepped out the side of the train to a small platform and called "Yonder there... Hello!"

While going through the routine of braking, stopping and shutting down the train, he had lost track of the light that had waved him to an urgent stop. The engineer grimaced at the thought of leaving the protection of his dry surroundings and called again, "Yonder out there... What seems to be the problem ahead?" He heard or saw no response—only the sound of the hard rain that pinged off the hot steel engine broke the silence of the night. He swallowed hard and glanced over at his fireman as three armed security men stepped into the engine. "What seems to be the delay, gentlemen?" the first security man inquired officially.

"We had some sort of track warning signal waved to us." He paused. "I don't ... seem... to see.... the signal... man... now, though," the engineer responded slowly as he stared out the front. A few seconds of silence went by and the engineer mumbled something and swallowed hard once more.

The three security men gave each other a quick glance and the first one nodded to the other two to return to the area of the train which they were assigned to protect. The engineer reached for his overcoat to step outside as the three security guards opened the door to return rearward.

It was at that second from outside and behind them that it happened. As the engineer opened his door, a sizzling, short fused full stick of dynamite flew onto the floor of the engine room at the feet of the engineer, the fireman, and all three security men, none of whom got out quite fast enough.

The explosion was deafening to the two thieves outside the train, but with one lucky toss at a very lucky moment, Otis and Franklin had taken out all five of their objectives on the seven-car freight train.

The Gold was theirs!

It had been as easy as that, but as fate would have it, only one man would carry it off the hill on that stormy night. Only one man would know, that night, the whereabouts of the 162 pounds of Confederate treasure that had been locked up for 38 years in a Kanawha County bank vault, and then was waiting to be placed in a Washington, D.C., museum for a temporary show. And only one man would know the truth that night—who killed five men in cold blood so quickly, and with not a moment's remorse. Only one man would know because the killing wasn't over. One more had to die. They were partners no more.

The treasure would now belong to only one man as a single gunshot ended a night of murder and greed and number six fell dead on the tracks of the C& O Railroad.

CHAPTER TWO
Present Day

Josh and Eddie's fishing poles laid flat on the rocks of the sandbar. Lines were limp and catching fish was not happening today. School was out for these guys and the heat of summer was upon them. When fishing was slow, stone skipping was the pastime—each boy trying to out-do the other. It required finding the perfect flat river rock and was considered a skill you must develop as a young boy where they came from.

Skip…. skip…. skip…. skip…. skip.

"Five! That's not good enough!" Eddie shook his head.

"Let me try again," Josh said while searching the sandbar for the perfect flat river rock. "Here we go."

Josh Baker reared back and let loose with a swinging, sidearm throw—flinging the rock perfectly flat across the surface of the calm river.

"Yeah!" Josh said, throwing both arms up into the air and proclaiming himself King of the Elk River Stone Skippers. "Eight!"

Eddie shook his head. "That was seven, my friend."

Josh acknowledged with a lopsided grin and flung another rock across the still waters of the Elk River—this time for distance. The boys were quiet for a moment, leaving only the bugs and frogs along the riverbanks to disturb the silence.

"Throwin' rocks in the river probably does nothing for attracting fish, does it?" Eddie said, laughing a little.

"They're not biting anyway," Josh mumbled, shaking his head. "Sometimes I think there's about ten fish in this whole river." He picked up his rod and tightened his line again, studying it carefully. "Then there are people who will tell ya there are catfish up by the dam that could swallow your leg."

Eddie grinned. "I don't believe that or half the stories on this river. I'd have to see those fish for myself." He paused for a moment, looking across the tranquil waters on that warm summer Saturday morning. "It's like the Wills Creek Monster story your aunt tells, or the Braxton County Monster or those UFOs they saw up near Flatwoods—just a bunch of tall-tales." He picked up another stone and gave it a fling. "Same thing with the leg-swallowing fish. Show me one, and then I'll believe it!"

Josh nodded in agreement. "But my aunt swears by that monster story."

"Maybe we should go up to the dam and find out about those fish then!" Eddie smiled and lifted his eyebrows.

Eddie returned to his fishing pole, reeling in and repositioning his bait, hoping for a bite.

Josh Baker and Eddie Debord were best friends and had been since first grade. Josh was a couple inches shorter than Eddie, with sandy blond hair that flowed straight to the bottom of his ears and touched the collar on his T-shirt in the back. Eddie wore his light brown hair short on the sides and off his collar in the back and, like his friend, always sported a T-shirt and Levi jeans or basketball shorts in the summer.

They had grown up in the same area of Blue Creek together and shared the same interests. They were both dutiful students, and they both enjoyed being outdoors in West Virginia. It was a splendid place to grow up. They had rivers to fish and swim in on sultry summer days. They had hills with endless trails made by the whitetail deer, and the hunters who searched them out. These trails could lead you into the next county if you could hike that far.

The riverbanks that flank the mighty Elk River are a blend of sand and mud and decayed leaves and trees that have fallen and create a slippery mix on the steep banks that lead down to the river. If you don't watch your footing, it will send you down the bank on your fanny in a hurry. The mix also has its own scent that stays with you even if you go away for many years and come back. If you grow up on the Elk River, the river never leaves you. Not the scents nor the culture nor the life lessons learned along these muddy banks. It's in you for your entire life. You are an Elk River Boy.

Eddie and Josh liked it all! They loved to fish and hunt and run up and down the riverbanks on their bikes. They loved to take their backpacks with only a tent, sleeping bag and a little canned food and head up into the hills to rough it for a weekend, to sit around a campfire and talk about whatever: fishing, sports, school, girls, anything. That's what these country boys did.

Their resourcefulness was also something to admire. There was the one time they took all their gear, all their food and enough water for a one-night camp-out but forgot to take any eating utensils. No forks or spoons. They had plenty of food but nothing to eat it with. So, being the young improvisers that they were, they simply found themselves two sticks about an inch in diameter, cut them to about eight inches long and carved themselves a fork to eat their canned stew with. It may have been a problem for some other kids, but not these two young country boys. They were, at 14 years old, true adventurers!

The two boys stood over their poles quietly for a few minutes, patiently waiting for a nibble, when Josh Baker's pole suddenly bent nearly double.

"Look at that!" Josh yelled out. "Oh, yeah!"

"Man, Josh, whatta ya got?" Eddie said calmly, running over to his friend.

Josh had grabbed his pole from the forked stick that acted as a rod holder and gave a yank to the line. It didn't give an inch as the drag on his old Zebco 33 whizzed—giving line to the fish and the running room he wanted.

"Don't lose him, Josh!" Eddie yelled "Give him the line, give him the line!"

"He's taking it... I don't have to give it to him! He's taking it!" Josh exclaimed, wide-eyed.

"Loosen your drag!" Eddie yelled.

The fish took Josh's line down the river in front of the sandbar and then back up the river repeatedly, pulling and tugging as Josh struggled to get a yard of his line back. After a couple of minutes, Josh's forearms and biceps began to tire.

"Just hope he doesn't wrap you around a log," Eddie said as Josh gave a big pull on his 10-pound test line.

This fish was enormous, maybe the biggest he had ever hooked here at the sandbar, and it was a fighter. Josh couldn't help but think that maybe an upgrade to his reel would be a magnificent idea for Christmas this year... and maybe a line upgrade as well. Back and forth, up and down the river, the fish took his line, looking for a rock or tree trunk to wrap around and break the fisherman's line. This clever old fish had not gotten so big and old by being brainless. Josh fought back with all he had, waiting to see who would make the first mistake.

"Man, Eddie…. this sucker is bi--".… SNNNAAPP!

Josh's line fell limp on the water as a look of disbelief immediately fell onto his face.

"Nooo!!!" Josh screamed out in defeat. "I can't believe it… I can't believe it! How BIG could that fish have been? I can't believe it!"

"Wow," Eddie said, shaking his head, "that was a monster."

Josh was catching his breath with his hands on his knees and his rod still in his right hand.

Eddie laughed. "Hey…. maybe that was one of those leg-swallowing catfish from up at the dam, Josh."

Josh looked at Eddie and they both laughed as the defeated fisherman just shook his head.

"Ya never know. The spring floods stirred the fish up a little, that's for sure. Maybe some big ones washed downstream." Josh paused, looking up and down the river. He looked at the banks of their river and the warm sun that cast its glow onto it. Josh figured it was a good day, anyway. Josh reeled his limp line and shook his head, still feeling bitterly defeated.

Eddie just grinned and gave Josh a few quiet seconds then said, "I think it was a big bass, Josh."

"I'm ready to go." Josh surrendered. "It was a musky."

The two freshman friends collected their fishing gear and headed across the sand and rock bar that arced out into the water. To the left of the sandbar was the old limestone train trestle built long ago to cross over a stream that flowed out of the hills. The trestle had replaced an even older wooden bridge that carried the train over the stream prior to 1902. During the construction of the trestle, the engineers figured out a way to keep the tracks open and the trains rolling while they replaced the old wooden structure with the new permanent stone trestle. The stream, over the years, had washed sand and rock out of the hills and deposited them into the Elk River, eventually creating the sandbar (more of a rock bar but they called it a sand bar) that the boys spent many hours on every spring and summer. On the right side of the sandbar was a steep path that led up to the railroad tracks of the C&O Railway about fifty feet above the river.

Josh and Eddie had just started to pack up their boat to head back across the river when they heard the whistle of the train.

Eddie looked at Josh, grinned and asked, "Got any change?"

The two boys dropped their poles and ran up the bank via the path. At the top, Josh fumbled through his pockets and pulled out a nickel and two pennies. Eddie took the nickel and he and Josh carefully placed the coins on the center of a rail. They could hear the train but not see it, so it was still over a mile away, up past the curve. The two boys scurried back down the bank and waited by their fishing gear for the train to go by. As the coal-hauling beast bore down on them, they could feel the ground rumble under their feet for about a minute as nearly a mile of steel and coal roared past them. When the caboose brought up the rear, the two boys ran back up the bank to search for their newly pressed coins.

"Where'd they go?" asked Josh.

"It's always a game of hide and seek," Eddie replied, beginning the search.

Josh pointed, "Oh, here's a penny. Flat as a pancake."

"Yeah…. here's the other penny over here. Do you see the nickel anywhere?"

Josh Baker shook his head.

The two boys searched the perimeter for the remaining coin. Sometimes the enormous steel wheels of a train would flip a coin quite a few yards. As the boys continued looking for their illusive prize, they spread out further and further from each other until they were encompassing an area of about fifty feet of railroad track.

"I think it flipped over the bank," Josh conceded.

"Yeah… yeah, I don't see it anywhere. It had to have flipped into the weeds somewhere. Oh well…" Eddie agreed while still looking down and around.

"We put it on the rail about here, so let's look down over the bank a little before we give up," said Josh.

"Alright," Eddie agreed. "Then I'm gonna go get some lunch."

Josh and Eddie stepped off the rock foundation that lay under the railroad ties and looked for the coin where the rocks ended, and the weeds began.

"Oh, look Eddie, one of those glass things."

"Insulators," Eddie said.

Josh leaned over and picked up the mushroom-shaped glass insulator used long ago on the high line poles to insulate the wires from the wood cross members they were mounted to. They were abundant along railroad tracks and roadways where old electric and phone lines used to run high overhead. Years later they became abundant at flea markets.

The boys searched, but to no avail.

"We're not gonna find that nickel, Josh," Eddie said, half laughing and shaking his head.

Eddie was plenty ready to give up and go home to eat lunch.

The two boys stood and scanned the riverbank from their perspective up by the railroad tracks. Down and to the right was the sandbar and Josh's small boat. To the left a little was the river side of the trestle that ran under the tracks and let the small stream that ran out of the hills, split the sand bar and flow into the Elk River. Straight down was the river. One slip down the sandy, muddy mixture and you were wet.

Josh's eyes caught something in the weeds close to the river's edge near the sandbar.

"Eddie what's that?"

"What. Where?"

"In the mud, down there just to the right of that small patch of milkweed. Looks like it's sort of orange or red on top."

"Ah, I see it," said Eddie. "I don't know."

"Let's go check it out."

The two boys traversed the bank down the path and then walked the sand bar along the water's edge until it met the muddy riverbank. There they once again spotted what they saw from up on the tracks.

"I know what that is," said Eddie. "My uncle has one of those painted silver and sitting on his porch for decoration. It's an old five-gallon can that was used for transporting milk back in the day. Uncle Cue said they would fill'em with fresh milk and deliver them by truck to stores or homes or whatever. I guess they're pretty old."

"Let's pull it out of there," Josh suggested.

"It's a muddy old can, Josh."

Josh looked at Eddie. Adventure races through the minds of adolescent boys when they find treasures like this. They paused, looking at each other for a second. They had nothing else to do!

"Okay, let's pull it out of there," said Eddie.

The two boys carefully walked along the steep riverbank, doing their best not to slip until they reached the old milk can.

"This must have washed down river this spring, too." Josh said, while positioning himself on the bank so as not to slip.

"It still has the lid on it." said Eddie.

Josh and Eddie grabbed a handle on each side of the can and pulled. The mud easily gave up the old container. They carefully retraced their steps back over to the sandbar, each boy still holding onto one handle of the milk can. They sat it down with a clank on the flat river stones.

"Let's take it over there and wash it off," Josh said.

The two friends dunked the can in the river and wiped the sandy mud off the old treasure they had found.

"You could give this to your uncle Cue and he could have a matching set," Josh teased.

"Actually, he would like that!" laughed Eddie. "He really likes to collect old stuff. You've seen his basement."

"Look how tight the lid is," said Josh. "It's clamped on," he continued.

Eddie nonchalantly gave the can a little shake back and forth and both boys looked at each other puzzled, as they heard a soft flump, flump, flump from within the can.

"What the heck's in it?" Josh asked curiously.

Eddie shook the can once more. Flump, flump, flump. They paused.

"Let's open it!" they said together.

Eddie grabbed a large rock and began beating on the old rusty clamp that held the lid on tight. Bam, bam, bam, bam, bam. Over and over he pounded until the clamp started to give a little.

"Give me a whack at it," said Josh.

Bam, bam, bam, bam, CLANK. The rusty clamp finally let loose and snapped apart. The boys pulled it off and then thought about how to get the lid loose, since years of oxidation had sealed it tightly to the can.

"OK, I got it," Josh said. "Eddie, you're bigger than me. You hold the can as tight as you can in a bear hug, and I will put this long stick over here through the lid-handle for leverage, and twist. But you will have to hold it tight!"

Eddie looked at Josh.

"OK, I'll bear hug this wet, muddy, sandy, stinking can so you can take the lid off, Hero," Eddie shot back, not so enthusiastically.

"It's the only way to get it off, Ed. Down here, anyway. Don't ya want to see what's inside?" Josh asked, lifting his eyebrows.

Eddie said nothing. He grabbed the can and sat himself down on the sandbar. He then sat crossed legged and put the can between his legs where he could not only bear hug it with his arms, but squeeze it with his legs, giving him a double lock on the can.

Josh brought the long stick over and ran it through the lid handle as planned and walked forward until the stick was firmly leveraged.

"Ready?" Josh asked.

"Ready."

Josh tightened the tension on the stick by pushing on it with his leg, being careful to increase pressure, but to not twist the container out of his friend's vice-like hold. Josh pushed more and more, as Eddie's face got redder and redder.

"Hang onto it, Eddie. You're doin' good." Josh encouraged.

Josh increased the pressure on the long stick ever so slightly and both boys noticed the lid begin to twist. Eddie looked at his friend, saying nothing while still clenching the can with all his might, nodding to say, "Keep going... don't let up." Josh Baker did just that and the lid continued to twist, little by little. As it did, Josh lifted on the long stick as he pushed it to try to pry up and get the lid to come off.

"It's working, Eddie... hold on to it."

A couple of seconds later, and with a fooop, the lid popped off and fell to the sandbar with a clank.

Eddie fell over in exhaustion and Josh fell forward with the sudden release of the lid and both boys rolled on the rocks and sand, but their efforts were not in vain—the lid was off.

Josh picked himself up and stepped back over to where his friend was lying, still bear-hugging the milk can. Eddie sat up and both boys examined the top of the can. Josh Baker wrinkled his nose a little and said, "What is this stuff around the rim?"

Eddie, still catching his breath, touched the gooey stuff with his finger and sniffed it. He took his thumb and rubbed it against the other finger to test how slippery it was.

"It's like wax," Eddie said.

"Wax?" Josh questioned, as he performed his own viscosity test. "Why would this lid be waxed?"

"To seal it.... so water or air can't get in." Eddie figured.

No one spoke for a moment. Both boys were thinking the same thing as they looked at each other and then at the top of the can. The only reason a person would water seal and lock a container is because there was something in the container that needed to be protected. Something important. Something vital. Legal documents or papers or maybe a keepsake for generations to pass down. A will, possibly, or a personal diary. Things that would be kept in a safe at home nowadays. Birth certificates or death certificates or insurance papers.

The two boys' hearts pounded as they slowly stood up and peered over the rim and down into the can.

"Pull it out of there, Josh," Eddie said, as if he were a little spooked to put his arm down into the dark hole.

Josh shook the can back and forth again as before and again, flump, flump, flump. Josh took a deep breath and slowly lowered his arm down into the old milk container. He went down to about his elbow and looked at his friend as he grasped the soft, cylindrical-shaped object inside.

He pulled it out slowly and the two boys again looked at each other as their hearts pounded faster.

Josh had in his hand a rolled piece of animal skin type material with a single piece of leather bootlace wrapped around it and tied in a simple knot.

"What in the world could this be?" Eddie asked, as both boys looked at it in amazement.

Josh, still holding onto the unknown treasure, lifted his other hand up to the bootlace and pulled on the loose end. As he did so, the knot fell loose and the rolled-up animal skin was untied for the first time in many, many years.

As Eddie took one end of it, Josh held the other and the two friends slowly unrolled the mysterious scroll.

"What is this thing? It's like deerskin or something," Eddie said. "Or part of one."

Eddie knew a deer hide when he saw one, as his father was an avid hunter and always bagged his trophy every November. Eddie had joined his father the past few years as they headed north to the high country in search of white-tailed deer but had yet to harvest his first buck. Still, he would always be there to help his dad skin their trophy and quarter the meat.

Josh remained speechless as they continued to unveil their treasure. As they unrolled it, an inch at a time, their eyes grew wider and wider. They couldn't believe what they had discovered along the muddy banks of the Elk River, right in their backyard.

CHAPTER THREE

Very much aged but in good condition was, what looked to be, a deer-hide that was tanned and preserved by someone long ago. The skin was dry and wrinkled and its edges ragged and rough. The boys stared in amazement at this document that had not been unrolled in decades.

"What is all this writing on it?" Josh questioned.

"I don't know… It's weird. It's like a list. And down here is a sketch of something," Eddie said.

Josh squinted to better see the writing, "Can you read it?"

Eddie shook his head and looked around at the shaded riverbank, "Kind of hard to see in the shade."

"This is cool… what if it's something historic and we found it?" Josh asked.

"Don't get your hopes up, Buddy. If it were important, it wouldn't be in an old can. It's probably just an old farmer's list of crop records or a moonshine recipe or something," Eddie replied.

Josh laughed, "Yeah. Well, why don't we take it up to my house and look at it in the light, anyway?" he suggested.

"Let's go to my house," Eddie said. "We'll get some sandwiches. I'm starving."

The two boys picked up their fishing gear and their newfound treasure and headed towards the boat to cross the river. Something caught Josh's ear and eye at the same time as they walked past the tunnel under the train tracks. Josh spotted something large through the darkness in the foliage on the other side. It moved quickly and was gone. Josh thought it must have been a deer and said nothing to his friend.

Back at Eddie's house the two boys lugged their fishing gear into the garage, sat the can down, and put the deer-hide up on the workbench under the four-foot fluorescent bench light.

"I'm gonna go get some food. I'll be right back," Eddie said, while heading for the side door to the house.

"OK," Josh replied, as he untied the scroll once more.

Josh Baker rolled it out and placed a heavy open-ended wrench on either side to prevent it from rolling up. His eyes squinted as he studied the writing. His head turned from left to right, looking at it from fresh angles, hoping it would give him a new perspective. He looked it over for a few minutes, turning it this way and that and looking at the sketch at the bottom right-hand corner.

In the upper right-hand corner was a group of numbers that Josh figured could be a date, but it didn't look like enough digits unless one or two was lost to years of fade. He moved closer and turned the document to get a better look. The ink was jet black and had smeared just a little, after writing and storing it for all these years. The numbers Josh thought could be a date, read: 9104.

"Hmmm," he studied.

Eddie returned with two paper plates and two waters. His gourmet lunch included peanut butter and grape jelly sandwiches, potato chips and a piece of fresh chocolate fudge made that morning by Mrs. Debord. He sat them down on the end of the workbench and dug in.

"What did ya' learn?" Eddie asked, with a mouthful of sandwich.

"It's kinda smeared, but what I can read is written in phrases, like a poem. It doesn't make a lot of sense." He paused while Eddie chewed. "We have seven lines of smeared words and some numbers, a set of numbers in the upper right corner, and this drawing in the lower right corner."

Josh looked back to at the numbers in the right-hand corner. "Does that look like a date to you?" he asked.

Eddie moved over in front of the bench where the document lay and, while holding his sandwich, looked up and studied the figures.

"9104." he paused. "No. Doesn't look like enough numbers to be a date," Eddie said. He scanned the deer hide while Josh moved back into study position.

"But…. what if it means 09-01-04?" Josh asked.

"No." Eddie paused. "I mean, I don't think we have the Dead Sea Scrolls here, but I do think it's older than 2004."

"I was thinking more like 1904."

Eddie shrugged his shoulders. "Is that how they wrote dates back then?"

"Maybe. Or maybe that's how whoever drafted this wrote his dates."

"Or her dates."

Eddie took another bite. He was more skeptical than his friend. "You're really reaching, man."

"Well, what do you think we have here, Ed?" Josh asked with that trademark lopsided grin on his face.

Eddie shrugged and rolled his eyes. "Are you going to eat that sandwich, or am I?"

Josh picked up the peanut butter and jelly masterpiece and as he did, a flash caught his eye once again from outside the rear service door to Eddie's garage. It was over the riverbank—just a brief flicker of movement and then it was gone. Josh, once again, said nothing to his friend about it.

Eddie Debord's house sat along the riverbank of the Elk River. It was a modest three-bedroom house all on one level with an open floor plan inside and a two-car garage with a rear service-door. The house sat atop high ground and their yard tiered a couple times downward until it met the river. The riverbank was lined with trees just above the water's edge and it dropped near vertical to the water, where Eddie's father had constructed a fishing dock. A path led down to it.

Josh lived three houses down from Eddie and had a similar yard layout. The house was an old cinderblock construction, two-story with three bedrooms and a two-car garage. The two boys were very content with their homes and yards and with their proximity to the river and to each other.

The sandbar was directly across the river from Josh Bakers' boat dock. Sometimes, instead of dock-fishing, the two friends would take the Baker's 12 ft. Alumacraft V-bottom boat, and row across to their favorite fishing spot. The sandbar allowed them a larger casting area and room to move around.

Josh glanced back at the old deer hide and stared at it with enthusiasm.

"Well, it's something. We just have to figure out what," Josh said, as he began to eat his sandwich.

"Let's do this. Let's get a piece of paper and write all the letters and numbers that we can read that aren't smeared or streaked. Then we will see if we can fill in the rest of the letters by using some logic," Eddie suggested.

Josh shrugged and then nodded. Eddie went over to a desk that his dad had in the garage and pulled out a legal pad and a pen.

The two boys started at the top with the numbers 9104.

For the next few minutes, Josh and Eddie studied the writing and wrote only the letters they were absolutely sure of while leaving blanks for the letters that were illegible. With his sandwich in his left hand, Josh did the writing while Eddie looked on. Occasionally they would confer on a letter and only when agreeing, would they write it down. After about twenty minutes the boys had the seven lines of the strange, riddled document on modern-day paper.

Josh then looked down at the lower right-hand corner of the hide, laid the yellow paper on top of the deer hide and did his best to trace the little sketch in the corner near the ripped edge, not knowing what any of the lines or symbols meant.

After he completed that sketch the boys looked it over, sighed and then agreed to make another copy so they each would have one. That completed, they took their copies and looked them over.

They had a document that looked something like this:

Whe-- -teel --r--s r-n

St---ms f-ow fr-- hil-- -igh

A southern -ewel rest-

Fr-m - -ain- n-gh-

San- -s a -aul-

Key -rom -he doo-

In -n I- -an- -ank

"That third line is the best," Eddie said.

"Yeah... no doubt," Josh agreed. "A southern -ewel rest-. It's gotta be 'Jewel', right?" And R-E-S-T and an S on the end, Rests. A Southern Jewel rests. What is that?"

"Not sure," Eddie replied with a half grin.

CRACK!!!

The two boys jumped as the sound of something hard broke the silence as it whacked the back of Eddie's garage. The two boys rolled up the deer hide and ran through the service door to the backyard to investigate. There was a slight dent the size of one's fist about eight feet up the back of the garage wall. A little bit of paint had been taken off in the process and when the boys looked around, they found the projectile that had done the damage. A three-inch round river rock lay at the foundation of the garage with the incriminating paint chips still on it.

Eddie squinted, looked down toward the river and shook his head. "Who would do this?" Eddie ran down to the edge of his yard where it tiered off to the river and scanned the bank. He saw nothing. "They ran off quick, whoever it was," Eddie said, returning to the area of the garage where Josh stood biting his lip.

"Eddie, when we were leaving the sand bar, something caught my eye through the tunnel... a movement but I didn't think anything of it. It just made a move real quick like. And I heard it, too. Could have been a deer, even. Then again, just a few minutes ago while we were eating our lunch… something caught my eye through your back door down by that biggest tree on the bank.

"Was it a person?"

"I don't know. Can't say for sure."

"But why would anyone throw a rock at us?"

"Made any enemies lately, Ed?"

Eddie thought for a minute.

"Nope." He paused. "Not that I know of."

Josh scanned the riverbank once more, not ready to suspend his investigation just yet, but Eddie didn't seem too concerned about it, so darned if he would be either.

"Ya know, it could have been that jerk, Radcliffe, messing around. He has nothing better to do than cause trouble," Josh said.

"Coulda been." Eddie shrugged one shoulder.

Josh glanced over at the door to Eddie's garage.

"Ed, is your garage lock still busted?"

Eddie nodded. "Yeah. Well, it's not busted, it just turns in circles."

Josh shrugged a shoulder. "That means it's busted, Ed. Why don't I take this over to my place, just for safekeeping? I mean, ya never know." Josh picked up another piece of fudge.

Eddie nodded. "Okay. You need some help?"

"No, I can get it," he waved him off. "Mom wants my room cleaned today."

Josh walked over to the bench, rolled up the deer-hide and placed it back into the can. He then pushed the lid on tight and grabbed his copy off the yellow legal pad lying on the bench.

"Alright, I'll see ya a little later, then," Eddie said.

Josh headed out the garage door with the old milk can in one hand, his fishing gear in the other and fudge in his mouth. Josh had a big imagination and his mind was not on the heavy load he was hauling, but on their newly found adventure.

CHAPTER FOUR

That evening Josh Baker lay silent in his bed with eyes wide open. His second-story bedroom window was open and the sounds and smells of a summer night drifted in. He could hear the crickets by the hundreds along the riverbank and the owls, too. Occasionally a firefly would drift high enough for him to see. It would flicker a hello and then disappear.

In the far distance, he heard his favorite night sound of all. A coal train chugging out of the hills of Blue Creek and making its way down the straight stretch across the river from his house. He could hear it two miles away and, as it got closer and closer, it got louder and louder until it was directly across the river and Josh could hear the clackity, clack, clack of the big steel wheels on the tracks. He would listen to it until it disappeared into the night, heading who knows where. He never tired of this, never thought the train noise a nuisance. It was comforting to him and he liked it.

He then thought of the deer-hide and the strange wording on it. Was it even complete or was it part of a bigger document? What did it mean by A Southern Jewel Rests? And the numbers. Was that a date or was it something totally different at the top? The drawing would have to be studied, just to make any sense of it at all.

Josh couldn't help but be intrigued by the document and imagined it was something very important. He also considered it could turn out to be a nothing. Something a couple kids scrawled while playing a game many years ago—kids like him and Eddie. But even if that were all that it turned out to be, it would still be cool. A time capsule—a message from kids generations ago. *Hey, here's what we did for fun!*

He lay there and pondered it all for a while, rolling ideas around in his head and then reached over to the table beside his bed and flicked on his old two-dollar Hallicrafters Ham radio receiver he picked up at the flea market last summer. With his low budget radio, he could lie in bed at night and listen to far-off, distant voices and wonder, literally, where on earth they might be. He would hear networks from ships at sea reporting weather conditions or Sargasso drifts. The receiver, with the help of a copper-wire antenna strung between two trees outside, would pull in transmissions from all around the world. Occasionally he would hear broadcasts and chatter from exotic-sounding places like Bimini, Cuba, Bermuda, Mexico, or the China Sea. There were languages he didn't recognize and for Josh, that was fascinating. For those moments, when he lay in bed at night, he could leave his little town and take a cultural vacation far different from where he lived.

Tonight, however, it would be "Mystery Theater" on the AM band that he would listen to as he crawled deeper into the sheets, never admitting to anyone that the show creeped him out a little. The eerie voices of the radio actors and that creaking door crackled through the single speaker until the end of the show when the culprit was always revealed with symphonic music and high drama. Creepy, but he liked it!

CHAPTER FIVE

Eddie Debord's eyes flew open at the first smell of bacon in the morning. He glanced over at his clock to see that he had slept a little later than normal and felt very refreshed. Summer break is outstanding when you are fourteen years old.

He and Josh had a plan to go to the library later that day, but for now, breakfast was the priority. Eddie absolutely loved his Mom's good old-fashioned country breakfasts. On this morning, and before church, he would dig into pancakes with butter and thick-cut bacon. Scrambled eggs and hash browns would be on a separate plate, (so the syrup wouldn't touch them), and a tall glass of orange juice would wash it all down. Jo Anne Debord was Eddie's favorite chef, and that's just the way it is with boys and moms.

Eddie threw off the sheets and swung both legs around to the floor and bounced out of bed to go brush his hair and teeth and wash his face. A shower would have to wait.

On this morning, eight-year-old Amy beat Eddie to the table by about five minutes. Being the little sister and the early bird, Amy had rights to the first stack of buckwheat pancakes that came hot off the griddle and she let Eddie know that.

Amy wrinkled her nose to tease him as she shoved in another mouthful.

Eddie's father was already up and outside doing early garden work before church on that warm Sunday morning. He would hoe weeds or pull ripe tomatoes or anything else that needed done to keep his garden neat and healthy.

Everyone consumed their fill of Mrs. Debord's breakfast, then Amy and Eddie pitched in to help their mom clear the table and load the dishwasher. It was then time to get ready for church.

Josh Baker and Eddie Debord stepped outside of the church and squinted a bit from the bright sunlight that warmed the balmy June day. The boys had a plan to ride their bikes to the library, by way of the old railroad tracks that ran parallel to the highway on their side of the river. The rails and wooden ties had long been removed and now it was a great path for biking, motorcycles, quads, and the occasional horse rider. Pretty much anything that wasn't street legal could be seen on the old railroad path from time to time.

The library was about a five-mile ride for the boys and was nothing new. They would often ride nearly the same distance just to go to the Dairy Queen, which was in the same area and would be a likely pit stop for the boys today after the library.

Josh and Eddie had an idea to research the library local archives for old newspaper clippings of anything that had the words "Southern Jewel" referenced in it. A small-town library can be a treasure trove of information when looking for something local. The deer hide document they had found had strummed a major curiosity chord in them and they wanted to know more.

The two boys had agreed to meet at Josh's house after Sunday lunch and be on their way. Eddie showed up at around 12:45 and they saddled up on their bikes and headed out. The library would open at 1:00.

"I brought a notebook in my backpack to write stuff down on, in case we find something." Josh said.

"Good idea."

The ride took the two boys out of their neighborhood and headed them south down WV State route 119. The boys took occasional diversions off the railroad path to swoop down into a ditch or two that acted as a natural "half pipe." They would run hard down into the ditch about 10 feet and pedal like crazy up the other side, doing their best to pull a wheelie as they came up out of the deep trench. These drainage ditches were often well worn from teenage boys doing teenage things.

The old railroad bed rocks that were laid down under the railroad ties to give foundation and stability to the tracks, had been long scavenged by people with pickup trucks looking to fill in holes and low spots in their unpaved driveways. Miles and miles of bedrock were hauled away, over the years, and left behind was the dust of many tons of coal that was transported along these tracks in days gone by. The railroad bed was now a mix of black dust and dirt which made a real nice smooth riding surface but did nothing for chrome rims or clean shoes.

They rode on as they felt the summer heat on their backs and at about the halfway point, they stopped and chugged down about half of a bottle of water each.

"We're gonna smell nice for the library crowd." Josh laughed.

Eddie nodded, catching his breath. "Let's get going."

Break time was over and once again the two friends were on their way down the path that once carried coal trains to far away destinations but now provided a path for two boys searching out an adventure. There were no steep grades to speak of on their ride and the two boys made excellent time getting to the library just before two o'clock.

They parked their bikes in front of the building and walked towards the front door, noticing that the library was open until 5 o'clock that day. Three hours. Plenty of time.

Josh did a quick sniff test on his underarms before opening the door and Eddie tried to suppress a laugh and, instead, blew the last drink from his water bottle straight out of his nose. Both boys laughed hard as they stood outside of the door, with Josh hanging onto the door handle. Eddie pitched the empty bottle in the outside recycle can and, as Josh opened the door, he noticed that the front desk librarian was staring at them from over the top of his skinny reading glasses.

The boys were still smiling as they walked into a room of silence. In an almost whispered voice the librarian, whose nametag read "Elton Mansfield," asked, "May I help you, gentlemen?"

"Yes sir" Eddie replied. "Where might we find old newspaper articles, like from the early 1900s?" Eddie spoke it with confidence, as if he knew exactly what he wanted to find.

Elton Mansfield gave the two callow boys a curious look while cocking his head slightly. "Anything in particular you might be looking for?" he asked.

Josh bit his lower lip and glanced over at his friend. They didn't want to tell anyone what they were looking for or why, at this point. They didn't want to be heckled for considering ridiculous ideas or dreaming too wildly about something that was probably nothing more than a recipe for corn liquor hidden away by a long-dead mountain farmer.

"Just current events type stuff for the early part of the century, I guess," said Eddie. "It's school stuff."

Eddie knew he had screwed up as soon as he said it. School had been out for two weeks.

Elton Mansfield's head turned sideways as one eyebrow went up. "OK," he said, still wondering what the boys were up to. "You will need to go downstairs to the microfilms. There is a young lady down there who will help you get started. Her name is Giselle."

"Thank you very much," Josh said politely.

The two boys made for the stairway, taking two steps at a time on their way down. They found the young lady with the name "Giselle" on her nametag. She was young and pretty and the boys didn't mind taking instruction from her at all. In a few minutes they had signed out the films they wanted and were winding their way through old newspaper clippings of events in the early 1900s.

They flipped past very old articles on coal operations in Braxton County where they were surface mining coal out of the hills instead of using the conventional method of tunneling deep shafts that took miners to unthinkable depths underground with toxic methane gas ever present.

There were articles on union organization talks amongst the ranks of miners and other labor groups tired of sweatshop work conditions and low pay. Unfamiliar terms like Wildcatters appeared in the headlines.

Headlines chronicled uprisings in faraway places like Russia and Germany. The world was about to change.

They whizzed past birth announcements and death notices, praying that something would catch their eye with the words "Southern Jewel."

The boys both smirked as they cranked past an article of a train robbery in Kanawha County in 1903 and wondered what would be on a coal train worth robbing.

They continued their search until 4:55 with no luck at all finding their Southern Jewel.

"We'll be locking up in five minutes, boys." Elton Mansfield's voice rang from behind. "I hope you were able to find what you needed," he said, once again raising an eyebrow.

"Yeah….it worked out good. Thank you," Josh replied, putting on his best reassuring grin.

"I will put that away for you if you like," Elton offered.

"Thanks, thanks very much," Josh replied.

The two friends climbed up the stairs with less enthusiasm than when they had bounded down them two-and-a-half hours earlier. As they walked outside and flipped the kickstands up on their bikes, Eddie said, "Why don't we go to DQ so this ride isn't a total bust."

"O.K… It was a shot in the dark though, ya know," Josh said. "Maybe that 9104 isn't a date. Maybe it's something else. I mean, we based this search on those numbers being a date. Could be we have to rethink this whole thing."

"Maybe this whole thing is nothing." Skeptical Eddie again.

Josh shook his head.

The boys rode down over the embankment on a dirt path and made their way to the Dairy Queen, a quick ride away. They both ordered up their desserts piled high with whipped cream and nuts and lots of hot fudge. After paying, they went to the side of the building that gave them some shade, sat on the sidewalk and leaned up against the cinderblock wall to eat their treats.

Eddie said, "So, here's what we'll do, Josh? We will go home and search the Internet for anything with the phrase Southern Jewel in it. If it's famous, it'll be there, right?."

Josh raised his eyebrows and wobbled his head back and forth while working a mouthful of sundae. "There might be a hundred things listed under that search… but I guess it's worth a try," Josh replied, shrugging one shoulder while taking another bite. "This might be a hard nut to crack, ya know?"

"Yeah… I don't plan to spend all summer on it. We have a lot of other things to do. I want to do some camping soon. I've got the itch." Eddie took his last bite.

Josh nodded while eating. "I cleaned out my backpack Friday. I still had a can of tuna in there from last summer."

"Gross."

"Also, I still have my fork that we carved from a stick, remember?"

Eddie grinned while nodding. He then pulled the yellow legal pad out of his backpack that had his copy of the hand-written version of the document on it. He laid it on his lap and studied it while Josh worked his ice cream all the way to the bottom of the plastic cup. The two boys said nothing for a while. They sat there enjoying the summer, their snack, and their teenage freedom. With the sun on his face, Josh felt as if he could take a nap.

"Ready to hit the old dusty trail, partner?" Eddie said, doing his best Roy Rogers.

Josh laughed, and the two friends were on their way to the Baker's house to see what they could dig up on the Internet about the illusive Southern Jewel.

CHAPTER SIX

Josh and Eddie came to a sideways, tire-screeching halt just inside Josh's garage, propped their bikes up on the kickstands, and hurried inside to re-hydrate with whatever they could find in the Baker's refrigerator. Josh grabbed a Gatorade for himself and one for his friend, and the two boys headed into the den to power up the PC and see what they could find. Josh tapped a couple keys and waited while the computer woke up and refreshed itself.

"We should go fishing tonight," Josh said. "Just off the bank down here. What do you think?"

"Be a good night for it," Eddie agreed, nodding slightly and turning both corners of his mouth down.

"Mom!" Josh called.

Emily Baker walked around the corner from the kitchen, wiping her hands with a small towel. "Yes? Hi, Eddie"

"Hi Mrs. Baker," he responded.

"Do we have any chicken livers in the freezer?" He asked.

"Umm… I think, in the garage freezer if you want to check. Why?"

"We might fish tonight."

"Oh… OK," She paused. "Don't forget bug spray."

Nighttime fishing is extra fun for young boys who grow up along the banks of a river. The quiet of the night along the riverbank is pleasant, the conversation among friends is always fun and the sounds of the animals are peaceful.

They might hear the constant chirping hind legs of the crickets and the croaking bull frogs all around them. Sit there long enough and they will hear something scurry down the riverbank and into the water not far away. Most likely a muskrat, or a beaver, or even a mink. They will hear it but won't see it. It knows they are there.

If they make the mistake of leaving their bait too close to the water's edge at night, they may have to contest a 10-inch river turtle for what's left.

When they can find one, the boys will drag an old used tire down to the fishing spot at night, and light it on fire about fifteen feet up the bank from where they are fishing. A little motor oil usually helps initiate the inferno. The burning rubber compounds put off a heavy black smoke that the boys swear keeps the bugs away. It also burns very hot, so on the cooler nights it will even help to keep you warm. Elk River ingenuity.

Boys will tend to be boys along the river at night, too. Many a boy has puffed his first cigar while night fishing…. just to keep the bugs away. And many a young fisherman has vomited his guts out after trying Red Man Chewing Tobacco for the first time in his life. They always swear they will never try it again.

Peeing in the river is another thing exclusive to nighttime fishing for young boys. Pee and giggle. There is just something funny about it!

The computer up and ready to go, Josh clicks on his browser icon and waits momentarily for it to link up. He grabs a sheet of printer paper from underneath to make notes and pulls a Bic from out of the penholder on the desk and lays it in front of his monitor.

In the "search" box he typed: southern jewel. *Enter.*

"While it's thinking, I'll go take those livers out before I forget," Josh said.

The Wi-Fi did its thing and the search results were coming in. The page flashed on the screen and Eddie's eyebrows went up as his eyes widened when he saw it—86 pages.

Josh hurried back from the garage and took his seat in front of the monitor.

"Oh man," he said. "This might take some time."

"Unless we get lucky and what we are looking for is on the first page," Eddie said.

"Wish I knew what we are looking for. I guess something with the words 'Southern Jewel' in it and we need it to reference West Virginia in some way, right?"

"Right. Let's get with it."

Josh took the mouse slowly rolled down the list of search results. The two friends glanced past "Southern Jewel Recipes" and the "Southern Jewel Flower" as well as the "Southern Jewel Seven Day Wine Tour." There was the "Southern Jewels Tour of Stately Homes" and there was also financing available for anything you see at "Southern Jewel Used Car Lot" in Macon, Georgia. For many minutes, the boys were glued to the screen.

Page after page, they hoped something would catch their eye, and with each page they eliminated, their spirits sank and their hope diminished. Eddie began to think more about that night's fishing plans than looking for a "Southern Jewel" whatever on the vastness of the Internet.

They rolled on past jewelry stores, homemade apple butter and palm readers, all associating themselves with Southern Jewel, somehow.

After page sixty, Josh's enthusiasm fell from his face and he was just going through the motions than trying to study what he was doing.

Eddie sighed and shifted in his chair as the search got boring and monotonous. After a few more minutes, he wasn't even looking at the screen anymore

They were down to the pages where "Southern" and "Jewel" were often separated by about four or five other words. Often, but not always.

Josh shook his head slightly, as if he were ready to throw in the towel on this adventure when something at the bottom of page 64 caught his eye. He sat up and squinted at the screen with a spark of newfound enthusiasm as he read a small bit that made his eyes spring to the full-open position.

WWW.OURCONFEDERATEGOLD.ORG

.... the true southern jewel of the south, supposedly disappeared from a freight train after all five crewmen were murdered in central West Virginia circa 1903.....

"Eddie! Eddie, look here!" Josh said in an excited whisper. "Look at this!"

Eddie's head swung from its drooped down, rested position, as he sat on his chair with his forearms on his knees, to an upright sitting position once again. Eddie read the search result that Josh was pointing to on the screen.

"Hmmm…" he paused. "Click on it."

Josh clicked on the link that was hi-lighted and once again the Wi-Fi went to work.

What popped up on the screen next would change their young lives—a website entitled *"LEGEND OF THE SOUTHERN JEWEL."*

It was a very tacky looking home page with shiny gold bars for a background and little sparkles that blinked on and off. On the left side of the page was a row of tabs to various pages on the site: HOME, LEGEND, FACTS, IMAGES, and REFERENCES.

"Legend," Eddie said, directing his friend.

"Yeah."

Josh clicked on the LEGEND tab and, once more, and they waited. In seconds it was on their screen. What had consumed their thoughts ever since they had pulled the top off of that old milk can down on the sandbar—what had kept Josh thinking and dreaming since he and Eddie deciphered "Southern Jewel" on the animal skin document in Eddie's garage, and what had led them on a 10-mile bike ride only to come up empty-handed at the library, was now before them. The story of the Southern Jewel read like this:

The Legend of the missing stash of Confederate Gold has been around for about 140 years now and has been told and re-told many times. We, here at "Legend of the Southern Jewel" site, have done extensive research and tapped an unlimited supply of resources that come in to us every day. Our most reliable and often-used resource is, most definitely, the Library of Congress and The National Archives, which are all open to the public to educate themselves as much as they like. We also work off of tips and information from visitors to our site. (Feel free to leave a message on our message board.)

The story goes that towards the end of the Civil War, around the winter of 1864, Jefferson Davis, Robert E. Lee and other top generals and government officials of the Confederacy, including the Secretary of War, gathered and discussed their realistic outlook on the war, and what they should do about it. The south had lost a quarter of its population and farms and homes were now being looted and burned as the Union Army gained more of a foothold from every battle that took it further into the southern states. Even when losing a battle, the Union Army had the resources to re-provision and continue their march into Confederate country.

The Southern leaders agreed to fight on, but to put in place a backup plan to regroup in a matter of time and invade the north once again. For this they would need finances, and what the south had was a vast supply of old Spanish gold that had been "salvaged" from ships that had run aground on the barrier islands and reefs along the southern coast in the very early years of our country. The government had set up a "legally questionable" Naval operation to "rescue" stranded ships that were hard aground, and for payment, the cargo went to local and state governments in the south. Many times, the cargo was precious and often it was gold.

The Confederacy also had a supply of gold on loan from France for the purpose of supporting their Confederate currency. Printed currency, without gold to back it up, is just useless paper. This gold was supposed to be returned to France after the war. That didn't happen, and maybe that's why they don't like us today.

There are many rumors of where they hid the gold. Some say it was stuffed into cannons and buried at the site of the Battle of Bull Run, around the Stone House, where Union General Pope *made his headquarters. Judith Henry was the only civilian killed in the first battle, and some even say a portion of the gold is buried with her. Some say they buried it at Virginia Military Institute where it could be guarded constantly. Others say it was shipped to Georgia where it turned up missing after a wagon train hold-up.*

The most common belief is that it was, in fact, scattered to several locations throughout the south to prevent the entire lot from being discovered all at once, should someone be lucky enough to discover its whereabouts. This is most likely the truth since it is backed up by hints and clues within the articles and documents left behind by the short-lived Confederate government and available in the National Archives, as mentioned.

Josh and Eddie looked at each other and kept reading.

One portion of the Confederate gold was discovered near the end of the war in Vicksburg, Mississippi. In desperation, the Confederate army stuffed it into one of the hand-dug caverns carved out in the sides of the hills of Vicksburg. They could not transport the gold out of the city because of the siege that was in place. Upon discovery of the gold, the Union Army put it onto a train and shipped it to a bank vault in central West Virginia, where it was safely stored until after the war. This gold was a real prize for the Union Army and was dubbed "The Southern Jewel".

Josh Baker and Eddie Debord gasped in unison as chills ran through their bodies. At that moment, their emotions bounced between fear, excitement, and an overwhelming feeling that they were in way over their heads on something they knew nearly nothing about. They continued.

This is where the strange part begins, as we have discovered here at "Legend of The Southern Jewel".

The gold became strangely forgotten and sat in the Hillsburg, West Virginia bank vault for many years until a special section of the Smithsonian Institution was made ready for it to be temporarily displayed. They placed the gold on a train one night in

1903, along with armed guards, and it was to run nonstop to Washington D.C. The gold never made it. As a matter of fact, it didn't even make it to its second checkpoint. The train was held-up, most likely by a large band of southern sympathizers who had some inside information on the shipment in transit. Yes, the true Southern Jewel of the south supposedly disappeared from a freight train after all five men on board were murdered in central West Virginia circa 1903.

The government denies the gold ever existed, most likely to avoid the embarrassment of losing it. They say they have no record of it ever existing and call the entire thing a hoax. We know better.

Josh and Eddie were numb. Their bodies were covered in chill bumps and Eddie even felt slightly nauseous. Josh's right hand was shaking at the mouse as he stared at the screen with a blank expression. Eddie shook his head slowly and tried to say something, but no words came out. The boys had found what they were looking for, the meaning of "The Southern Jewel." And it was way bigger than they could have ever imagined.

Josh leaned back in his desk chair and looked straight ahead. "The article at the library…. do you remember?" He asked quietly.

"The train robbery in 1903... the one we laughed at."

"We have to go back. We have to go back to the library," Josh said.

One thing was for sure, there would be no fishing tonight.

CHAPTER SEVEN

Eddie showed up at Josh's house just before 9:00 the next morning, ready to make the ride down the old railroad bed again to the library. The boys would need to find the microfiche once more that had the article that, just yesterday, they had dismissed as a "coal train hold-up," and gotten a chuckle out of.

It's true that they hauled coal out of these hills for many years, but that particular train on that particular night was a freighter and was carrying very special cargo. If they could find that article again, and the story matched what they found on the Internet, then they would have a very interesting little prize in that old milk can in Josh's garage.

Off the boys went again, out of the neighborhood, down the dirt trail, through a couple of ditches. They pulled a couple nice wheelies, landed on their back tires and got back on the old black railroad bed that would take them the five miles to where they needed to go.

The boys pushed their ride a little harder because they knew there was some information at the library that could be very beneficial to them. They stopped only once for a drink and when they pulled up to the front door of the library again, both boys turned up a 16-ounce bottle of water and killed it. They caught their breath for a moment and proceeded into the library.

Elton Mansfield recognized the boys right away and said, "Hello boys. More school work?" He smiled, looking up from his paperwork.

"No sir," replied Josh. "All pleasure." He smiled too.

"We need those films again," Eddie said.

"Well, you know what to do, right?" Elton answered, looking over his glasses and turning both palms up.

"Yep. Go see Giselle," Josh replied.

"She's downstairs."

The boys walked toward the stairs and Elton Mansfield said, "Uh, fellows?" He paused and his expression turned curious. "Is there something in particular you are researching in the early part of the century that I could help you with?"

Josh and Eddie paused and glanced at each other once again.

"No," Josh said. "We're just looking up genealogy stuff."

Elton didn't buy it for a minute, but whatever they were doing was none of his business anyway, as long as it was within the rules of the library.

"Feel free and help yourself. If we can help you in any way, let us know." He smiled again and went back to his paperwork.

Josh and Eddie bounced down the stairs as before and walked towards the newspaper archives.

"He's a little different, huh?" Josh commented.

Eddie smirked and nodded in agreement.

The boys thought no more about Elton Mansfield when they saw Giselle.

Long, straightened, auburn hair and green eyes, and looking very pretty. She was returning books to the shelves from a cart when she spotted the two boys looking her way.

"Oh, hey guys." She said, like they were old friends. "Back for more, huh?"

"Umm, yeah." Josh paused. "Could we get those early 1900s films again? The ones we had yesterday?"

"Sure," she said happily, "let me get them for you." Giselle paused and looked at Josh. "Is your last name Baker?"

Josh nodded. Giselle smiled softly and turned to get the films.

Eddie elbowed Josh, and both boys grinned, Josh raising his eyebrows a bit.

It hit Josh at that moment. *Giselle O'Conner*. Josh's father was friends with Tom O'Conner, Giselle's dad, and Josh remembered her from three or four years ago when the dads got together for a trout-fishing trip up on the Cranberry River with another mutual friend. Four years ago, Giselle had been all knees and elbows and looked very little like what he saw in front of him. Josh remembered the O'Conner's were a good family and very nice people.

He told Eddie the story while Giselle was searching for the films that the boys needed.

This Giselle O'Conner was seventeen years old and just out of high school. She lived within walking distance of the library and planned to kill a couple months this summer by working there until she started college in August at the University of Charleston.

She walked back over to where the boys were standing and handed the microfiche to Josh and said, "They hadn't been put away yet. Still over there on the cart." She paused. "Soon these will all be on hard drive and microfiche will be a thing of the past.

The library is in the process of it now. But it's expensive and funding for us is not a big priority for this county."

"That'll be cool when it happens." Eddie said.

"Yeah, then you will be able to log into our site and do your research at home. What are you guys looking up, anyway?" she asked nonchalantly.

Eddie and Josh looked at each other and then back to the very cute Giselle. They hadn't told a soul what they had found and had planned on keeping it that way, but isn't it amazing what pretty eyes, gorgeous hair and a gentle smile can make a young boy consider? Reveal the biggest secret of his life! Giselle was looking at them and slightly cocked her head and half grinned when the boys hesitated.

Eddie drew a deep breath and looked over at Josh once again and then back to Giselle, eager to spill the beans to someone. "Can you keep a secret?" he asked.

"Sure," she said, shrugging one shoulder. Her expression grew more curious.

The boys were both thinking the same thing. Giselle was much more knowledgeable of the library and the way it worked and could probably speed up their search and maybe be able to reference other information that would help them, too. They could use all the help they could get. Plus, she was darn cute!

"You got time to sit down for a few minutes?" Eddie asked again.

"Wow!" She half laughed. "Sure. What's going on?"

Josh started out. "A couple days ago, me and Eddie were fishing down below our house, across the river on a sand and rock bar. We were goofing around and getting ready to leave when we looked back down over the riverbank and saw an old milk can.

One of those old ones about this tall used a long time ago to haul milk around, I guess."

Eddie said, "You see them on people's porches and stuff now days."

Josh continued. "We pulled the can out of the mud and it still had the lid on it. We carried it over to the water and washed it off and, while we did that, we heard something inside flopping around so we figured *'hey... let's open it up.'* So we did."

Eddie said, "It took some doing, but we got it opened and inside there was this old deerskin that had been tanned a long time ago. It had writing on it."

Giselle shifted in her seat and leaned up on the table, now becoming more interested in the two boys' story.

Eddie continued. "Josh and I took it up to my garage and spread it out to see what we could read." He paused. "This is where it gets cool. We wrote down everything that we could make out. Some of it was smeared or faded and there was also a little drawing at the bottom."

Josh reached into his backpack and pulled out his copy of the document that was written on yellow legal paper. He put it on the table, flattened it out with his palms, and turned it to where Giselle could see it. Her expression turned back to curious again as her eyes squinted and her mouth opened. Her eyebrows had flattened out, losing that natural arch, and her brow furrowed a bit as she read what the boys had written from the old document.

The boys let Giselle look for a moment and then Josh said, "This part right here is what caught our attention first... *Southern Jewel.*"

"What is that?" Giselle asked. "*Southern Jewel.*"

"We had no idea either," Josh answered. "That's why we came here yesterday, just to see if we could find out what that meant. See this up here? It's a date, we think. 9104. September 1, 1904. We figure that was when this deer hide thing was drafted," he shrugged.

"How do you figure that?" She asked, sort of skeptically.

The boys glanced at each other once again and then Eddie said, "We found nothing here yesterday with *'Southern Jewel'* in it for the early 1900s."

Josh interjected, "At least we didn't think we did."

Eddie continued, "So we went to Josh's house and thought we could do an Internet search for it."

"Did you find anything?"

Josh pulled out the pages from his backpack they had printed from the "Legend of The Southern Jewel" website.

"This is what we found on the computer," Josh answered.

Giselle took the papers. She read the part about the story of the gold that was discovered in the caves of Vicksburg, Mississippi, by the Union Army and how it was shipped up north to be stored in a West Virginia bank vault until it could be temporarily displayed at the Smithsonian.

Giselle's eyes widened, and she drew a quick breath when she got to the part after that. The gold was dubbed *"The Southern Jewel."* She looked over at the yellow paper. "Southern Jewel."

She continued to read and came to the part in 1903 when, *on a stormy night while the gold was being transported by train to Washington, D.C., a band of southern sympathizers had somehow stopped the train and killed all five men aboard taking the gold for themselves.* She read over the part about the government denying the gold ever existed and slowly shook her head.

Josh said, "What we found here yesterday was an article we thought nothing of at the time. An article about a train robbery in

1903. We laughed about it at first until last night when we got to this part here." Josh pointed to the printed papers and tapped his finger on the lines about the train robbery in 1903, where the supposed southern sympathizers had held up the train and taken the gold, leaving five men dead. "We need to find that article again and read it this time to see if it matches up with what we found on the website," Eddie said.

Giselle O'Conner stared at the boys for a moment while thinking deeply and trying to put all of this together, trying to figure it out for herself at the same time. "So what do you guys think you have here with this animal skin thing? A treasure map?"

"Not sure, but if the two stories match up, then we have something pretty interesting at least, don't ya' think? We just have to figure out what it is," Josh replied.

"Let me ask you a question," she paused, "Why did you tell me this?"

"Well, you asked, and we figured you might be able to help us gather information, since you know your way around a library pretty well," Eddie said. "And you did say you could keep a secret."

There was silence for a moment.

"It's very intriguing," she said, thinking for a bit.

The boys still weren't sure that they had made the right decision by telling her.

"Well, I guess I'm in whether or not I want to be. Right?" She added. "OK, let's start cranking through these films."

"We're pretty sure it was the last one we looked at yesterday, whichever one that was," Josh said.

Giselle looked at the micro film containers and then said, "If you looked at them in chronological order, then it would be this one here."

"Let's try it," Eddie said.

Giselle sat down at the projector and loaded up the film. Josh and Eddie squeezed in to get a look at the articles whizzing by. They all looked familiar since the boys had just scrolled through them yesterday, but nothing really jumped out at them. She continued cranking, and the boys continued skimming the write-ups from a long-forgotten paper.

A few minutes went by and they were getting a little stare crazy again from gazing at the screen and then Josh said, "STOP... hold it!" He had gotten a little excited and had shouted a little too loudly, and a few people sitting downstairs looked over at him. Josh held up his hand a little to apologize, but something had caught his eye and he knew they were close.

"The articles about the union organizations and rallies were real close to the train robbery article!" he said. "Go slower now."

The boys leaned in a little closer and Giselle slowly turned the handle until Eddie and Josh said simultaneously, "There it is!"

"It's not a very big write up," Giselle commented.

Giselle zoomed the article and read:

5 DIE IN LOCAL TRAIN ROBBERY

-Officials are unsure of cargo stolen-

Kanawha County Officials are unsure what was onboard the freighter of the late night Hillsburg train that was held up just south of Blue Creek on the C&O line last week. They reportedly found all five crewmen on board, dead at the scene.

"It seems a little curious to us," a local official stated. "These trains run through here regular and usually it's just coal they are haulin' and sometimes a freight car or two." When asked what was so curious about this situation, the official went on to say that normally, he thought, they only carried a crew of two: a fireman who shoveled coal into the boiler, and the engineer. "Why there were five men on board, we don't know at this time," he said, "and what would be on board one of these trains worth killing five men over? It's possible it might be wildcatters that killed them fellows kind of random, but it seems a little extreme, even for them crazy union organizers."

The Railroad had no comment at first, but later said that three of the men on board were "in training" with C&O.

Curious rumors have begun to surface that the train may have been hauling the old Confederate gold that has been legendary in these parts for years. The gold has supposedly been stored in a cement and steel vault in Hillsburg since being discovered in a Confederate cave in Vicksburg during the War.

The three kids rose and looked at each other, then read on.

Local Sheriff, Dan Bloom, laughed when asked about the rumor. "That has been an old wives' tale around here since I was a young boy," he said. "It don't exist and we don't need that kind of nonsense interfering with our investigation of this incident. We have enough ground to cover without chasing crazy, made-up stories about secret gold."

Bloom had nothing else to say on the matter and took no more questions on the train robbery.

The Kanawha Chronicle will continue its investigative reports on this story as information becomes available.

Giselle and the boys sat in silence for a moment, collecting their thoughts and putting it all together in their minds.

"This is *very* interesting now," she said.

"Well, there it is," Josh said. "I mean, I would say that the article we have here and the one we pulled off the internet have a lot in common, wouldn't you say?"

"Oh, absolutely they do," replied Giselle.

"I wonder if there are any other articles about the robbery on film," Eddie said.

"Well, the paper said that they will continue to report on the story so there might be more," she replied. "And… I'm wondering what the rest of the skin means. We haven't deciphered the entire thing yet," Josh added.

Thunder rumbled in the distance as Josh noticed the light coming through the small basement windows was diminishing.

"Is it supposed to rain today?" he asked.

"I think it's going to whether or not it was supposed to," Eddie replied.

"We better get home."

"Man, I wanted to keep looking!"

"You guys take off and I will look for more later," Giselle said. "I need to get back to work, but I will look for more when I get time. Give me your number and I will call you if I find anything good, okay?"

"Alright. Yeah, we better get out of here," Josh said.

Thunder rumbled once again in the distance. Josh and Eddie got up to leave and Giselle said, "Hey guys." She paused. "I appreciate your trust." She smiled.

The boys looked at each other. "We appreciate your help," Josh returned.

Josh wrote his number down on a piece of paper and gave it to his new friend. Giselle stuffed it in her jeans pocket and gathered the films once more to return them to the shelf.

The boys bounded up the stairs, past Elton Mansfield and out the door to where their bikes were parked. Thunder once again rumbled as they mounted up and headed over the hill on the dirt path that led to the old railroad bed. No time for ice cream today.

Josh couldn't wait to hear from Giselle tonight—for more reasons than one!

CHAPTER EIGHT

By seven o'clock that evening, the rain had come and gone, and Josh hadn't heard from Giselle. He stepped out onto his back porch and noticed the river had risen only slightly after the rain and that it was a little muddy. Perfect for catfishing!

He called his best friend and fishing buddy, Eddie Debord, and, in a few minutes the two anglers were sitting on the boat dock with bare feet dangling, and two fishing lines anchored on the bottom of the slightly swift Elk River.

The chicken livers that they had thawed out two days ago had not gone to waste. As the heavy sinker kept the line in one place, the bait would float up about eighteen inches off the bottom and no catfish in their right mind could refuse a good chicken liver.

The sun was about forty-five minutes from setting and the bugs and mosquitoes were making their presence known and so were the frogs. The boys sat there watching the current take an occasional log or piece of debris downstream and, looking at it, they both wondered out loud how far it would go. Would it get stuck just around the bend or would it make it all the way to the Kanawha River?

If a log could make it that far and get into the deeper and wider waters, maybe it could even make it to the Ohio River. And, if it could make it to the Ohio, then it's a sure thing it would make the Mississippi. This is where it got tricky because only the clever Elk River logs could make their way down the Great Mississippi River and through the series of lock systems that were set up to control *The Old Man*. But, if successful, an adventurous log would then find itself at the mouth of the Mississippi and the northernmost point of the Gulf of Mexico, and, from that waypoint, that old Elk River log could then explore the world.

There is a lot of time to think when fishing and, as twilight fell, Josh wondered the same thing about himself. Would he stay here on the banks of the Elk River, or would he make his way downstream one day? Was it possible to leave and one day come back? Would he ever get the desire to roam or would he be as content all his life as he was right now, 14 years old, sitting on the muddy banks of the Elk River with a line in the water and his best friend beside him.

Josh decided then and there that he would do his part to keep their great friendship together, because one good friend, one honest friend, was one of the greatest things that a person could have.

"Hey Ed." Josh broke the silence and spoke slowly, "Do you think there is gold around here somewhere?"

Eddie paused a moment, thinking about it, and then spoke, "What would you do if you went to all the trouble of holding up a train and stealing all the gold and then killing off five guys to top off the night?"

Josh thought for a moment and said nothing, just shrugged his shoulders slightly.

"I don't know about you, but I think I would go spend some of it. Live it up a little. Make it worthwhile before I went to prison."

"Yeah… But if that happened, why do we have this animal skin with clues on it? If there is no treasure, then why a treasure map? Why would someone go to the trouble of drawing it up and sealing it, if there were nothing to find?" Josh replied.

Eddie nodded. "Good point. But are they clues? We really don't know what that skin is."

"I think we need to study it and see if anything else jumps out at us," said Josh. "We will need to decipher the entire message to know."

"HEY GUYS!!!"

Both boys just about jumped off the dock and into the water.

Giselle O'Conner stood on the bank above the boat dock with her hands on her hips.

"You scared the fire out of us! What are you doing here?" Eddie blurted out.

Giselle was laughing at the two friends' reactions to her carefully timed interruption, pulling it off just as planned. Giselle was now in jeans and a Fender Guitars T-shirt with a pink Adidas baseball hat. Again, the boys admired how easy on the eye this girl was, no matter what she wore.

"My Dad remembered where Josh's Dad lived and told me how to get here. Any luck?"

"We haven't been down here long. We just got our lines set. How about you? Did you find anything else?" Josh asked.

"Well." Giselle studied the steep bank for the best way down to the dock. "Is this slippery?"

"Yeah… it can be. You might wanna watch your step." Eddie said.

"Are there snakes?" she asked, taking a couple well-placed steps.

The boys just looked at each other. Girls.

"Hang on, Giselle," Josh said. "I'm gonna come up and light that tire. Then I'll help you down."

Eddie rolled his eyes as he reached down and cranked his reel a couple of times.

Josh shimmied up the bank, grabbed a small can of used motor oil and glazed it over the old used Goodyear that lay on the bank above the boat dock. The tire was placed in a well-used fire pit that the boys had made of old bricks. The oil would allow the fire to catch slowly and not have the explosion factor like gasoline. Much safer.

Josh struck a match and tossed it down on the tire and after a few seconds the oil fire came to life and smoked dark blue. He then tossed on two logs that Eddie had brought from his dad's woodpile.

"That thing will burn?" Giselle asked.

"Oh yeah. It will burn for about two hours," Josh replied.

"Cool."

"Keeps the bugs away."

"Oh."

"Alright, you going down?" Josh asked.

"Yeah, I'll go down, if you don't let me fall."

"I'll hold on to your hand. You go down first and I'll hang onto you."

Giselle grabbed Josh's left hand with her right hand and started down the bank. Josh held back on her so she wouldn't slip as he dug-in to the bank with his bare feet and held tight to her hand. Josh held it a moment longer, just for fun, and then let go as they both stepped onto the dock. Josh stepped over to his pole and gave the reel two cranks to tighten the line.

"Thank you, Josh," Giselle smiled.

Eddie said, "So did you find out anything else at the library?"

"It's weird," she answered. "After that first article that we found, there was no more mention of it in the papers at all. That seems funny to me because back then this area was just a small little place, and a train robbery would be BIG news. You would think it would be in the papers for weeks. But no, there was no other article at all... except one little minor thing about an empty wallet found at the scene."

"That's big! What did *that* say?" Josh asked.

"I wrote it down." Giselle pulled a small slip of paper from her pocket and then read:

"The wallet of a Blue Creek man was found at the scene of last week's train robbery. It is said to have belonged to a guy named Arthur Otis," Giselle continued, *"a mountain man who lives mostly self-sufficiently."*

The tire caught fire and cast a glow down onto the dock.

"But here's the thing," she continued. "The article goes on to say that Otis could not be found for questioning."

"Yeah... he took the gold and split!" Eddie commented. "It's like I was telling you a little bit ago, Josh. You make a heist like that, you leave town."

"And that was about it. The article said that he was, most likely, one of the southern sympathizers who was unfortunate enough to leave his identity behind and that he would eventually be apprehended and questioned."

Eddie noticed the end of his pole slowly pull down… just a little.

Josh said, "How did they know whose wallet it was? It's not like they had drivers' licenses back then, right?"

Eddie's pole relaxed for a second and then was pulled toward the water about three inches again and held there.

Josh looked over as Eddie sat down on a cinder block and got into fishing position. "Current?" he asked.

"I don't think so," Eddie replied.

"Well, I guess his name was in there somewhere. Maybe it was carved into the leather."

Eddie's pole relaxed again.

"Could have been," Eddie said, while watching his pole.

"Yeah… think of all the saddle makers back then. I imagine leather work was common, and they were probably good at it, too," Josh said. "We did some in shop class last year."

Eddie's line pulled once more toward the water, only this time about six inches, and he reached down to grab it.

"Not yet!" Said Josh.

"I know, I'm not."

"Well, anyway, I'm sure they probably made a positive identification before they put it in the paper. I mean, maybe there was just something in the wallet with his name on it. Simple as that," Giselle said.

Eddie's pole relaxed quickly this time and then *boing, boing, boing!* The fish was off and running with the chicken liver. Eddie grabbed his pole and quickly jerked backwards to set the hook and the fight was on.

The fish immediately ran downstream with the current and Eddie stood up to adjust his position to land the monster that had swallowed his chicken liver. The boys were using their heavier catfish rods tonight strung with 10-pound test monofilament line, so line strength shouldn't be a factor in landing this one, unless it turned out to be one of the big "leg swallowers" from upstream.

"Watch your drag," Josh offered, excitedly.

Eddie's line whizzed out as the big fish ran with his bait about twenty yards and then turned to come back. It's a fish's trick to get slack in the line and then shake the hook out of his mouth. But Eddie was ready for him. As soon as he made his turn, Eddie quickly cranked his reel to take up any slack the fish had gained. Seeing that Eddie was an experienced fisherman, Mr. Catfish then turned toward the shore and swam hard.

"Oh, here he comes, Eddie. Crank it, crank it, crank it!"

Giselle stepped toward the front of the dock behind Josh to get a better view of the action as Eddie retrieved ten-pound line as quickly as he could. The whole time the fish was swimming toward the dock, he was shaking his head back and forth to throw the hook out of his mouth. Unsuccessful, the fish then turned and headed straight towards the other side of the river. When the tension on the line reset itself, Eddie's reel screamed as the drag control let the line spool out to prevent breaking.

Giselle piped up, "He's headed towards the sandbar."

Josh turned around and looked at Giselle, a little surprised that this girl was even paying attention to what was going on as Eddie fought hard. Giselle sensed what Josh was thinking.

"Hey, I fish," Giselle said. "And you better hope he doesn't go over there and wrap it around a rock."

Josh knew she was right and so did Eddie. Eddie reached down and tightened the drag just a little on his reel. It was time to get the line back in. The cat would tire soon and it should be just a matter of reeling him in. The fish swam to their right, downstream almost to the spot where, just a few days ago, Josh and Eddie washed the mud off an old, red milk can across the river. Just a few feet off the sand and rock bar the cat broke the top of the water with his tail, which is unusual for a catfish whose environment is primarily on the bottom of the river. This fish wanted off.

"He's stretching my line," Eddie laughed nervously, while trying to gain some ground on the big guy.

"Yeah, pull on him Ed. Your line will hold," Josh said.

Eddie pulled back on his rod, and the fish gave in. Eddie reeled in the slack and did it again and again until he had the fish coming his way. Eddie was making steady progress and got the fish within twenty feet of the dock until he turned once more to head out to sea. Eddie would have nothing of it and pulled back hard on the rod as the fish gave in and Eddie turned him back toward the dock and reeled him in little by little. Josh lay down on his belly on the dock as Eddie reeled him up close and Josh reached down and grabbed the monster cat, being careful not to get knifed by the very sharp fins.

Josh pulled the fish up and onto the dock and Giselle looked on, very impressed. While Eddie held the rod, Josh reached into his tackle box and pulled out a pair of long-nosed pliers and extracted the hook. Eddie laid his pole down and lifted the fish to claim victory.

"Look at his mouth. He's been caught before." Giselle said, noticing the other hole in the fish's mouth.

"I could tell that when I was fighting him. He knew just what to do, that's for sure." Eddie was excited.

"Lemme get the scale," Josh said.

Josh reached in and got the scale from his box and hooked it on the fish's mouth. The big cat pulled the scale down a good way as all three kids looked on.

"Nine and a half pounds," Josh said officially. "Nice fish, man."

"What's he, about twenty-eight inches or so?" Eddie asked, smiling big.

"Yeah, he's big," Josh said, smiling too. "Wow."

The catfish flipped its tail hard. The boys were very excited about the catch but knew they needed to get it back in the water to fight again another day.

Eddie jokingly said, "Goodbye, Mr. Fish. Thanks for the fight." He then leaned over and carefully placed the fish back in the water and with another flip of his tail he was off! Eddie washed his hands off in the river and stood up, still smiling big and proud.

"Good job," Giselle said, smiling too.

"Man, that's fun," he said, wiping his hands on his jeans.

Josh picked up his rod, reared back and flung his line far out into the water once again, and then bent down and placed the rod in its holder. The three were silent for a minute as Eddie baited his hook and threw his line out far to the right of Josh's. The fire above them had grown large and had provided that glow on the riverbank that gave them light and kept the bugs in check.

If one could stand on the sand and rock bar and look back across the river at the three friends, one would see the picture of Americana—three young people on the dark riverbank, illuminated by only the fire, enjoying each other's company and the surrounding nature. No iPad, no cell phones buzzing text messages, and no annoying ring tones to spoil the sounds of crickets, frogs and things that splash into the water at night. Just three friends doing what was meant for kids from West Virginia to do; enjoy the beautiful, outdoor life in a simple, wholesome, country style.

Softly, Giselle said, "Hey Guys?" She paused a moment. "We need to find out who Arthur Otis was."

They all stood silent once again with the fire crackling above them.

CHAPTER NINE

The boys had fished until late at night and had taken full advantage of summer vacation by sleeping in the next morning. Giselle had left at about ten o'clock to go home because she had to be at the library the next morning by nine. The three had made plans for the next day to go search town records for a man named Arthur Otis. This was Giselle's' idea, for she knew this information was public record. The boys both knew having her involved with their adventure was paying dividends already.

Josh heard the phone ring as he lay there with his head buried in the pillow at ten-thirty in the morning. A few seconds later his mom called upstairs, "Josh? Josh, are you up?"

"Not really," he called back, with his head still buried.

"Honey, it's Giselle O'Conner. I'll tell her to call you back."

"NO! I'm up! Hang on, hang on!"

Josh flung the light blanket over and sprung out of bed. Walking out of his bedroom, he rubbed his face and slapped himself with both hands to wake up. He met his mom halfway down the stairs as she handed him the house phone from the kitchen and gave him a curious look but said nothing more.

"Hello?"

"Did I wake you up? What a light-weight you are," she teased.

"We were out there 'til, like, one in the morning," he pleaded his case.

"I know," she laughed. "Your mom told me she heard you come in late. I'm just kidding. But hey, listen, the town records are in the building beside the police station and Mayor's office right there at the Blue Creek Bridge. I'm getting out of here at two o'clock today. I thought that I could drive right to your place and we could walk up there. It's not far."

"Yeah, OK. That sounds good," he said with a yawn. "Do you know how to find all that stuff?"

"Never done it before, but how hard could it be, right?" she said. "They'll tell us how. Mr. Mansfield said the records go way back to the origin of the town and everyone who has paid taxes here or was born here or died here would have some record on file. They have all the construction records of every building that has ever been put up here, so if Arthur Otis lived here, we should be able to get some information about any living descendents he may have, and then maybe we can learn something from them about the *Southern Jewel*."

"You didn't tell Mansfield anything, did you?"

"No, no, no. I just asked him how to go about looking up dead people in town records. That's all," she replied.

Josh thought *what an excellent thing it is having her on the team*.

"Alright. I'll call Eddie and have him over here at two o'clock, ready to go."

"OK. Hey by the way, did you guys catch any more after I left?"

"Yeah, we caught 'em all night. Nice ones, too. Nothing as big as the first one, but they were all nice!"

"Good. Hey, I have to run but I will see you guys at two or a little after, OK?"

"OK. See ya at two."

Josh clicked off the phone and went into the upstairs bath to brush his teeth and hair, and to get ready for the day.

At about twelve-fifteen the phone rang again at the Baker house. Mrs. Baker glanced at the caller ID and saw it was the county library. "Hmm," she said. "Hello." She paused. "Oh yes, hang on just a second. Josh… it's for you."

Josh hopped up from his seat at the computer to get the phone.

"It's Giselle." His mom smiled.

"Hello."

"Hey," Giselle said on the other end of the line. She was whispering so no one could hear her. "I had to wait 'til Mr. Mansfield went to lunch to call, but I think he's a little more than curious about what you guys have been looking up here."

There was a moment of silence while Josh thought about what she had just said. His stomach knotted just a little.

He said, "Well, he asked if he could help us the other day. Why? What happened?"

Josh noticed that his mom glanced over at him and, as casually as he could, walked out the back door and onto the porch.

"You know the three microfiche films we were scanning the other day?" she asked.

"Yeah."

"He had the same exact films down here a little bit ago, cranking through them. I saw him as I walked past to return some books to the children's area. Numbers 150, 151, and 152."

He paused. "Out of all those films he was looking at our three?"

"Yeah." She hesitated. "And Josh?"

"What?"

Josh heard her take a deep breath and then release it.

Slowly and softly she said, "He had that yellow piece of legal paper you were showing me."

Josh's stomach knotted a lot.

"Oh, no." Josh's mind raced.

Giselle said, "Remember how you guys left here yesterday when it began to thunder?"

"Yeah... Oh my gosh. I left it lying right on the table, didn't I? I forgot all about it. Oh man!"

"Yeah, and I had left the microfiche area when you guys did to go finish restocking upstairs, so either someone found it and turned it in to him or Mr. Mansfield found it himself."

"I didn't even realize it wasn't in my backpack. I haven't been in it since we left."

"Well, what's done is done. I just wanted you to know," she said.

"But why would it interest him?" Josh asked.

"I don't know. We can talk about it when I get there. I need to get off the phone; I'm supposed to be watching over the place."

"OK," Josh said with no exuberance. "I'll see ya in a while."

"Alright, bye."

"Bye."

Josh's heart was in his stomach, and his head was now spinning. What did this all mean? Why would a local librarian be curious about vague words written on a yellow piece of legal paper by two teenagers? Most of the writing on it was rows of unfinished words. The only legible line on it was *Southern _ewel*, and that would mean nothing to the average person in a library unless that person was a local historian. And how could they find out why he was curious about their research? They couldn't really just come out and ask him, because they didn't want him to dig any further or try to trick any information out of them. Maybe he was just curious, and that was all. Maybe that would be the end of it. Maybe not.

Josh decided to call Eddie and have him come over a little early so he could break the news to him. Mrs. Debord told Josh that Eddie was out with his father today but expected him to be back soon and that she would have Eddie call him back. Josh thanked her and hung up.

Josh hoped that Mr. Mansfield didn't know enough to figure out what the three were up to. Prior to Giselle coming on board their team, the boys had decided not to let their parents in on their little secret. Parents just seem to have a way of squelching a good adventure for reasons known only to them—usually it had something to do with safety. The boys were afraid that their moms and dads would want to let the proper authorities investigate the matter, if there *was* anything to investigate, and he and Eddie would be left out of it altogether. They figured at the proper time, or if things got crazy, they would reveal their secret. Giselle had agreed to this as well. But now the team had suffered an information leak and Josh couldn't have felt worse about it.

At ten minutes 'til two, Eddie showed up at Josh's door. Mrs. Baker told Eddie that Josh was in the garage and Eddie thanked her and then walked around to the side door. Josh was putting air into his bike tires when his friend walked in.

"Hey," Eddie said casually as he walked in. "Mom said you called. I thought I would just come on over."

"Hey, Ed," Josh said as he pulled the hose from the tire. "Giselle called. I guess I messed up. I left my yellow copy at the library yesterday and Mansfield found it."

Eddie's eyebrows rose a bit as he thought for a second.

"So. What could he get out of it?"

Josh shrugged and walked over to roll up the air hose.

"Something caught his attention on it because Giselle said he was scanning through the very same films that we were scanning. Why would he do that?"

"Wow." He paused. "I don't know. What could have caught his eye?"

"The only thing I can figure is the *Southern Jewel* part. With just the 'J' missing, it's not hard to figure out. I mean, *we* figured it out!" Josh said.

"What would it mean to him, though?"

"Beats me."

Eddie thought for a moment while his friend wrapped the hose and then opened the valve on the bottom of the air compressor to release the unused air and free any water that accumulated in the tank's bottom.

"Don't worry about it. Let's just keep on doing what we are doing. I don't think it's a big deal," Eddie reassured his friend.

"Probably right."

"Were your tires low?" Eddie asked, changing the subject.

"Both of them. We've ridden a lot of miles lately." Josh grinned. "Ya wanna check yours?"

"No. I'm good."

Josh hit the button beside the door to the house to raise the double garage door and, at that moment, a gorgeous, silver, Pontiac Grand Prix pulled into the driveway. Giselle pulled off her sunglasses and tucked them away. As she opened her door, the boys walked over.

"Nice," Eddie said, looking over the well-designed Detroit model.

"Yeah, and the car looks good, too," Josh added. He said it with no forethought, then immediately turned red as a beet as Giselle smiled and winked at him.

The car had a flawless silver and black paint scheme with charcoal grey interior. Not a bad ride at all for a seventeen-year-old. The deal she had made with her parents was to go to a local school so they would not have to pay for dorm expenses, and they would buy her a reliable car to get to and from school for the next four years. The deal was good for all involved.

"We're walking, right?" She asked.

"Yeah, but it seems a shame," Eddie said, looking over the impressive lines of the car.

Josh and Eddie's parents had a very strict rule forbidding them to ride in cars with anyone under twenty-one years of age unless they approved it. Since the boys couldn't tell their parents where they would drive off to, they could not seek approval. They had an extra bike to offer Giselle, but the section of railroad bed that they had to travel down still had the rails and ties in place, so riding a bike was out of the question. They had to hoof it. The good news was, it was only about a mile, so off they went.

The three walked through the neighborhood, past the elementary school where they would jump on the railroad tracks that would take them all the way to the Blue Creek Bridge.

Just past the school, Josh said, "Hey, on the way back we should stop at the truck stop and get a big plate of fries. I got a few bucks."

"Sounds good," Eddie replied, as the team walked on.

Ryder's Truck Stop was no bigger than most people's family room on the inside. Across the two-lane road was a wide spot where the trucks parked, and there was always at least three big rigs sitting there with their diesel engines idling. They had the best fries on Elk River Road and were only a dollar a plateful. It was just one of those little hole-in-the-wall joints that most people who lived up the river knew about. A stop on the way back would be mandatory.

The kids continued to discuss their dilemma.

"So, did Mansfield do anything else weird today besides get into our business?" Eddie asked with intentional sarcasm.

"No, I don't think so. And I kept an eye on him for the last hour or so, but I didn't see him go back down to the records room at all," Giselle reassured him. "I can't really follow him around though, ya know? I don't want him to catch on that I know he knows."

"It's creepy, man. Why would he have retraced our steps? Why would this be of any interest to him at all?" Josh wondered out loud.

"Well, with no more information than he has, he probably won't get any further than he already has gotten. I mean, unless he goes to the Internet and searches the way we did," Eddie said.

"But why would he unless he had already heard of the legend of the *Southern Jewel?* You know what I mean? If it is something that he has knowledge of, then that piece of paper would have caught his attention for sure!" Giselle added.

The three friends continued to step from one railroad tie to the next as they made their way down the straight stretch toward the bridge and Town Office.

"What are the odds of us finding this old milk can, figuring out a piece of a code that was in it, and then some guy who has been looking for it for years stumbles on to our notes? What are the odds?" Eddie pleaded.

"Yeah, I agree," Giselle said. "The odds would be astronomical. Like hitting the lotto. But people do it."

Josh shook his head, "I'm not going to worry about it anymore. We have to have more information on this than anyone. You can bet the people at 'The Legend of The Southern Jewel' website would love to have what we have."

"No doubt," Giselle replied.

The railroad tracks ran parallel to the highway and only about 10 feet away from it. Josh looked up to see a bike coming their way down the side of the road, dangerously close to where cars zoomed by at 50 miles per hour.

"Oh man," Josh said with regret. "It's Radcliffe."

Brad Radcliffe was the kid in town responsible for most of the juvenile disobedience that went on. He picked fights. He stole bikes. He threw rocks at cars going down the road at night. He was just a bad seed. If something was stolen, broken or vandalized, he was most often thought of first. Sadly, his anger came honestly, as he grew up with an abusive, alcoholic father who took his own shortcomings out on his family in a verbally abusive manner. His mother displayed the same psychological scars as Brad but did her best not to show it. At times, people, even the kids, felt sorry for Brad Radcliffe, but his mean and hateful manner pushed people away from helping him or trying to befriend him. He had a real tough outer skin for a kid of sixteen.

Radcliffe braked to a stop. The boys braced for a verbal confrontation.

"Hey Giselle. Whatta ya hanging around these pinheads for?" he asked sarcastically, nodding towards the two boys. "Kinda young aren't they?"

"What's it to you, Radcliffe?" she calmly replied. It wasn't her nature to be mean to people.

Brad shrugged. "So when you gonna take me for a ride in that Silver Bullet of yours?"

"When pigs fly!" Josh piped up, having had just about enough of Radcliffe already.

"Shut up, ya little twerp," Radcliffe said.

"No, you shut up, Radcliffe!" Eddie shot back.

Brad Radcliffe threw his bike to the ground and stepped around it towards the three kids.

"Oh, come on," Giselle said. "What are ya gonna do? Kick our butts for walking down the railroad tracks? Is your life that pathetic, Brad?"

Radcliffe had nothing to say to that as the silence was broken only by a passing car, his mind reflecting on his home life for a brief second. He had had an unpleasant day with his dad. His frustration was evident.

He looked at Giselle and then the two boys, and, for a moment there was that look in his eye that said, "Yes.... my life is that pathetic." He realized that there was no reason for any violence on the railroad tracks at that time and bent over to pick up his bike by the handlebars. His belligerence returned.

"You guys are lucky she's with you," he said.

"Hey, Radcliffe," Eddie said, as Radcliffe climbed back onto his bike. "Were you throwin' rocks at my garage a couple of days ago?"

"What are you talkin' about, Debord? He looked at Eddie strangely. "I got better things to do than throw rocks at your stupid garage!" He shook his head and rode away. "See ya, Giselle." Brad Radcliffe had had a bad day at home, and it showed. Josh and Eddie knew that, too.

Eddie was strangely convinced that if Radcliffe had thrown those rocks, he would have had no problem telling him. There was no doubt about that. But if *he* didn't do it, then who did?

The three walked on and soon entered Blue Creek's humble-sized Town Office.

CHAPTER TEN

A little bell jingled at the top of the door as the three friends entered the building, signaling a middle-aged Mrs. Anderson, who sat in a back room at a computer, that the office had visitors.

She looked out at them over the top of her reading glasses and said, "I'll be right with you."

"Thank you," Giselle replied politely.

The Town Office sat in a row of three two-story buildings attached to each other, all being constructed of old clapboard-style siding and all three painted the same light grey color. All three were local government buildings, with the Town Office sitting between the Sheriff's Office on the right and the Mayor's Office on the left. Once inside, one could access any of the three offices. The doors between them were always open, so officials could wander between them to carry out business or just to get a fresh cup of coffee that Mrs. Anderson always had ready.

The inside of the offices had that scent of age to them—old construction that is somehow comforting and welcoming.

From the Town Office buildings, you could look directly across the bridge that crossed the Elk River and see the original

General Store that was constructed when the town of Blue Creek was established. An old brick structure.

"May I help you?" The pleasant but very busy Mrs. Anderson asked from behind an open window.

"Yes, thank you." Giselle returned the politeness. "We need to look into town records to search an old name, if we could please."

"OK. Sure. How old are we talking here?" Mrs. Anderson asked.

"Sometime around 1903, 1904," Giselle replied.

To the left of the three kids, visible through the doorway to the next office, stood a heavyset, older gentleman who was a little above average in height. He had what was left of a large cigar in his mouth and was thumbing through a thick book at the front desk of the Mayor's office. The sizeable man leaned back a bit and looked over at the three kids when he heard Giselle's voice. Eddie recognized him as Mayor Billingsworth.

"Okay." She paused briefly while biting her right cheek. "Now, did you want tax records or birth and death certificate records or what?"

"Let's start with birth and death," Giselle answered.

"Sure. Step through that Dutch door over there and I will meet you in the records room. Oh, would you do me a favor and put your names on the sign-in sheet too, please?"

"Sure. Thank you," Josh chimed in.

The kids signed their names and then stepped around the right side to a half door that Mrs. Anderson opened for the three to walk through. They entered a room full of tall, green and tan, four-drawer file cabinets. The cabinets looked old and appeared to have been painted a few times.

"Okay," Mrs. Anderson said cheerfully. "Early nineteen-hundreds start here, in these green ones, and then they just go in order to the next cabinet. It's all public record and you can help yourself, but we ask that you don't carry anything out of here. Rather, we ask that you bring it out to me and I will make a copy, okay?"

"Sounds good. Thank you very much," Giselle replied with a smile.

"OK, and if you need any help or have any questions, just shout."

"Thank you," Eddie said.

The team looked up and down the drawers where Mrs. Anderson had pointed and found the one marked 1900-1905.

"One thing," Giselle said. "If we are looking for the birth record of a man who was at the scene of a train robbery in 1903, we need to look a lot earlier than 1900."

"Oh, that's true," Eddie agreed. "We should probably start around 1850, right?"

"Let's try that," Giselle agreed. "Arthur Otis, 1850. I am kind of amazed that they have records that go back that far. I mean for this little town?"

The three kids began their search through the endless files of Blue Creek citizens. They were lucky in one way. Mrs. Anderson was a skilled organizer, and everything was in order, year after year. All they needed to do was take each year and look in alphabetical order for the last name Otis.

In 1850 there was a man named Zeke Otis, but no Arthur. In 1851 plenty of babies were born but still no Arthur Otis. They found that in 1852 Zeke Otis married a lady named Othella Burdette. But there was still no Arthur Otis. The kids searched on, as each file for each year grew thicker as the town grew more populated.

After a few more minutes of thumbing through file after file, Josh exclaimed, "Got it!"

He pulled out a file folder that was labeled, "Otis / Arthur B."

They took the file over to a little table and opened it up to see what they could find on the man who had left his wallet at the site of a train robbery in 1903.

The first document was a duplicate copy of his birth certificate signed by Dr. Abraham Jackson, March 9th, 1855. It showed Zeke Otis as the father and Othella Burdette Otis as the mother. There were a few other documents in the file such as his Army registration paperwork in 1878 and his documents for being locked up in 1885 for the brutal beating of a man in a tavern over a game of poker. And that was about it. The kids were looking for more.

"Shouldn't there be a death certificate?" Eddie asked.

Giselle got up and walked back over to the file cabinet and pulled two citizen files and thumbed through them as the boys continued to look at Art Otis' file.

"Yeah. These all have death certificates in them, too," she said.

"Why wouldn't his?" Josh asked.

"Wait. Look here," Eddie said, pulling out a piece of hand-written paperwork that appeared very old.

"What's it say?" Giselle asked.

Eddie read:

ADDENDUM TO FILE

The death certificate of Arthur B. Otis has never been available to Public Record due to his apparent disappearance from the area of Blue Creek, West Virginia, in 1903. It is believed that Mr. Otis fled the area after being involved in the train robbery that occurred at that time, but that has never been proven. Please refer to Tax Records for information on properties and surviving relatives. As of April 14, 1920, Arthur B. Otis' whereabouts are unknown.

"OK. Where are the tax records?" Josh looked around.

"Tan cabinets," Giselle responded.

The three friends looked up and down the drawers until they found the year 1900. They then slid open the drawer and Eddie dragged his finger along the tops of the files until he came to the O's. He then pulled out a handful and went through them until he found a file on "Arthur Benjamin Otis." The kids opened the file and started their search to find out what they could about this man. They couldn't believe all this information was available so easily.

"OK, now we are getting somewhere. It's all here," Giselle said. "It looks like he paid an annual tax amount of $7.87 on a place that is referred to as 'Tater Holler Homestead.'"

"That's for the year 1900," Said Josh. "Let's look in the year 1903 now, the year he disappeared or took off or whatever."

"Good thinking," Eddie said, and he went back to the file cabinets.

A few minutes later they were looking at the Arthur B. Otis file for the year 1903. It didn't take them long.

"OK," Giselle paused. "There's no record of any tax being paid on his property in the year 1903. Makes sense if he's not around, he will not pay his taxes, right?"

"Yeah. Now what about survivor or descendant information or whatever it's called?" Josh asked.

Giselle was impressed with his vocabulary, considering he was only fourteen years old, and gave him *that* look. As well as accomplished adventurers, Josh and Eddie were both bright for their age.

The kids started rummaging through the few papers that were in the 1903 file until they came across a slip of paper that caught their attention.

It read: *For 1903 tax information on Tater Holler Homestead, see: Emanuel B. Otis file.*

"Who is Emanuel B. Otis?" Josh asked.

Giselle chuckled, "It's gotta be a relative, right? Let's look it up."

The very next file in the drawer was the tax file for Emanuel B. Otis. The sleuths were following the paper-trail.

Inside it were the normal tax record documents for the normal Blue Creek taxpayer. And then there was an extra document with a legal draft attached to it. It read:

1903 taxes on homestead property owned by Arthur B. Otis of Tater Holler have been paid in full on this day, Aug 29, 1903, by Emanuel B. Otis, surviving son of Arthur B. Otis. Therefore, the Homestead property of Tater Holler becomes the property of Emanuel B. Otis. If at any time in the future Mr. Arthur B. Otis returns to said property, the latter will have to settle back tax payments with the former to re-take possession of said property under the supervision of the court of law.

The county tax commissioner signed it, 1903.

"What……. does…… all…… that……. mean?" Josh asked slowly, a bit befuddled.

Giselle explained slowly. "It's just a bit of legal talk that says Arthur's son Emanuel paid his taxes for him and took possession of the house or homestead or whatever it was at the time. In other words, he paid his dad's taxes and moved in. And if Arthur ever comes back, he has to repay all the taxes that Emanuel paid in order to legally re-claim his property."

"Alright, so we found out he has a son named Emanuel. We can keep digging from there and find out if Emanuel had kids, right?"

"It should be right in this file or back over in the green cabinets," Eddie said.

"Have you guys ever heard of Tater Holler?" Giselle asked.

"Yeah, I think I know where it is. If I'm right, it's about five miles downriver from our house. It's takes off to the left just a little past the river shoals," Eddie answered. "My dad used to go deer hunting with old Tom Maynor up there. It's a pretty wide holler and runs a long way up into the hills. Ya' can't really get there by car. I mean, ya can but you have to go down the road and come into it from the back side of Hickory Holler on old, old dirt roads. It's not easy to get to."

"Hmm," She said. "Well, I'll keep looking here if you guys want to go back to the green files and see if you can find a son or daughter of Emanuel Otis."

"OK," Josh said.

When the two boys turned around, they were startled to see Mayor Billingsworth standing at the opening of the Dutch door, filling the space of the opened door pretty much to the max. He looked at the boys saying nothing, as he chewed his cigar and rolled it from one side of his mouth to the other and then casually walked away from the door and stepped towards the Sheriff's Office. His size 12 cowboy boots clumped heavily with each step on the hardwood floors. The three kids all looked at each other, shrugged and went about their business of finding the descendants of Arthur Otis. Josh scanned the green cabinets while doing some figuring in his head. He was trying to determine an approximate year to look for a son or daughter of Emanuel Otis. He reasoned a twenty-year bracket from 1900 to 1920 for starters. He thumbed across the years, looking in the "O" section of each one, for a man or woman with the last name Otis. A few minutes of searching went by and then they found something. In 1912 a baby by the name of Martha Otis was born to Emanuel B. Otis and Margaret Turner Otis. In that same file was her death certificate for the year 1982. The boys studied the file for a while, took some notes, and then tucked it away. They continued to look. In 1916 a baby boy was born to Emanuel and Margaret Otis, whom they named Matthew. They dug through his file and also found a death certificate for the year 1989.

Deceased Otis's would do them no good. They needed to find one who was still alive. Giselle finished with the tax files and came over to lend a hand to the boys' search. Once again, they needed to determine a bracket of years to start their search for descendants of Matthew Otis. This next generation would surely have to produce a living relative of the infamous Arthur B. Otis.

Giselle suggested, "Why don't each of us take ten years apiece, starting with 1936, and go from there? Matthew would have been twenty years old in 1936, so that is a reasonable place to start, right?"

"Sounds good," Josh chimed in.

The kids dug right in and continued their search. Each young detective doing his or her part to find a living Otis to talk to about the old red can and *The Legend of the Southern Jewel*.

A few more minutes went by and Josh's stomach was audibly growling when Eddie said, "Got one!"

Josh and Giselle turned to see what Eddie had come up with and noticed Sheriff Collins looking at them, this time through the

Dutch doors. Sheriff Collins was a bit more courteous, however, offering the kids a smile and a tip of his hat. His shoes didn't make a sound when he walked away. Neither did the old boards under his feet. Former detectives could do that.

Josh and Giselle turned back to Eddie.

"Whata ya' got Eddie?" Josh asked.

"Okay, 1948. Baby born to Mathew Otis and Teresa Hinkley Otis. They named him Burl Arthur Otis."

Eddie flipped through the papers in the file. The usual stuff, but this time…. no certificate of death.

Giselle said, "Hey…. this one could be alive still! Let's look through here really carefully and make sure there are no brief notes or riders or addendum or anything."

Josh and Eddie didn't really know what all *that* fancy talk was, but once again, they were glad that they had recruited their new friend.

They went through every legal document in the file and everything was in order as it should be and there was no sign or mention of a death certificate at all.

"OK," Giselle said, "We have a possible living descendant of Arthur B. Otis. Now we need to know where he lives. Back to the tan cabinets."

This would not take long. The three friends went right to the current year tax files and fingered their way to the "O" section.

"Burl A. Otis. Here we go. Let's take a look!" Eddie exclaimed.

The three kids were now getting a little excited about their interminable day of looking through files and trying to find a living relative of Arthur Otis. They laid the file out on the little table and gathered around it. Josh flipped open the front cover and right there on top, on an official Blue Creek Property Tax document, it was.

Burl Arthur Otis

*Rural Route 120, Tater Holler Homestead...22 acres......
Taxes paid... $218.00*

Eddie and Josh's jaws both dropped simultaneously as Giselle reacted, "Oh my gosh!"

Josh said it slowly, figuring it out as he went along, "Burl Otis lives in the original Tater Holler homestead that his great-great-grandfather Zeke Otis settled in the mid-1800s! Wow... that is so cool."

A genuine sense of accomplishment overcame the three as they smiled, looking at the file, proud of their sleuthing skills. They sat there in silence for a moment and then Eddie said, "Dude... we gotta go there! We gotta talk to this guy."

Josh looked at Eddie in agreement, with a "let's go" grin on his face.

"I wouldn't bother if I were you," boomed a voice behind them.

Startled, the three turned around and, once again, there stood Mayor Billingsworth, filling up the top portion of the Dutch door. "What interest would you kids have in a crazy old mountain man moonshiner like Burl Otis, anyway?"

They paused a minute as the Mayor rolled his cigar around in his mouth a little.

Eddie spoke up. "Oh, uh... We were just doing some research, that's all."

Sheriff Collins stepped up beside the Mayor, paused a second and said, "What kinda research would you be doing on a no-good family like the Otis'"?

Giselle defended, slightly irritated, "No good? How can you say they are no good? We just traced their family tax records from the 1850s up to the present and the only time they missed paying their taxes, another family member stepped up to pay it for them."

"Sure. Moonshine money paid all them taxes. Not an honest dollar in a century came from that bunch. Whata you kids know about the Otis', anyway? Why are you prying into their business?" the Mayor questioned, squinting one eye.

Giselle offered them this, "We are just doing some research on early Blue Creek settlement and we got the Otis' name sort of randomly from someone. We thought it was as good a name as any to look up." She shrugged one shoulder to give her excuse nonchalance.

Sheriff Collins and Mayor Billingsworth looked at each other, both knowing a suitable cover when they heard one and both wondering what the kids were really up to. The two officials realized, however, that all the information the kids had uncovered for themselves, *was* public record and that their curiosity in what the three friends were up to would have to end right there—for now.

"Well... OK." He paused. "Just remember to put things back as they were when you leave" the Mayor said. He then looked at Sheriff Collins as he walked away and gave him a quick shoulder shrug. They both walked in the same direction towards the little room with the coffeepot.

"What was that all about?" Josh asked. "What do they care what we are doing?"

"Who knows," Eddie replied. "These guys don't have much to do, ya know. Why don't we make some copies and get out of here?"

"Yeah, I don't know of anything else we need here. We have a family tree that we traced to a living descendant and we have an address," Giselle added.

The three friends took the latest tax document they found with the address and the birth certificates of Burl Otis, his father, grandfather and great-grandfather, Arthur B. Otis, to Mrs. Anderson to make copies.

"Can we have you make some copies for us?" Giselle asked her politely.

"Oh, um… ya know what…. Can you run a copier?"

"Sure." Giselle replied. "I work at the library."

"You guys come on back and help yourselves if you like. I have a deadline I am trying to beat today and heaven forbid if I go over it." She gave a head-nod toward the Mayor's office.

"Gotcha," Giselle replied with a smile. "We'll just be a second."

The three kids walked to the back room where the copier was and made the four copies they needed. They copied the birth certificates first and once finished with them, Giselle took them back to the records room to put them back in the files and put the files back in the cabinets where they belonged. Eddie and Josh were making the copy of the tax record as Giselle walked past the front window and was startled nearly out of her shoes when just outside the door, they all heard the unmistakable sound of tires screeching just a split second before a loud *CRUNCH*!!!

Everyone in the offices ran out to see what had happened, including Josh and Eddie. An older lady in a big old 1973 Chrysler New Yorker had rear-ended a Ford pickup truck that had stopped in the middle of the road for whatever reason. All occupants were fine as Sheriff Collins handled the situation with the help of a deputy who arrived soon afterwards. The kids watched the formality for a little bit and then made tracks for home.

"We got everything we need, right?" Giselle asked.

"Yep, all set," Eddie said. "Let's go get some fries at Ryder's."

"Sounds good."

CHAPTER ELEVEN

The three friends sat at the counter of Ryder's Restaurant, each with a plateful of crinkle cut French fries and a large puddle of ketchup. Ryder's made them the best and no one really knew why, but they were great. Maybe it was the oil or the quality of the potatoes or a combination of both or maybe it was just the atmosphere of the quaint little restaurant, but these fries were unbeatable and for one dollar you could get a full plate of them. As the kids ate, they chatted about the things that had happened up to this point and the information that they had gathered.

They had discovered a milk can that had probably been lost for decades. One containing, arguably, the biggest secret in West Virginia history. A map of clues to the *Southern Jewel*, a huge stash of Confederate gold that was robbed off a train on a stormy night in 1903. The document was drafted and placed inside the milk can for safe keeping in 1904. And, most likely, in case something happened to the person who had hidden the gold and drafted the map, another generation could discover it. Which is just what had happened!

They also knew that a wallet that belonged to a man named Arthur Otis had been left at the scene of the crime, which immediately made him a guilty man or at least a "suspect of interest." Arthur Otis disappeared immediately after the robbery, and that did nothing for his case either.

They knew that Elton Mansfield seemed to have an interest or at least a curiosity in what they were sleuthing, and they knew that a living descendant of the man who left his wallet on the train tracks on that night in 1903 lived about five miles downriver and then straight up the mountain who knows how far. They knew something else too—they wanted to go find him!

"So, now we need a plan," said Josh. "We have to get up Tater Holler to talk to Burl Otis."

"I have freshman orientation downtown the next two days so you guys will be on your own. I expect you to keep me updated though," Giselle said. "So… what's the plan gonna be?"

"You know that camping trip you've been wanting, Eddie?" Josh asked. "I was thinkin' how about we take the backpacks and go for a couple days."

Eddie nodded his head in approval as he chewed and swallowed a mouthful of fries.

"I've never even been up that way before. Do ya think there is a place to pitch a tent?" Eddie asked. "Besides in the middle of the woods, I mean."

"Well, if nothing else, there's usually an oil well site to camp near if nothing else," Josh replied. "You just have to listen to the pumps all night."

"Yeah, if they're running."

This region of West Virginia was full of oil wells with pumps busily pulling crude out of the seams of the hills. The drilling companies came in with all their equipment and huge drill bits, sometimes up to fifteen inches in diameter, and drilled over a mile deep, searching out the black gold. Once the hole was drilled, they ran a four-inch diameter pipe all the way to the bottom and cemented it into place. Once that was done, they set in place the pump jack that would, with the help of a small engine, rock a plunger type device up and down inside the four-inch pipe, sucking the crude out of the ground and into a storage tank on sight. It made for a noisy campsite, with the engine running, but sometimes was the only flat spot that could be found with enough brush cleared away to keep the snakes out of one's tent. There was usually a well site about every mile along the old oil roads that crisscrossed through the mountain region.

"We'll find somewhere to camp. We always do, right?" Eddie replied. "Do you think this guy will talk to us? We don't know anything about him."

"He's gonna be around sixty-five years old, if he was born in '48," Giselle said, just offering information. "How are you planning to find out where his house is up there?"

"You think we could map it on the computer?" Eddie asked.

"Map Tater Holler Homestead?" Josh asked, cocking an eyebrow at his friend.

"Probably just have to go search the place out, huh?" Eddie conceded. "Do it the hard way."

"You mean the fun way!" Josh smiled, itching for more adventure. "Here's another problem," Josh said, shoving a fry into his mouth. How are we going to get downriver to the point where we cut up the holler?"

"What about your boat?"

"It's a deep-V. It won't go over the shoals down there. It's also light-gauge aluminum and Dad would have a cow if we brought it back with a hole in it."

"I got news for you," Giselle said. "If you put a hole in it in the river, you won't be *bringing* it back!"

The friends all laughed at the reality of what Giselle had said, all indulging in their fries once again. Each one was thinking about how they could overcome this obstacle and be able to get downriver five miles and explore Tater Holler in search of Burl Otis, the man whose great-grandfather left his wallet at the site of a train robbery in 1903.

"What we need is something with a real shallow bottom, something that will float right over the shoals. I think that the rocks are about a foot to a foot and a half below the surface of the water down there. A flat-bottomed Jon boat would be ideal, but I don't know anyone who has one who would loan it to us," Eddie thought out loud.

"Me neither," replied Josh, shaking his head and eating his last fry. "A rubber raft would work, too."

"Until you hit one sharp rock," Giselle said. "Blub, blub, blub." She made a sinking motion with her hand, then laughed.

Josh looked at her and shook his head. "No, we need something that can take a hit or two and keep floating," he said, "and it's not like we can ask for a ride, either. Then we'd have to tell the whole story and we can't do that... not yet. Can't ride our bikes either. Not down the railroad tracks."

Eddie said, "We could just cross the river behind your house and then hike the five miles to Tater Holler, ya know, walk the tracks."

"Last resort. That's a long walk carrying packs," Josh replied shaking his head.

"We'll figure something out. You guys ready? I gotta get home," Giselle said.

"What's the rush?" Josh asked.

"Probably got a date," Eddie teased.

"No, my Dad is doing some maintenance stuff on my car tonight before I drive back and forth to school every day. Oil… and…. some other stuff."

Josh and Eddie just looked at each other.

"He said to have the car back in the garage by six o'clock. He is starting right after dinner."

"Alright, well I'm ready," Eddie said.

The three spun their counter stools around and hopped down to leave the best French fry joint on Elk River. Giselle reached for the old door handle and as she did so a beefy trucker pulled the door open from the other side. As he opened it, he tipped his greasy Peterbilt hat at her, offering her the right of way. Giselle thanked him and the three walked out of the restaurant and continued their way back to Josh Baker's house, where she had parked the newly named *Silver Bullet*.

"So when are you guys planning to take this camping trip? I mean, are you going sooner than later or what?" she asked.

"I don't know. We have to see what we can come up with for getting to Tater Holler first and then we're good to go, or at least I am," Josh Replied.

"Oh yeah… me too! Hey, it's summer vacation. Not too much to work around as far as schedules go." Eddie said.

"Well, keep me posted. Let me know what's going on. You have my cell number, right?"

"I got it," Josh confirmed proudly.

"We'll call ya," Eddie said.

Arriving at Josh Baker's house, the two boys watched Giselle hop into her fabulous looking Grand Prix, lock her seatbelt, back out of the driveway and head home, her dual exhaust rumbling slightly as she took off. Both boys were thinking the same thing but said nothing. They enjoyed her company and man, was she cute!

"Josh is that you, honey?" his mom called from inside the house.

Eddie laughed at the honey part, and Josh smirked back at him.

"It's me, Mom," he returned.

Mrs. Baker walked over to the door. "Are you hungry? We have pot roast, almost ready, with potatoes, carrots and corn bread. Oh, hi, Eddie. You're welcome to eat too if you'd like."

"Hi, Mrs. Baker. Thanks, but we just killed three plates of fries and I am stuffed," Eddie replied, putting his hands on his stomach.

"Yeah, me too, Mom. I'll have some later, though. It smells great."

"Okay," Mrs. Baker said, a bit surprised that teenage boys would turn down such a hearty meal. It wouldn't take them long.

"Later it's serve yourself, ya know," She said, giving them the eye and reminding them that the kitchen closes after dinner, for service, that is.

"That's fine. We'll fix it," Josh said. "Hey, let's take a cruise down the riverbank on the bikes," he said to his friend.

"Let's go."

The boys enjoyed riding their rugged bikes down along the sandy banks of the Elk River. There was a trail that followed the terrain of the rolling banks that took them across small streams that emptied into the river and then back up and through a huge patch of milkweed plants that grew six or seven feet tall, maybe an acre of it, and then through a wooded area where the boys had built their tree house a year earlier. Of course, all the boys who lived in the area would take the liberty of sharing the tree house without the courtesy of asking, but what could they say? It wasn't even built on their property.

The two friends rode along, enjoying the pleasant fragrance of the honeysuckle and the lilacs that grew in abundance along the river banks in the summertime, while watching the falling sun sparkle on the ripples of the river like diamonds. Occasionally, Eddie would look back to make sure his friend was still back there and then resume hard pedaling.

As they rode along, Josh was taking it all in. The scents, the sights, the feel of the bike as it dug into the dry, sand/dirt mixture. His mind went back a few days to when, just across the river, they had pulled a muddy can from the bank of the river that held in it a message from the past. There was no doubt about it now. Someone had drawn up a document, of sorts, that was meant to be a message for someone. But who? Was it a treasure map? Treasure maps, he knew, were more myth than reality. In all the years of all the pirates who are so well known: Blackbeard, Long John Silver, Captain Morgan and so on, not one documented treasure map was ever found directing a lucky soul to an "X" in the sand. It was all fiction. So he thought, wouldn't it be a bit of a reach to even think he and his best friend, Eddie, had stumbled on to the world's first, real documented treasure map that would lead them to the proverbial "X"—the Confederate gold known as the *Southern Jewel*?

Josh was running it through his head when suddenly Eddie abruptly squeezed both hand brakes as hard as he could and slid to a sideways halt. Josh slid in behind him, running his tire into Eddie's spokes.

"Man! I almost ran you over!" Josh said.

Eddie held up one hand to quiet his friend and then pointed down the riverbank about fifty yards. Heading down over the bank was Brad Radcliffe with a long, narrow pole about twelve feet in length, and about fifteen empty one-gallon milk and water jugs. As he made his way down the path, he looked this way and that to see if anyone was following him or watching him. He couldn't see Josh and Eddie for the bush they had quietly pushed their bikes up behind and had no idea they were there.

The two boys weren't sure what Brad Radcliffe was doing at the water's edge with milk jugs and a long pole, but they were certainly curious enough to stick around and find out.

CHAPTER TWELVE

Brad Radcliffe made his way down the narrow path that led to the water's edge, moving the milkweed aside as he lugged the long pole and empty jugs behind him. The jugs were all strung together with what looked like a long length of old cotton sash cord and the long wooden pole was stripped of all its bark and was straight as an arrow, maybe twelve feet long and two inches in diameter.

Just off the riverbank was a small version of Josh and Eddie's sand bar, like the one they spent so many hours on every summer. This one only went out into the flow of the river about ten feet, however. Again, a mix of flat river rocks and sand — it was just big enough for Brad Radcliffe's project. As he reached the area at the end of the path down the bank, he lay his jugs down and dropped the long pole behind him. The boys watched through the bush as Brad took a deep breath and stepped over to a brown tarp that was tied down to small trees with the same type of sash cord that had been used to haul the jugs down the bank. It was covering something that was nearly twice as long as it was wide. He untied the cords from the trees as Josh and Eddie decided it was time to get a closer look. They stepped from behind the bush and moved closer to where they could see what Brad was up too. They were about twenty yards away now, but a Honeysuckle bush hid them from Brad.

Brad untied the last cord and then grabbed the tarp by the edge and flipped it like a bed sheet to uncover what lay underneath.

Both Josh and Eddie lifted their eyebrows at the same time as their mouths dropped open. They instantly knew what they were looking at even though they had never seen one before. Brad Radcliffe was constructing a Milk Jug Raft!

Brad had three sheets of ¾ inch plywood that looked to be secured together underneath with lengths of two by fours. Each sheet of plywood was four feet by eight feet. Two of the sheets were laid side by side lengthwise, and then the third sheet was laid across the front of the two others to add four additional feet to the length of the raft. The whole raft would measure eight feet wide by twelve feet long.

Underneath he had secured milk jugs for floatation. There had to be at least one hundred jugs already attached to the sheets of plywood with very little room for more. From what the boys could see, Brad had drilled about a gazillion small holes in the plywood to run the string through to attach the jugs to the wood. Not the most highly engineered vessel in the world, but it did look like it would work.

Brad had come down here today to attach the remaining jugs to his own private little river raft. Before he could start, he had to flip the raft up to be able to get to the underside. The boys watched as Brad grabbed one side of the raft and heaved as hard as he could to lift the raft up and put a short log, maybe three feet long, under it like a kick stand on a bike. Brad tried over and over to pull off the maneuver, but once he got it up in the air, he couldn't get the log over and in place with his foot. He tried standing the log up, lifting the edge of the raft up into the air and then sliding the log over with his foot but every time, the log would fall over onto the sand and rocks.

Josh and Eddie looked at each other and decided without words to go down and give Brad a hand. The boys stood up and made a deliberate noise so that Radcliffe would know that they were there. Brad looked around to where the boys were coming down the bank and was surprised at what he heard.

"Need a hand?" Eddie asked as they stepped onto the small sandbar.

Brad hesitated for a moment, not knowing why the boys were there or what they wanted. He looked back at his work and said, "I'm trying to get this edge propped up so I can get under it." He was a little out of breath from all the previous tries. "Whata you guys spying on me?"

Josh ignored the comment, looked the raft over and said, "Brad… this is awesome! What a great idea."

Brad gestured with his hands, shrugged and replied, "Just a little project." Brad was maybe a little embarrassed.

"Let's get it up," Eddie said.

Eddie and Brad grabbed the raft and easily lifted it as Josh took the log and securely wedged it underneath. Teamwork. The boys could see that there was just enough room underneath for the jugs that Brad had hauled down the bank a few minutes earlier.

"Where did you get this idea, Brad? This isn't like you to do something like this," Eddie said.

The old Brad returned for a second as he glared at Eddie because of his comment. Eddie felt that he probably deserved it.

"It just came to me," He said nonchalantly. "I was fishing from the riverbank one day and about six jugs went down the river all tied together with rope, probably from a trot line that broke loose upriver, and I thought it would be great to put jugs under some plywood for a dock for fishing off. The flotation is great as long as the caps are glued tight."

"Yeah," Josh agreed.

"And then I thought on it some more and figured, why not a raft?" he continued, "Then I could get up and down the river to the really good fishing spots, 'cause, ya know, I don't have a boat, anyway."

Josh and Eddie looked down and then over at each other, both picking up on a different side of Brad Radcliffe that they had never met before and feeling like they should have let him in their own little fishing club long before today—but man, the belligerence of this guy sometimes. Brad had never owned a boat, nor had his dad or uncles or anyone else in his family. It's a wonder he liked the sport of fishing at all. He was never taught to fish, never learned about the great outdoors from any father figure in his life.

"So I started saving the milk jugs, and it wasn't going very fast, ya know, I was only getting a couple jugs a week out of our house. And then a light bulb went on. I thought, *Recycle day*! Building a raft out of jugs is recycling, right?"

Josh and Eddie looked at each other and shrugged a *yes*.

"So on Monday last week, I went out real early before most people were up and raided their recycle bins for jugs. Jackpot, man. All I wanted. I picked out the ones with the caps still on them and then I strung them together with cord and hid them over in the weeds over there. Then I started bringing them down here and tying them on. It only took me two weeks to get one hundred jugs. All I needed."

"Where did ya get the wood?" Josh asked.

"Up where they are building the church. They have a stack they used for forming concrete. The guy said I could have a few if I wanted. They are perfect too, with some cement still on them. I figured they wouldn't be as slippery."

"Wow." Josh was amazed. "This is a big raft, Brad. How are you going to get it up and down the river?"

"Down the river won't be a problem. I just have to attach a tiller with a rudder on the end for steering, and then when it's time to come back up-river I will pole it. The river is shallow enough."

"Might be hard. You couldn't do it with a fast current fighting you," Eddie figured. "Upstream, I mean. You might need some help."

"No way!" The old Brad again. "The reason I am building this is so I can single hand it! Go alone!"

Josh and Eddie glanced at each other, not about to put up with Brad if he got an attitude with them.

"Well, you're going to have to put a sail on it then," Josh returned fire.

There was dead silence as Eddie looked at Josh as if he'd been struck with brilliance. Brad looked at both of them, wondering what they were thinking and if they were plotting against him telepathically.

"Josh, you've got it," Eddie said.

Brad listened.

"Think about it," Eddie said with a laugh. "This river runs pretty much southeast except for a few bends and turns. In the summer, the wind comes right out of the south to southwest. We know that from fishing, right?"

Josh shrugged. "Yeah."

"So, you rig up a square sail, like on the old ships, pirate ships, the old Galleons, that you can rotate a little to suit your wind direction. The wind blowing out of the south, southeast, southwest or even out of the west, will blow you right back up the river with a little help from the pole."

Josh and Brad looked at Eddie with curious looks on their faces.

"What do you know about sailing?" Josh asked.

"I read a lot of books, buddy!"

Brad said, "Could you guys help me with that? I mean, I don't have the slightest idea…."

"We'll help," Eddie said. He had something in mind. "In exchange."

"Exchange for what?" Brad responded, turning up his palms.

"We need the first ride down the river. Five miles to Tater Holler."

Josh's head turned toward his friend with a grin and he thought *you're a genius!*

"You got it!" Brad agreed.

Their dilemma of how to get down the river was solved. They just wrote themselves a free ticket to go see Burl Otis.

Now, they had a raft to complete. A sailing raft!

The boys all jumped in to finish attaching the jugs to the bottom of the plywood, all excitedly conversing as they worked. This was a new Brad Radcliffe that the boys had never seen before and they wondered how he could be so arrogant a few hours ago and so much easier to get along with now. Actually, creative and industrial. They had, at the very least, become business partners.

Once the jugs were finished, they lifted the raft again to remove the "kickstand" and lower it onto the small sandbar. Brad then tied a rope to one corner and the boys all looked at each other.

"Well, should we?" Brad asked.

"Let's do it," Josh said.

The boys all grabbed a corner of the raft and lifted. It was lighter than they thought it would be. All the jugs underneath created a false sense of mass. They walked it over to the water as Brad waded in with his corner. As he waded in deeper and deeper the raft held itself up! Brad was up to his waist when the whole raft was floating on its own. The boys all had huge smiles on their faces as Brad let out a whooping "WHOO YEAH!!! IT FLOATS!!! IT FLOATS!!! YEE HAA!!!"

Brad waded out of the water and climbed on board his new river vessel. He walked from one edge to the other and then from one end to the other. It was a defining moment for him.

"Stable!" he said, "Really stable! We have to make a sail now!" Brad was excited.

The raft sat as level as could be as Brad walked over its deck and it didn't sit down in the water more than five inches. It was extremely buoyant.

Eddie reached down with his foot and shoved Brad off from the bank so he could get the feel of it in deep water. Josh held onto the rope. Brad smiled bigger than anyone had ever seen him smile before. He put his arms up in the air like a prizefighter that had just won the title belt. Brad had something to be proud of and the boys were proud of him for it. At this point they had forgotten the incident on the railroad tracks a few hours earlier.

After a couple minutes, Josh reeled the raft back into the bank and Brad jumped from his new vessel, back to the small sandbar with the boys.

"We have to think about the sail," Eddie said. "What we need to do next is make the tiller and rudder."

"I got a hatchet. I'll go up on the bank and get another pole, a shorter one for the tiller handle and then I was just going to screw it to a piece of plywood cut to look like a rudder," Brad said. "I have another half sheet up on the bank. There's a hand saw up there too."

Josh said, "Me and Eddie will cut the rudder, and you make the handle, how's that?"

"OK," Brad said. He then paused before heading up the bank. "Hey, guys?" he said in a humble tone. Brad looked down at his feet for a second and then looked them right in the eye, "I, uh… appreciate your help on this, and all. I… know I probably don't deserve it, and uhhh, well… thanks. Sorry about calling you pinheads, too."

Josh and Eddie laughed.

"Hey man. No problem," Josh said. "Let's make a tiller."

The three business partners now teamed up on a steering mechanism for Brad's river raft. Brad chopped down a small tree about two inches in diameter and then took the handsaw and cut it to three feet long while the other two boys marked out the shape of the rudder on the half sheet of plywood. Sawdust was flying as the team worked to fabricate the steering system for the raft and it wasn't long before they had it all cut and shaped.

To make the tiller attach to the rudder solidly and not come apart, Brad ingeniously cut a slot in the end of the three-foot pole about three inches long and ¾ inch wide. The tiller handle will slide over the rudder and screws and wood glue will fasten the two together. Josh made two trips to his garage and back to fetch tools and supplies for the project as the other two boys engineered and thought out the design.

After about an hour, the tiller/rudder project was complete. They had a well-designed, sturdy, very functional way of steering the raft. Eddie had even come up with a way of locking the tiller in place to keep a straight-ahead course without having to constantly keep a hand on the tiller—sort of an autopilot for Brad's raft.

Brad was ecstatic. He was grinning most of the evening and couldn't be any happier with his raft and the two guys who stopped to help him. He was a different person that day and felt good for it.

Nightfall on the riverbank stirs up a multitude of bugs, frogs and things that go splash in the water. As the sun goes down the critters come out. And tonight was no different as crickets and bullfrogs sang back and forth to each other from bank to bank.

The boys had worked until they could hardly see what they were doing and then called it quits for the night. They weren't out of energy or enthusiasm. Young boys have plenty of both—they were just out of daylight.

"I have an idea for the sail design," Eddie said. "Shouldn't take too long in the morning if you guys want to meet back here. We're going to need about three more long poles, some thin, but strong, rope and some material for the sail."

"Well, I'll get the poles, no problem," Brad said as he looked up the bank at the dark profiles of hundreds of tall thin trees standing there like sentries watching over his project.

"Dad has lots of rope I can grab, too," Josh said. "Nylon stuff, I think."

"That would be perfect. Strong and thin," Eddie replied. "I'll think about what we can use for sail material and try to come up with it for tomorrow. With any luck we could test sail by noon."

"Awesome," Brad smiled. He probably wouldn't sleep that night.

The boys left the riverbank and made their way back to their respective houses, excited about tomorrow's plans to launch the raft for a test sail. It wasn't Josh and Eddie's raft, but they were pretty enthused about it, nonetheless.

Josh took his mom up on the pot roast offer and, after filling himself on that, he showered and hit the sack. Tired from a full day of private detective work and shipbuilding, he lay down and flicked on his two-dollar ham radio receiver to the AM band, and once again tuned in to another captivating episode of Mystery Theater. He didn't make it to the second scene. Sleep comes easy after hard work.

A few houses down, Eddie pulled the yellow copy from his backpack and crawled into his own bed. With a small light on, he studied each letter, each fragmented word and each line. Trying to fill in the blanks, he took one word at a time and ran through the alphabet. It was a great idea, albeit time consuming, to help solve the puzzle but it only took about five minutes of this before he zonked-out with the yellow copy still in his hand.

CHAPTER THIRTEEN

"Josh, get out of bed! The Sheriff's here!" Emily Baker commanded.

"What?" Josh rolled over sleepily, squinting from the morning light coming through his window.

He looked at his clock on the bedside table: 8:01 a.m.

She yanked the covers off him. "What are you kids into? Tell me before we go downstairs."

"Nothing. Holy cow, Mom! What's going on?"

"The Sheriff is here and wants to speak with you and your father and me. Are you doing anything illegal? Tell me now."

"No. Gosh, Mom," Josh said.

Still bleary–eyed and his left arm half asleep, he rolled out of bed to go throw water on his face. His mom followed.

"Are you sure?" she asked sternly.

"Mom, you know better," Josh replied as he turned on the cold water and made a bowl of his hands.

"OK." She exhaled hard, realizing that mostly, what he was saying was true. "Well, get ready and come on down and we'll see what this is all about," she finished in a calmer voice.

Josh washed his face, quickly brushed his teeth and pulled a comb through his hair a couple of times, getting ready to go greet the Sheriff. He recalled Sheriff Collins and the Mayor at the Town Offices watching over what the three of them were doing, but they were looking up information that was public record. True, they didn't want anyone knowing what they had stumbled across, but it was hardly illegal.

Josh pulled on fresh jeans, a T-shirt and clean socks and headed downstairs. Sheriff Collins was standing at the front door with his hat in his hands speaking with Mr. Baker.

Mrs. Baker was standing to the side of them and all three smiled at Josh as he came to the bottom of the stairs. Sheriff Collins had already reassured the Bakers that their son was not into anything illegal, thus the smiles.

"Mornin' Josh," the Sheriff said with a Chamber of Commerce smile. Josh sensed a different personality today. He was acting a little friendlier and had a very different face on. The Sheriff spoke with a strong mountain accent.

"Good morning, sir," Josh replied respectfully.

"I'm sorry to get you up so early this morning, Josh. I have to head up to Clay County in a little bit and I just wanted to make sure I caught you before we both got busy today."

"It's not a problem at all, Sheriff," Mr. Baker assured him.

Josh looked at his dad.

The Sheriff reached into his pocket and pulled out a piece of paper and unfolded it. "You guys left the original in the copier at the office. I got your name off the sign-in sheet."

Josh's heart skipped a beat as he looked at the tax records for Burl Otis.

"I'll get right to the point, Josh. I'm not sure what your business is with Mr. Otis, you and your friends that is, but I just wanted to warn you that if you don't know him he can be a, uh, let's say, hard man to get along with. Now, it's your business and all, I just wanted to forewarn you of that."

Josh's mind raced for something to say. The right thing to say.

"It's just a little history thing on the town, sir. Nothing more. My friends and I are already a little bored this summer and are just looking stuff up, that's all."

Emily Baker smiled.

The Sheriff continued with his mildly disguised interrogation.

"Oh, that's fine, Josh. Umm. But his tax records?" The Sheriff paused a bit and gave Josh one raised eyebrow. "I mean, it is public record and there is nothing illegal about the information you were looking up, but we at the office were just a little curious why you would collect personal information on a man like Burl Otis, you understand." He gave Josh the eyebrow again. "Mr. Otis might have something to say to you if he knew you were checking up on him, ya know."

"Yes sir."

"And I am just looking out for your safety, you realize."

"Yes sir." He paused. "Really, it's just a project we're doing. That's all. Just looking up some town history and early settlement information." Josh said.

"Oh, that's fine." The Sheriff smiled and looked at the Bakers. "I wish more young folks would take an interest in our town and its history. I would have a lot less youthful indiscretion calls to check out. Less trouble when kids are kept busy, ya know." He smiled again.

The Bakers smiled back proudly and Mr. Baker put his arm around his son who stood beside him.

"OK, I won't take up any more of your time here, folks. I gotta get up to Clay and take care of some business, but I appreciate your time this morning."

"It's no problem at all, Sheriff. We appreciate your looking after the safety of the kids," Mrs. Baker said.

"Well, that's what I'm here for," He said, putting his hat back on. He looked back at Josh and winked. "If there is anything I can help you with, come and talk to me, OK?"

"I sure will," Josh replied.

The Sheriff bade the Bakers a wonderful day as he stepped out the door into the garage and proceeded to his cruiser. Josh thought it a little strange that he had made a special stop on a busy morning to show concern for Josh's safety.

Josh couldn't believe that they had left the tax record in the copier but remembered well how it had happened. They had just made the last copy of what they needed when the two vehicles out in front of the Town Offices decided to try to occupy the same twenty feet of pavement. He remembered the screeching tires and the sudden crunch. In all the excitement, they had forgotten to go back in and put the tax record back into its file. Apparently the next person who needed to make a copy was the Sheriff. What luck!

As Josh turned to head upstairs, he thought he heard the clank of something metallic in the garage but gave it no thought and reformatted his mind for a day of sail design.

About an hour later, with a belly full of breakfast, Josh rode out of his garage on his bike, headed down over the river bank, past the honeysuckle and lilacs, through the milkweed patch and arrived at the small sand bar area where he was greeted by his friends who had beaten him there by about thirty minutes. Josh walked down the bank with about one hundred feet of a flexible, but very strong rope that he had grabbed from his dad's garage, and noticed a large, lightweight painter's tarp and a bag of various hardware supplies lying on the bank beside three new, long poles that had just been cut.

Josh dropped the rope off of his shoulder, beside the other supplies, and said, "Hey, guys." Josh gave Eddie a look and mouthed silently, "I need to talk to you."

Brad turned around. "Hey, Baker. What kept you?" he joked.

Brad was all smiles again this morning.

"Had to do something for Mom and Dad," he replied. "Did you guys get anything done or were you waiting for me?"

"Ha Ha," Eddie said. "We put it back in the water and figured we could finish it out there. Once we add the sail system, it's going to get heavier and, hey, it's stable enough to work on, anyway."

"Yeah. True. Why keep lifting it, right?" Josh replied.

"Right."

Brad was out on the raft adding screws and construction glue to the tiller system as Eddie looked over the poles and the nine-foot by twelve-foot lightweight painter's tarp. Josh walked over close to Eddie. "The Sheriff was at my house at 8 o'clock," he whispered. Eddie's eyes widened as he glanced out at Brad. Brad hadn't heard Josh because he was using a cordless, battery-powered drill to secure the tiller system. As Brad drilled, Josh spoke to his friend.

"We left Burl Otis' tax records in the copier yesterday. Remember the crash outside?"

Brad drilled some more, as Eddie thought about it.

"We didn't go back inside," Eddie recalled. "We walked off and left it right in the copier." He paused as Brad stopped drilling. Brad resumed.

"What did he want?" Eddie asked.

Josh looked at Brad. "He said that Burl Otis is a mean old dude and that he is concerned for our safety. He said that if Otis knew we were in his business, he would have something to say to us."

"The Sheriff is concerned for our safety because we were looking up tax records?" Eddie asked, disbelieving. He paused and thought. "Doesn't sound right, does it?"

"I didn't think so either. He was a totally different person this morning, too. Real warm and cozy. Remember yesterday, the way he was?" Josh asked.

"Yeah. Him and the Mayor."

"I think we're ready to do the sail now!" Brad called out from the helm. "This is done!" Brad said it in a proud tone and without knowing it, ended Josh and Eddie's private conference.

Josh and Eddie looked at each other, both knowing they could talk more about it later, and started grabbing poles, wood blocks, all the hardware, and the large paint-covered tarp to go fabricate their sail for Brad's raft.

The design was basic but well thought out and the materials they had on hand would work perfectly. The main mast would stand about five feet back from the front of the raft and be centered side to side. They would secure it to the deck of the boat with blocks of wood around the bottom of it and screwed into place. Once in place, it would stand about twelve feet tall.

Four ropes would come from the top of the mast, running to each corner of the raft to keep the mast from falling over in any direction. Once the mast was in place, the boys would attach the "yardarms," two horizontal poles on the mast, about seven feet apart, onto which they would attach the sail. The top arm could be lowered and raised with a single rope or line.

The boys jumped right in on the final phase of Brad's raft project as Eddie sort of took charge and called out directions. Neither of the other two seemed to mind, since the sail system was Eddie's design, anyway. The three "business partners" all worked together drilling, screwing, cutting, tying, securing, rigging and finally, attaching the sail onto their sturdy, new river craft. In a couple of hours, they were done. To the three boys, it was a work of art.

"Man, just look at it!" Brad exclaimed proudly. "It's way better than I ever imagined!"

"It *is* very cool," Eddie admitted.

Josh was wide-eyed in amazement, standing back on the shore looking at it and shaking his head. "What a cool project. Ya think it will work?"

"Only one way to find out, I guess," Eddie said. "Let's get it out there and head downriver."

Josh walked over to the pile of supplies and grabbed an old life ring with a long length of rope attached to it and tossed it up onto the raft. He had snagged it from his garage that morning, figuring that it might be a good idea to have some type of a lifesaving device on board in case the maiden voyage didn't turn out so well. They had all seen Titanic!

"Are ya ready, Captain?" Josh asked, looking at Brad.

Brad's chest puffed up a little and at the same time a bit of a nervous look came over his face. Perfectly normal for a rookie river pilot, of course. He would, for the first time, be piloting his very own river vessel and be responsible for the safety of two crew members. He had never had to be responsible for anything in his life. It was a real defining moment for Brad.

"I'm ready!" He said confidently. "Untie the dock lines!"

As Eddie stood on the raft with one hand holding onto the newly constructed mast, Josh untied the line that secured the raft to the riverbank and tossed it onto the deck of the boat. Eddie then grabbed it and coiled it up into a neat circle on the left or port side of the vessel. Brad took his position at the helm, disabled Eddie's autopilot system for the time being, and took hold of the tiller with a confident hand.

With the Captain at the helm, Josh then pushed off of the bank with one foot as he stepped on board with the other. That gave them enough momentum to get out a few feet and into the flow of the river.

It was a perfect day for a test float—just a slight down-river current with a warm summer breeze blowing back up the river. The boys could float down a few hundred yards and then turn it around, hoist sail, and hopefully let the breeze carry them back to where they had started.

As the raft made its way out to the middle of the river it picked up a little speed. Not much, maybe something a little faster than walking speed, but enough to where the water flowing under the raft and through the maze of jugs made a pleasant gurgling, sloshing sound, letting the crew know that they were making way. The boys all smiled.

Brad pulled the tiller this way and that a few times and the raft responded beautifully by turning left and right. The rudder seemed perfect. Not too big and not too small—very manageable for sure. They had done a great job engineering and constructing the steering mechanism for Brad's milk jug raft.

Once out in the middle of the river, Brad turned it and pointed the front, or bow, of the raft straight downriver. He then reached down and enabled Eddie's autopilot system to see how it worked. Just two ropes, really, that ran off the tiller and tied off to two points on the deck. It would hold the tiller in a straight-ahead position and give the Captain his hands to do other things on board. It, too, worked great.

The boys couldn't be happier with their accomplishment, and their faces showed it. There were grins all around.

As the three headed down river, Josh's mind drifted away for a bit, to the old can and the document inside. How it had fallen into their lap and how it was changing their lives. It had helped Josh and Eddie make a new friend in Giselle and had indirectly had a hand in changing the attitude of a town bully. Time would tell if the change was permanent or not, but so far the boys cautiously enjoyed each other's company. Business partners, at least. It also occurred to Josh that they had only scratched the surface of decoding the document they had found. They had deciphered the *Southern Jewel* part of it, and that had given them a lot of information, but what about the rest of it? There were more lines and a little sketch to study. Josh made a mental note to himself to revisit the document before they went camping and to take a copy with them. He also made a note to call Giselle and fill her in on what had been going on the past couple of days and to let her know of their plans of how to get downriver to Tater Holler.

"Let's drift down to the deep hole where the rope swing is and then turn it around and see how this thing sails," Brad said.

"Sounds good!" Eddie said with a smile. "Josh, I'll need you to help me pull this sail up."

"No!" Brad snapped. Josh and Eddie both looked at him, knowing that at any time, he could break out of his pleasant mood and return to his old habits. He paused. "I just mean… that I wanted to do it all by myself so I could… you know…"

"You want to be able to single hand it." Eddie finished.

"Yeah." He paused again. "Can you just call out what to do to me and see if I can do it?"

"Sure," Eddie said. "You're right. That's a good idea."

Brad sort of looked away. "I didn't mean to snap at you like that. I really do appreciate all you've done."

"OK, that's cool," Eddie returned. "I'll call out what to do."

Brad nodded, a little embarrassed.

Brad's transformation, if there would be one, would take some time and a little patience.

Josh pondered over Brad's passion to be so independent. Why did he not want any help sailing his raft, only help with building it? Was Brad planning an escape like the lonely log that would make its way from river to river and finally end up at the ocean where there are no boundaries? Had he had enough of his father that he would ditch his hometown by way of water and leave everyone behind? Or did he simply enjoy fishing by himself and didn't want any partners when hunting for the big one?

Either way, it was Brad's raft and he could do with it whatever he wanted. Josh just wanted a ride downriver on a flat-bottomed craft, to go talk to the guy who might hold some secrets to a 1903 train robbery.

The boys drifted quietly for a few hundred yards and watched as a muskrat slid down the bank and into the water. Turtles sunned themselves on logs and a nice bass busted top-water about twenty yards in front of their raft. Josh wished he had a fishing pole with him. As they drifted in and out of the shade of the trees that grew tall along the riverbanks they could feel the heat of the summer sun come and go on their skin.

As they approached the turnaround point, three boys on the riverbank were hauling in the rope swing that was tied high into a tree. It hung over a deep hole close to the bank and made for marvellous fun in the summer heat.

A young man grabbed onto the swing and walked it as far back as he could and then ran forward until he ran out of river bank and was out over the water. His momentum carried him outward and when he reached the point over the deep hole, he let go and with a loud *"whhooo yeah,"* did a perfect back flip and came down feet first. His friends laughed and applauded his efforts.

Josh, Eddie and Brad laughed too and envied the other three boys a bit as they took advantage of the river's cooling effects on a sultry summer day.

"Are you ready?" Eddie asked.

"Yeah, let's do it!" Brad said.

"OK. Now, what we will do is, pull up the sail and tie it off before we turn. The sail will probably act like a brake until we turn, which will work out just fine. And then after we turn, the sail should fill up with wind and carry us back upstream… I hope," Eddie said.

"What do you want me to do?" Josh asked.

"Just hang loose with the life ring in case all goes wrong," Eddie replied.

The boys all laughed.

Eddie stood by the mast as Brad held his position at the helm and Josh moved to the side of the raft, out of the way of the sail rigging that would be hoisted.

"OK, ready? Go ahead and grab that line right there…
aaannd… HOIST!"

Brad pulled firmly on the single line that the boys had rigged
to lift the top yardarm and the sail that was attached to it. It pulled
up smoothly, just as designed.

"OK, tie it off by doing figure eights around that cleat right
there," Eddie said.

Brad did what Eddie called out and in seconds the sail was
up and secured. Eddie showed Brad how to finish the knot to make
it lock itself.

"Alright, ready to do a one-eighty?" Eddie challenged.

"Ready," Brad replied.

"OK…. Ready… COME ABOUT!" Eddie called out.

Josh smirked a bit at Eddie's newfound sailor slang.

Brad eased over on the tiller causing the raft to begin its turn
and, hopefully, start heading the other way. As the raft swung
around in a tight turn, the southeast breeze made its way into the
homemade and very colorful sail as it puffed to life and
immediately began pulling on the mast and the rigging lines. The
force transferred its way through the sail system and after a brief
pause the raft began to move again. The boys were ecstatic. Their
sailing raft was moving upriver! They would not even need to use
the pole to help themselves along! She was sailing on her own!

The sail arced out beautifully and amazed them at how much
force it created with such a small amount of fabric. They could
even turn the entire sail system to optimize the wind at the best
angle to take them faster upstream.

Josh turned around to see the three kids on the bank now
looking at them as the rope swing hung limp. It was their turn to be
envious. They looked on in amazement as the boys made their way

upriver on a homemade vessel with no motor at all. Just the power of the wind carried them along, overtaking the strength of the current.

In reality, they were all lucky, the guys on the raft *and* the kids on the shore. All six of them lived along the banks of the beautiful Elk River and were enjoying summer the way kids were meant to enjoy summer. Country style!

GISELLE O'CONNER

Only the light of the computer screen illuminated her room as well as her warm hair and green eyes that first captured Josh and Eddie's attention... but mostly Josh.

Giselle scrolled screen after screen looking for anything that might give her some more information about *Southern Jewel*. She couldn't figure out Mr. Mansfield's curiosity in the matter and was also confused by how the Sheriff and the Mayor acted at the Town Office. It seemed that everyone was looking over their shoulders now, which made the matter even more of a mystery.

Giselle had searched out some genealogical facts and had been digging for a couple of hours on the *Mansfield* name.

She found a branch of the not-so-popular-for-the-area name and traced it right down to a baby born about 57 years ago by the name of Elton Jacob Mansfield. Not so difficult. But it didn't tell her much, other than the Mansfields had been in the area for about 150 years. What was it about him that was so peculiar? She searched on and see what she could dig up on Sheriff Collins.

As the night went on Giselle researched the name and isolated it to the Elk River area. The genealogical website was full of the information she needed.

Sheriff Collins' father's name was Thomas Collins and his mother's name was Elizabeth. They were both from the area and their families had been there for generations, just like the Mansfields. That was the one thing that was beginning to be the common denominator — everyone who was looking over their shoulders had an extensive family history in the Elk River Valley. All of these families traced back to before the time of the train robbery. The Otis family, the Collins family, and the Mansfields. Curious and interesting, but maybe just coincidence.

.

Now it was Mayor Billingsworth's turn.

"Giselle?"

She jumped nearly out of her seat as her bedroom door eased open.

"Oh my gosh, Mom."

"Sorry, honey. Hey, we have to be at the University at 8:00 in the morning. Do you know what time it is?"

"Yikes," she said as she looked at her clock beside her bed and then confirmed the time on her computer: 12:53 a.m. "OK, I'm done for the night."

Her mom blew her a kiss and pulled the door back to its slightly open position.

Billingsworth would have to wait.

CHAPTER FOURTEEN

The test sail had gone beautifully. The raft was stable, steered well, and sat high in the water, which would be perfect for taking the boys over the shallow shoals. It was now time to go camping and search out a man named Burl Otis. Back to business.

Josh and Eddie had agreed to meet Brad the next morning at "Brad's Landing," as they called it, the area where Brad had put together his vessel and opened the door to new adventures in his life, and new friends too.

Eddie showed up at Josh's house at ten o'clock the following morning with his backpack full of the supplies he would need for the next couple of days — canned food, bottles of water, matches, beef jerky, a hatchet, a knife, rope, his tent and his sleeping bag to name a few. Josh was still busy stuffing his own backpack full of necessary items when Eddie walked into his garage.

"You still packing?"

Josh turned around to see his friend stepping from the driveway into the garage.

"Hey. I was thinkin' of takin' the deer hide," Josh said.

"OK" Eddie paused a second. "The real one? How come?" Eddie walked over to where Josh was provisioning his backpack and lay his down on the garage floor.

"I don't know. I just thought we could look at it while we are camping. Try to figure out more of it."

"You got room in your pack?"

"Yeah. I'll put it in this tube and then let it stick out the top of the backpack."

Josh walked over to the corner of the garage where the old red milk can sat and reached for the lid to pull it off. The lid lay loose on the top of the can and Josh thought this a little peculiar, remembering he had put it on tight the last time they had the document out, over at Eddie's garage. *The clank of something metallic.*

"Did you throw away that old can of tuna from last year?" Eddie joked.

Josh smirked as he lifted the lid off of the can and looked down into the emptiness and immediately his stomach knotted. His face was white as a sheet as he turned and looked at Eddie. He didn't have to say anything at all. Eddie knew something was wrong as he stepped over to the can to see for himself. It was gone.

"Oh man," Josh said, as his hand went to his forehead and he stared off into thought.

"Are you sure you put it back in there?"

"Oh yeah. Remember at your garage? I took it off the bench, put it in the can, and pushed the lid on tight. Just now, it was lying there loose."

"Do your parents know about it?"

"No, I haven't told them." He paused for a moment, thinking. "I have no idea who could have come in here and taken it. I can't believe this." Josh shook his head in disbelief.

"It would be awfully bold of someone to do, that's for sure."

"You still have your copy, right?"

"Yeah. I'll run back home and get it so we can study it, like you said."

"Eddie, we have to figure out who took this thing. Nobody knows about it but you, Giselle, and me. She wouldn't have come and gotten it, would she?"

"No, not without talking to us first. I don't think so."

"I guess we should have left it over at your place."

"Well, it doesn't matter. It's not your fault, Josh. Don't worry about it."

Josh said nothing, still in a bit of a daze trying to figure out who and why.

"I'll run home and get that copy," Eddie said.

"I'll be ready to go by the time you get back. Hey, bring some of that fudge."

Eddie grinned as he hopped on Josh's bike to make better time.

"I'll be back."

Still in disbelief, Josh continued his packing and scanning his memory for who could have known of the can and the document and who would have known enough to steal it.

In total, only three others could have any knowledge of what they had found. Elton Mansfield found Josh's yellow legal pad copy, but he would have needed to have had some knowledge of the can and the document in the first place to have any reason to come and steal it. Second was the Sheriff or someone else in the office, who had found the copy of Burl Otis' tax records in the copier. But that would be a stretch. They would have to have known the story of the Otis' and the train robbery. It was possible, but not likely. And then even less likely was Brad Radcliffe, who would have stolen it just for the sake of being mischievous. If it was Brad, though, Josh figured he would have returned it or at least confessed to taking it since Josh and Eddie helped him out so much on the raft. Brad would be more likely to steal tools or a bike or something he could use or sell. Not a deer hide from a milk can. Maybe *new* Brad wouldn't steal anything at all.

It was baffling, to say the least, but it was gone, and they were not likely to get it back.

Josh finished his packing and Eddie returned on the bike with the yellow legal pad copy of the document in his back pocket. The two friends grabbed their backpacks, closed the garage door, and headed down over the riverbank where they would walk about a half-mile to *"Brad's Landing."*

They walked along the muddy banks on their bike trail that led them across small streams that emptied into the river, and through the thick milkweed patch to where they had first seen Brad constructing his river raft. As they began dropping down towards the river, they saw Brad already down at the raft, double checking knots and neatly coiling up the ropes that controlled the sail on his raft. Neatness on a vessel is mandatory.

"Below, there!" Eddie called out in his best pirate voice.

Brad looked up over his shoulder, continuing his work, and acknowledged his new friends. "Hey guys! Ready to go?" he asked enthusiastically.

The boys made their way down to the water's edge, loaded their gear onto the raft and untied the line that secured the raft to the shore. Their downriver adventure was about to begin. It was finally time to go find Burl Otis and try to get some answers to some questions about a stash of Confederate gold that was robbed from a train one rainy night in 1903.

"OK Shove off!" Brad gave the command.

Once again, Josh put one foot on the riverbank and one foot on the raft and gave a hard push. Eddie grabbed the long pole and pushed them out into the current once again. Brad was at the tiller and Josh situated himself on the starboard or right side of the raft. Once they reached midstream, Eddie put away the pole, and the raft was under Brad's control. He held the tiller steady, keeping them on a very straight course down the middle of the Elk River. They had about three miles to drift and all three boys were settling in for a smooth, relaxing cruise. There was a steady, warm wind blowing in their faces, which would mean when Brad was sailing the raft back upriver by himself, he would have a perfect tailwind. It was a magnificent day.

They went a short distance and to the right was the tree swing that, a day earlier, was hurling three adolescent boys out into the cool river. Today it hung limp.

Josh watched a water snake drop from a tree limb into the river, and a turtle duck his head underwater.

They had drifted about a mile when Eddie spotted Tiny Brooks sitting on his small and sagging fishing dock. Tiny was an old black man that the boys liked very much. Nobody could tell a tale like Tiny Brooks, and he had a lot to tell. Tiny, in his early seventies, had seen and heard a lot of things that went on up and down the river. He was a fun man to set around a campfire with, and Josh and Eddie had done that a few times.

As they got a little closer, the boys all waved and Josh shouted out, "How many ya caught today, Tiny?"

"Hey, boys! I'm doin' alright." Tiny Brooks lifted a stringer full of nice-sized catfish that would most likely be on his dinner table that evening. He smiled big.

"Whatcha got there?" He nodded his head toward the plywood contraption with milk jugs tied to the bottom. Tiny sat there with old worn black pants cut off to just below the knees and an equally vintage khaki shirt. He was barefoot and wore an old Panama on his head with his favorite fishing lures hooked to it, along with extra hooks for bait fishing.

"It's my new raft!" Brad replied proudly. "My buddies helped me put it together!"

"Buddies?" Tiny mumbled to himself.

Josh and Eddie looked at each other and grinned, still not believing the change in Brad Radcliffe.

"That's a fine lookin' raft," he assured Brad while nodding his head. "Fine lookin' raft." Tiny looked at Josh and Eddie and then at Brad. He knew Brad and knew of his reputation very well. Tiny also knew Brad had a tough home life.

"Thank you, Mr. Brooks."

"Where you boys headed?" he asked, sitting up a little.

"Tater Holler," Eddie returned.

Tiny Brooks got a look of concern on his face and then stood up. "Why you goin' to Tater Holler? They's nothin' there." He stepped closer to the river.

Josh and Eddie looked at each other.

Josh responded, "We're just going to do some camping. Just a couple nights."

Tiny turned his head a bit in disbelief and pulled his eyebrows down as he studied their answer. "There's no place to camp up there, boys, unless you pitch on a well site. But that's not good camping." He paused a bit and put his hands on his hips as they drifted a little further downstream. "What else you up to?" He squinted.

They could get away with nothing with Tiny. He was too old and too wise and knew teenage boys too well, having been one once.

Eddie was chewing on his lip when Josh said, "We're gonna go find Burl Otis. Ya' know him?"

Eddie looked at Josh and hoped he knew what he was doing. He would take two more people into his confidence. Tiny and Brad.

Tiny Brooks' look of concern turned into a look of worry. "Why… would you boys be looking for Burl Otis? I hear he's a nasty old man. You boys know that, right?" When Tiny said it his nose and mouth wrinkled as if he had just eaten a lemon.

The raft continued to drift as Tiny now walked along the riverbank, talking to the boys out in the river. They got further and further away as Tiny's eyes stayed fixed on them.

"It's a real long story, Tiny," Josh hollered back. "We'll see you in a couple days!"

"I'll be back up this way in a couple hours, Tiny." Brad hollered. "Don't catch 'em all!"

Tiny Brooks stood on the riverbank with his arms down at his sides. The look of worry never left his face as the three adventurers drifted out of sight around the bend of the river.

"Hope you boys know what you're doin'," he whispered to himself.

The raft continued to drift until they came to the old one-lane bridge that spanned the river. The bridge was still in use, although ancient and rusty. Someone had painted it baby blue a few years back, which made the old iron structure a site to see and an icon on the Elk River.

As they drifted under the old bridge, cars crossed above them, and one could see the boards move that were used for the road decking. As the vehicles drove over, you could hear the *boom, boom, boom* as the boards rattled around under the weight of the heavy cars. A new bridge would be a marvelous idea sometime soon.

Once past the bridge, it was just about a half-mile to the shoals that they would have to navigate. It would be a proper test of the boys' seamanship.

Eddie said, "I think we will have to stay to the left side of the shoals. That's where the break is where we can squeeze over the rocks. It's the deepest there."

"OK," said Brad. "Josh, can you go to the front as a spotter and Eddie can get the pole?"

"Yeah" Josh and Eddie answered in unison.

"Hey Brad, you're getting the hang of this," Eddie assured him with a grin.

Brad returned the grin and nodded. His way of saying thanks.

"You'll have a hard time coming back across these rocks by yourself, though."

"I was thinkin' about that, too. I'll manage. I'll use the pole."

They said nothing at all for a couple of minutes as they floated closer and closer to the shoals. Brad began steering them to the left side of the river and spotted the gap they needed to squeeze through. It was about twice the width of the raft and, to make it difficult, they would have to go way to the left and angle back through it. The gap pointed from the side of the river to the middle and would take careful steering by Brad and poling expertise by Eddie. Josh's job as a spotter would be critical, too. They could not go over any sharp rocks or else they would puncture a row or two of jugs from front to rear. Maybe twenty jugs. If that happened, they would lose buoyancy and sink lower into the water and then they would hit more rocks. There could be no mistakes.

"OK guys, are we ready?" Eddie asked.

They were all a little tense as Brad blew out a breath of air from between his pursed lips, staring straight ahead all the while.

"We can do it." Josh fired up his team. "We're lookin' good."

Eddie had the long pole in hand as Josh got down on his hands and knees to get the best perspective of the water depth.

"It's getting shallow," he said. "Looks good though. Straight ahead."

Brad held the tiller with a steady hand as the water under them gurgled with turbulence and the raft rocked slightly in the light rapids.

"Two feet," Josh called out.

They were angled perfectly for the gap as Eddie kept the raft from drifting by sticking the long pole into the river bottom every few feet.

The raft now sped up just a little as they entered the more turbulent water of the shoals. Rocks showed themselves, jutting out of the water on either side of them, but straight away still looked good.

"A little right! A little right," Josh called out, spotting a large, submerged stone coming up.

Eddie poled them a little to the right as Brad held a steady tiller.

"A foot and a half! We're good. We're not hitting bottom! Hold it straight!" Josh called again.

"Very cool," Brad whispered as he beamed.

The raft was now moving faster than it ever had and all three boys' hearts were pumping hard with excitement and pure adrenaline.

"Less than a foot! Hold it steady! We're good!" Josh called out excitely. "I can't believe we're not hitting!"

They were now in the shallowest and fastest part of the gap and were still sitting high in the water and, even with all three of them on the raft, plus all the camping gear, they never touched bottom once. The water rushed through the jugs underneath and the raft wobbled and rocked to the motion of the river. The boys' balance never wavered, and they felt that they were one with the river and in tune with nature at its best.

It occurred to Brad, once again, that even with a pleasant wind, coming back the other way by himself, and with the sail up, would be challenging.

The boys rode the current for a few more yards, with Brad holding the tiller and Eddie working the pole to keep them centered while Josh did the spotting. The swift current suddenly spit the boys out the other side of the shoals and into the placid waters, more like a lake than a river. It was smooth and calm and as quickly as the rapids had begun—they had ended. The guys had done it!

"Whoo hooo!!!" the three of them cheered. "Yeah!"

"Nice job guys!" Josh gushed. "Wow!"

The kids were all grins as they all took a break and just drifted for a moment.

"That was a rush!" Brad said, still beaming. "That was outstanding!"

"That *was* fun," Eddie agreed. "I thought we were gonna drift left, and I was like *Oh... Man!*" Eddie illustrated by tilting his open hands at an angle.

"I looked back and Brad's face was as white as a ghost when we were in the shallow part." Josh laughed. They all laughed.

"Alright. Tater Holler... next stop!" Brad exclaimed, still smiling.

"It's just right up there, around where those trees are hanging out over the water," Josh said. He indicated an area that was about a half a mile away. Just a few more minutes.

The boys continued to drift and the warm wind continued to blow in their faces as they made their way to the landing point where Josh and Eddie would disembark and begin their land journey to find Burl Otis.

Brad steered the craft closer to the left side of the river, gradually making their way to the wide landing where the boys could step off. There was a dirt road that ran parallel with the river, just up on the riverbank a few feet. As they neared the landing, they could see there was a small stream that flowed out of Tater Holler. The stream ran under a small bridge that the dirt road ran across, and then under a small train bridge, then emptied into the Elk River, just above the landing. The landing area looked much like their very own sand and rock bar that the boys spent so much time on in the summer, but this one was much less shady.

Brad eased the raft up to the landing while Eddie slowed them down with the pole and, with a slight nudge, the raft eased to a halt perfectly at their river destination. The mouth of Tater Holler!

"Nice job… nice job," Eddie said, putting the pole back into its storage position.

Josh grabbed his backpack and tossed it over onto the bank. Eddie did the same and then turned to Brad and took a deep breath. Brad stuck out his hand to Eddie, and Eddie grabbed it and gave it a firm shake. "Thanks, man. It's an awesome raft," he said.

"Couldn't have done it without ya."

Josh patted Brad on the back with his bare hand one time. "We'll see you in two days, okay?"

"I'll be here, buddy!" Brad smiled. "Twelve o'clock noon, right?"

"Twelve noon," Josh confirmed.

The two shook hands and Josh and Eddie hopped off the raft.

"Do you want us to help set the sail before we go?" Eddie offered.

"No, I'm not headin' back right away. I brought my pole. I think I'll fish awhile here in the tailwaters of the shoals and then go meet up with Tiny."

"Okay… Don't miss the wind, though. It'd be a long pole home."

"You guys be careful. I'll see you in two days."

Josh and Eddie Picked up their packs and made their way up the riverbank to the dirt road that ran along the river. They stood on the road and looked up at the holler where they would be hiking. There was a path that led up into the holler that the boys could start out on but would probably have to deviate from it at some point to find Burl Otis. They looked back down at Brad who was getting his fishing gear ready when, from up in the holler, came a high velocity projectile. CRACK... CRACK... KATOOOSH!!!

CHAPTER FIFTEEN

A large stone crashed through the tree limbs, ultimately hitting the water about five feet from Brad's raft. Brad jumped and yelled up at the boys in disbelief, "Hey! Whatta ya doing?"

They paused, looking back up into the holler.

"We didn't do it," Josh shouted. "It came from up on the hill!"

"Who keeps throwing stuff at us?" Eddie exclaimed.

"I don't know. It came way across the tops of the trees up there. Whoever it is has a good arm." Josh replied.

"Could be, they weren't throwing at us," Eddie suggested.

"Yeah. Well, let's go." Josh wasn't convinced.

Josh would not waste any time on it. They had a long hike ahead of them and they both wanted to get back to the business of treasure hunting. They had taken two days off to help Brad with his raft and were itching to learn more about the night of the train robbery and what happened to that portion of the *Southern Jewel*.

Early that morning, Josh had called Giselle's cell phone and left her a message, updating her on everything that had been happening with Brad and his raft, and promised to call her when they got back from their camping trip in two days.

Josh and Eddie had a longstanding agreement never to bring cell phones camping with them, but Josh had waived that rule in case Burl Otis turned out to be the monster that everyone said he was. He would leave it turned off and only turn it on a couple times a day to check in with his parents, and would have it in the unlikely event of an emergency. Josh and Eddie liked this rule because the reason for going camping was not to sit around the campfire texting.

The two friends waved to Brad and stepped over to the beginning of the rustic trail to begin their journey up into the mouth of Tater Holler. Tater Holler was very typical of any holler in West Virginia. It was simply two large hills that came down to meet in a "V" at the bottom, and usually had a small creek or stream flowing down the middle where the mountain rain showers would run off and flow down to the river.

The path would lead them parallel with the stream straight up into the depths of the holler and, hopefully, to the original Tater Holler Homestead of Burl Otis. They really didn't know what to expect of Mr. Otis, but by all indications, and what people had told them, and the research that they had done themselves, he would be a mean, rough man who didn't really want to be bothered by the outside world, much less by two kids prying into his past. This situation would require their best finesse.

The two boys hiked their way up into the woods, Eddie keeping an eye out for a "stone thrower" as they walked.

The path was well worn at first, and the forest smelled great as they wandered deeper into the pines and oaks and hickory trees that stood tall and strong. Squirrels scurried up trees as they heard the footsteps of the two boys invading their habitat.

The stream flowed nicely with fresh, clean water for the boys to refill their canteens. The moist banks, just above the small stream, were covered with fern and rhododendron which helped provide wonderfully fresh air, and Josh caught himself thinking of how his mom loved both of these beautiful plants.

Their path took them about twenty yards up the hill from where the stream flowed and when that side of the holler got too steep or rocky, the path would switch back and run down across the stream and up the other side for a while. They had to be careful stepping on the slippery sandstone as they forded the streams. One twisted ankle would be the end of their adventure and, even worse, the other guy would have to help the injured off the hill. They knew this and took all their usual precautions such as cutting themselves a five-foot walking stick, about an inch and a half thick, for balance and assistance in negotiating the steep banks. A comfortable walking stick is a wonderful friend in the woods. The boys hiked on.

About an hour into their climb they dropped down to the stream to refill the water supply and take a momentary break. Eddie peeled off his backpack and set it on the ground. Josh did the same and, as they kneeled down to top off the canteens, they heard a heavy rustle in the leaves about a hundred yards up the hill from where they were.

"Deer?" Eddie asked.

By then, Josh was face down in the water, sucking in a big mouthful straight out of the stream.

"Probably," he said, coming up for air long enough to acknowledge his friend. He then scooped a big handful and washed off his sweaty face and hair. Eddie did the same.

"Didn't sound like he was running, though."

Josh chuckled a little. "He knows he can outrun us."

Eddie grinned and nodded.

"Why don't we break off from the path here and head straight up to the top and walk the ridgeline for a while? We could probably see more from up there and figure out which direction we need to go," Eddie suggested.

Josh snarled his top lip, looking up at the steep hill they would have to climb.

"I mean, the path is almost gone anyway, and it's getting pretty brushy. Whatta' ya' think?" Eddie added.

"Alright," Josh said, not very enthusiastically "we're giving up our water supply, ya know."

"I have sixty ounces in three bottles, and you have about the same, right? Plus the canteens?" Eddie asked.

"Yeah."

They heard the slow rustle in the leaves and sticks up on the hill again and both boys' heads pivoted to look. The sound was coming from up on the hilltop where the boys were planning to trek.

"We'll just follow that slow-moving deer," Josh joked.

Eddie grinned, but didn't laugh. A deer would have been in the next county by now, but he said nothing to his friend as they picked up their backpacks and began their climb. *Could be a fox or a raccoon,* he thought.

The assent was steep and slow as the boys gave it their all to climb up to the ridge which would give them a better perspective of the surrounding terrain, and the hike that still lay ahead of them. Their walking sticks really showed their worth, as they dug them into the side of the hill to push themselves up the steep grade. Josh and Eddie used the "grape vines" that grew up the sides of the trees and webbed the forest, grabbing onto them like ropes and pulling themselves up the hill.

The boys stopped occasionally to catch their breath and give their legs a break, and then would trudge on. After about an hour they reached the ridgeline where they both plopped down for a much-deserved break.

"Man!" Josh said, out of breath and throwing his backpack to the ground. "I'm pooped."

Eddie dropped his backpack in the small clearing and lay down, using the backpack as his pillow. "That... was a climb," he said.

Josh looked around while catching his wind, looking up and down the length of the hill they were atop. "Looks like a pretty well-worn path up here," he said.

"Yeah." Eddie raised his eyebrows. "Deer must run this ridge like crazy."

The guys took only a minute to re-energize and were up exploring their surroundings. They walked over to a muddy area that sat square in the middle of the path that ran along the ridgeline.

"Yeah. Plenty of deer tracks," Eddie confirmed his belief.

Josh wandered a few feet further ahead of him. "Hey, that's not all that's running this ridge, unless the deer are wearing boots." The mud was wet and the huge boot tracks were recent. Eddie walked over.

A fresh trail of flat-bottomed shoes or boots, at least a size 12, ran the length of the muddy section of the path on the ridge. There was no tread at all on the soles, which seemed odd.

"That's a big shoe," Eddie observed. "Probably a hunter scouting deer already," Eddie said, adding his deer-hunting knowledge he learned from his father.

Josh wandered around some more.

"But look here. Here are some old tracks of the same shoe. It's got to be. They're going both directions. The same shoe!"

"So, he scouts a lot."

"Hmm."

Over to the side of the ridge there was a clearing that the boys would have to knock down some small brush to get to. Josh pulled out a two-foot machete from his pack and stepped into the brush, hacking his way through it. He cleared a path big enough for him and Eddie to walk through and when they did, they were awestruck. The view was spectacular. They could see all the way down over the hill to the baby blue bridge that rattled with the traffic that rolled over it, probably a mile away.

When they looked to the right, they could see the Elk River snake its way up the valley where they lived, all the way to the island that split the river upstream from their house. They had never had this perspective of the hometown they grew up in and stood for many minutes gazing around and pointing out places and things that they were very familiar with. They could see across the main highway that ran up the valley, and into other hollers that forked off of the Elk River Valley. They could see Glennie's Hill, where they would sled in the wintertime, and Melton's Holler, another place where they like to hike and camp.

The two friends took it all in for a little while and then noticed the sun was getting close to setting behind the far mountain. They needed to get to a campsite within the next couple of hours or else they would be looking for one in the dark.

Josh pulled out his digital camera and took a few shots of the panorama and then the boys stepped back through the brush, Josh going first. Once they cleared the thicket, Josh Baker stood tall and stopped dead in his tracks as he drew a sharp, deep breath. Eddie stopped behind him as both boys froze in sheer terror.

CHAPTER SIXTEEN

The cougar stood over Eddie's backpack, pawing and digging at it, trying to get to the fresh food inside. The two boys were paralyzed with fear and Josh found it hard to breathe. Never in their lives had they been so scared. Mountain lions were indigenous to the hills of West Virginia, but seldom were they actually seen. They are nocturnal, mostly, night hunters that prey on smaller, weaker game animals. The two friends had never heard the eerie scream of a mountain lion that friends and family talked about when telling their best and scariest mountain stories. They had never even seen any tracks in the woods or along the streams or rivers, left behind by a prowling, stealthy, hunting machine like a mountain lion. And yet here they were, twenty yards from the most frightening beast they had ever encountered in the woods.

The cat was chewing on the canvas of Eddie's pack, shaking it, perhaps trying to get to the bacon or jerky that was packed deep within. It shook it violently and then dropped it and then picked it up with its mouth and shook it and dropped it again.

Eddie stood behind Josh and very gently reached forward and grabbed him by the shirt. He gave two short tugs to indicate they should step backward quietly and slowly. Josh was frozen in his tracks and his heart was beating a mile a minute. He couldn't move. Eddie tugged two more times, keeping his eyes fixed on the big cat that was mauling his pack. Josh stood solid in fear, and his eyes were as big as saucers.

The mountain lion had its back to the boys. It then swayed slowly over to check out Josh's pack. A warm breeze blew over Josh's shoulder and he cringed with the terrible luck of that happening. It was then that the cat stopped in his tracks and his nose went up in the air. He moved his head from side to side a bit and then locked in to one position and froze. The cougar had their scent.

Josh and Eddie knew they were in grave danger and terror, once again traveled through their bodies like an electric shock. Eddie breathed heavily, nearly hyper-ventilating.

The animal lowered his head a little, and the boys heard the deep, throaty growl of a predator who knows he has company. His movements were slow and calculated, eyes scanning the forest and weeds for the scent that he detected.

Terrified, Eddie pulled back on Josh's shirt as he took one step back into the thicket of brush and weeds.

Snap!

Eddie stepped on a small branch, breaking it, and instantly the cat's head spun around and its green eyes squinted and focused on a much easier meal than a tied up backpack. His eyes fixed on the two boys and never left them as its head lowered and it slowly turned its entire body to face its new meal. As it moved, the muscles in its legs and shoulders flexed and rippled. The mountain lion began a slow, steady and low crawl towards the two best friends. The cat was now in kill mode. Its mouth opened, and it stopped and crouched to pounce on the boys. The cat's weight shifted to his back legs. At that second, Eddie grabbed Josh and, with all his might, yanked him straight backwards in a desperate effort to run from certain death.

Simultaneously, as Josh and Eddie were flying backward, the big cat sprang and a huge plume of blue smoke blew out of the brush and weeds about thirty yards away, along with a very loud *KA BOOM!!!* It was the unmistakable sound of a black powder muzzleloader. It sounded like a cannon! The cat fell hard to the ground from his midair pounce and landed only a little more than an arm's reach away from where the two boys had fallen back.

Josh and Eddie lay stunned, hearts beating overtime, and eyes still as big as saucers as they stared at the vicious predator before them.

A low throaty growl came from the mountain lion as it exhaled its last ragged breath and closed its eyes. The predator now lay dead at their feet, when it was most apparent, a few seconds earlier, that it would be the other way around.

The loud sound of the fired muzzleloader echoed across the hills and the blue smoke puffed its way out into the clearing. Without moving a muscle, Josh and Eddie's eyes now focused from the enormous cat before them, to the area across the clearing where the life-saving gunshot was fired.

The sun was now sitting about halfway behind a thick, distant cloud and the light had dimmed. From where they were sitting, the shadows were lying across the clearing in a way that kept them from seeing into the brush and trees, to the origin of the gunshot. They listened intently but heard nothing. Josh looked over at Eddie and motioned him to get up. The two boys stood, Josh watching the cat as they did. They slowly stepped out a few feet to get a better look into the weeds across the way. The mountain lion's left front paw twitched one time and Eddie jumped to the left so fast he knocked Josh into a tree.

"Sorry," he whispered.

Josh grinned nervously from one side of his mouth and shook his head.

They stepped out into the clearing a little more to get some distance from the cat and, once again, looked around to see who it was that had saved them from an early grave.

Eddie looked around and then looked at Josh and turned both palms up in disbelief, shaking his head.

"Where would they have gone?" He asked.

There was a pause.

"Over here," a big, deep voice boomed.

Josh and Eddie's heads whipped around to an area one hundred and eighty degrees from where the gun had been fired. They gasped in unison.

"Just makin' sure I don't need a second shot!" the sizeable man said in a low, growling tone.

About twenty yards from them stood a huge, burly, bearded man with a muzzleloader that must have been seven feet long. Josh glanced back at the cat and then quickly back to the big mountain man that now stood near them. It puzzled the boys how the big guy had moved a hundred feet without them hearing one stick break from beneath his heavy feet.

The shooter took on the presence of a bear. He was a large man with slightly bulging eyes and a large round head and face. He was barrel-shaped and must have gone three-hundred pounds. His hair was long and black with silver, and his beard was the same. His eyebrows were thick and his skin was olive in color.

He wore a huge, long duster that fell to his knees and dark work pants and shirt underneath. Eddie thought this unusual for the summer, but of course, said nothing.

"They'll fool ya, ya know. Lay there 'til you turn your back and then make a last jump at ya."

Josh and Eddie looked back at the big cat that lay motionless and quickly stepped well away from it.

"Oh, he's dead. I got a good clean shot." He paused. "Didn't want to do it, but I didn't want to haul two dead boys off the mountain either."

The boys' breathing was just beginning to relax and their minds were taking in all that had just happened to them as the big man stepped out of the weeds and into the clearing.

"We… really appreciate the good aim… sir," Eddie said.

"Otis. Burl Otis is the name."

Josh and Eddie looked at each other in disbelief.

Burl Otis walked over to where the boys were standing. He towered over them. The boy's eyes widened as he stuck out a hand that looked like a bear's paw. Each boy shook his hand.

They couldn't believe it. All the research and all the deciphering and all the hunting and they just run right into him in the middle of the woods. Not only that, he saved their lives!

"What are you boys doing up here, anyway? It's not the best camping hill around," he said, with a look of curiosity.

"Well… we thought… uh… we like to rustic camp!"

Burl Otis gave them the look of a man who won't be fooled. He paused and looked around and then looked back at the boys.

"Ya know boys, this ain't the only cougar in these hills. And Tater Holler is pretty well known for its bear, too. Has a lot to do with the rough terrain, ya know. Steep hills, lots of caves and places for these big guys to hide." He looked at the boys. "You shouldn't be up in here in a tent at night."

Josh looked around at the darkening sky and shrugged.

"We don't have time to get off the mountain now," Josh said. "We gotta stay up here."

"Hmmm," Otis grunted. "Well then, you're just gonna have to stay at my place. You can sleep in the old bunkhouse."

Josh and Eddie looked at each other and, with a nod of approval, Josh decided to go ahead and spill the beans.

"Mr. Otis, uh… we actually… umm… came up here… to find you and… talk to you about something." Josh smiled nervously.

The big cat gave another jerk behind them. All three looked over at it. Otis walked over to the cat that now lay dead, grabbed him under his front legs and threw him over his left shoulder. Both boys gasped in amazement.

Burl Otis gave them a wry smile as if he already knew why they were up there and turned to step towards the path that would lead them to his house. The original Tater Holler Homestead.

"Follow me, boys."

CHAPTER SEVENTEEN

Brad Radcliffe heard a rustling in the brush behind him as he reeled in his line to re-cast and reposition his bait. He smiled when he saw Tiny Brooks emerge from the brush, pulling sticky burrs off his pants as he stepped onto the small, sandy area, where Brad had dropped the boys off just two hours ago.

"Ya doin' any good?"

Brad reached down and lifted a stringer with three nice catfish on it, each about three pounds.

"Yeah… nice. I knew there were some nice ones down here below the shoals. I hear there are even trout in here," Tiny said. With a wide grin, he continued admiring the fish. "Got enough for dinner," he laughed.

Tiny walked to the water's edge.

"I ain't never seen a trout come out of here, Tiny."

Tiny winked at Brad and said, "We'll get some salmon eggs and give it a try sometime." They shook hands.

Brad knew that Tiny would take him to school on trout fishing and he would look forward to it very much. Freshly caught trout cooked on a riverbank fire with butter and lime and maybe a little fresh dill weed. It was a West Virginia delicacy. It was a delicacy anywhere, really.

"I took a walk down here and help ya get this thing back up through the shoals." He paused for a moment, looking out at the river. "Let's get back upstream before evening falls and the wind dies," Tiny said.

"Man, I appreciate it. We have a nice breeze… let's do it."

"Let's do it."

Brad once again reeled in his line and placed his fishing rod and tackle box back on the raft.

"I was thinkin' about rod holders and a permanent mounted box for over here to hold my stuff," Brad said. Brad was very proud of his vessel and was full of ideas of how to fix it up even better.

"You could troll off the back of it if you had rod holders back there," Tiny suggested.

"Hmm." Brad liked it.

Tiny stepped on board as Brad untied the line and prepared to set sail. Brad took the long pole in both hands and moved toward the middle of the boat to shove off. With one good push Brad had the two of them off the sand and floating back out into the river. Brad gave Tiny the full tour of the boat and the quick rundown on how to hoist and set the sail. As they drifted out past where the trees hung over the water, they felt the breeze on their faces and Brad said, "OK Tiny, hoist the sail!"

Tiny Brooks pulled on the line that stretched the colorful sail all the way to the top of the sturdy mast. He then tied off the taught line to a homemade cleat secured to the edge of the raft. The sail still hung limp.

"Now, while I hold the tiller, spin that lower boom around to where the sail faces right over there, right where the wind is coming from." Brad pointed. "Then tie off that line when I tell you."

Tiny did what the Captain said and, as he turned the boom, the sail filled and Tiny could feel the raft begin to accelerate ever so slightly. The boom line he was holding slipped through his hand and he squeezed it a little tighter.

"OK. Tie it off!" Brad said.

Once again Tiny followed orders and Brad pulled hard over on the tiller to begin their upstream sail. Brad locked the tiller in a straight-ahead position and picked up the pole to help the raft along. It only took gentle poling to help propel them upstream at a respectable pace. Tiny, standing on the bow of the raft, turned his head around and once again flashed his brilliant smile, giving Brad his endorsement on a job well done. The summer breeze pulled hard on the sail and Tiny was quite impressed. Brad was smiling, too.

As they approached the shoals, Brad pointed to the gap and explained the strategy for crossing the shoals. Tiny would be on his knees, just as Josh had done, directing and calling out depths and dangerous rock sightings, and Brad would steer and pole when needed. A certain amount of steering could be done by using the pole as well as the tiller.

The crossing went flawlessly as they popped out of the upstream side of the shoals without a single milk jug dragging bottom.

"Ya know Brad, if you are going to plan on traversing these shoals very often, it might be worth our while to spend a day down here moving rocks and rigging up two homemade buoys to mark the channel. Make it about a foot deeper."

Brad reacted with surprise. "That's a great idea, Tiny. Did you say it might be worth *our* while?"

"I'll help ya out with it. Sure."

"How about tomorrow?"

Tiny Brooks grinned and looked toward the shore where a turtle was sunning himself. He thought about what a nice perspective it was to be out on the water looking back at the riverbank. Everything looks different from out here. He had lived along these banks all his life and sure, he had been out on a boat many times, but it was almost like being on stage, people watching you drift by until you got out of sight, especially when you were on a milk jug raft! He was enjoying himself very much on this big, roomy vessel. Tiny thought about how it would be if Brad had a motor on the raft, but no, this was better. This was peace and quiet. No artificial noise could be heard down here on the river. Just the wind in the sail, that's all. Who's in a hurry, anyway?

The speed was a little slower going back upstream, but not much. Brad wondered what kind of speed he could get going downriver with the sail up and the wind at his back. Might be fun to try sometime.

Tiny and Brad carried on a lot of conversation on the trip and Brad soaked up a lot of wisdom from the old river man. They talked about fishing, trapping, baseball, girls, and they talked about Brad's father, who Tiny knew of and knew of his problems. Brad opened up to Tiny, who seemed like an old friend, and Tiny listened when he needed to and gave advice when it was appropriate. It's amazing what a drift on the river will do for a bad attitude or a bad problem.

As they floated along, both river men heard the thunder of a gunshot somewhere behind them and way up in the hills. A fairly common sound in these parts. Just one shot, a clean shot most likely from a hunter with excellent aim and a big gun.

Brad's landing was in sight and both repositioned themselves to begin their approach to shore and to ready the lines to drop the sail at just the right time. Tiny's eyes caught something moving at the top of the bank at about the same time he heard the unmistakable hum of a golf cart. He then heard the click of the locking brake.

Sheriff Collins sometimes liked to cruise the neighborhoods of his jurisdiction on his city-owned golf cart to try to spot infractions of the law that may be a little harder to spot if he were in his cruiser. Boat licenses, or garbage violations or maybe truancy. (Boys around here liked to ditch school and go to the swimming hole late in the school year.) There weren't too many hard crimes going on in this area, so occasionally city officials had to assign each other "busy work" when there was no other work to do.

Collins looked down at Tiny and Brad with his hands on his hips but said nothing while his cart sat parked on Riverview Drive. He studied the craft without moving for a couple of minutes and it worried Brad that there might be a question about the legality of such a vessel. Like *I don't see a DOT sticker anywhere... ya got a license for that contraption?*

But Collins said nothing as he stood there staring from behind his dark sunglasses. As quickly as he appeared, he left. Brad and Tiny just looked at each other and shrugged.

Collins didn't realize it at the time, but he had just learned and seen with his own eyes how Josh Baker and Eddie Debord had made the trip downriver to a point where they could hike up the mountain, meet up with a man named Burl Otis, whose name they got from Collins' very office, and gain loads of knowledge on the very subject that was his own obsession—a huge pile of gold that was, according to legend, somewhere under his feet in his very own town.

Brad and Tiny secured the raft for overnight and the two had a brief parting conversation about what time to meet tomorrow for a day of dredging the Elk River by hand to clear a path for frequent raft traffic through the shoals below the bridge and into trout country. They shook hands and departed, both smiling from the positive mental effects of a beautiful river cruise on a beautiful day on a beautiful milk jug raft! Brad was carrying what he hoped would be tonight's dinner on a stringer over his shoulder as Tiny took one more glance up the bank where Sheriff Collins had been just a few minutes ago.

CHAPTER EIGHTEEN

The path led the three along the ridgeline and snaked its way around briar patches and thick underbrush. It was a well-worn path that Mr. Otis knew well, having shared it with the deer, bear and mountain lions over the years.

Otis paused for a second, looking up into a hickory tree at one of the biggest red squirrels he had ever seen. He thought about his gun, but he only had a slug bullet in it. If he hit the squirrel with it, there would be nothing left to eat! Without putting the cat down, he then looked down at the ground and picked up a stone about the size of a tennis ball. Josh and Eddie looked at each other, a bit puzzled. Otis took the rock, reared back and flung it with the steam of a major league pitcher at the big red squirrel on the limb of the hickory. The rock missed only by about three inches and then powered on through the trees and way, way over the hill, before coming to rest down in the holler. Otis turned and looked at the boys and shrugged one shoulder.

Josh and Eddie looked at each other and knew that it was Burl Otis who threw the rock down at the river's edge, most likely to try to dislodge another huge squirrel from its perch on a limb high up in a hickory tree. The two friends also figured that Otis had spotted them and watched as they traversed up the hill and, luckily, had been there to take care of the cougar for them. He saved their lives, but they would need to get to know this man very carefully. Maybe he could be nasty like Collins had said. But what an arm! And what an impressive shot!

They walked about a mile along the tops of the hill—the boys enjoying beautiful vistas and perspectives of where they lived that they had never seen before. The path then began a gradual slope down over the right side of the ridge that led them down to a bench or shelf on the side of the hill, an area where the hillside flattened out to create a perfect piece of land for a homesite.

Josh and Eddie could see the cabin from the top of the slope before they dropped over the side of the hill. It was a remarkably crafted log home structure. Not huge, but big enough to raise a family in. The wood was grayed with age and the three inches of mortar between each log looked beautiful in contrast. As they got closer to the home, Josh noticed that each end of every log was dovetailed to interlock with the next one on top of it. It was a well-built home, built by someone who knew how many years ago.

As they stepped off the path and into the naturally wooded yard, the two boys looked around to take it all in.

The Tater Holler Homestead looked like a pioneer village. It could have been a stage set with period actors walking across the yard making apple butter in a huge black pot on an open fire outside, or a blacksmith demonstrating how to prepare a horseshoe for mounting.

But there was none of that. This was a real, old-fashioned settlement house that had changed little in a hundred and fifty years with no actual road that came to it. If you wanted to get here, you had to do it the hard way! Hike. There were paths off the yard in all directions.

Burl had a large barn about thirty yards from the house, also constructed of log, and two sheds used for storing farm-type equipment for clearing land and being self-sufficient. Josh spotted the bunkhouse, a wood structure that stood to the side of the house built up on stilts about five feet high, with strong wooden steps leading up to the entry door.

On the other side of the house Eddie noticed a water well, complete with stonework and a little roof structure built over it. Hanging from the roof structure was a bucket for hauling up water. Josh pointed out to his friend about fifteen raccoon hides tacked to the side of one shed, stretching and drying in the warm air.

One could see here all the things that you would expect to see at a frontier settlement; a horse-drawn plow, a small blacksmith shop, a burn pile, and a house with a big shady front porch. As rustic and old-fashioned as it was, the boys loved it. The entire place was surrounded with huge oak and maple trees that gave the house and yard shade and protection from the wind.

"Well, this is it. Nothin' fancy, but I call it home," Otis said, laying down the 140-pound cat for the first time since he threw it over his shoulder.

"It's outstanding," Josh replied, looking around.

Otis grinned at the boys.

"You can throw your stuff on the porch if ya like. I'm gonna carry in a little wood for a fire."

"OK."

Eddie said, whispering, "This guy seems alright."

Josh shrugged, "He was nice enough to let us spend the night."

"Glad of that!"

Josh grinned and agreed as the two boys hurled their packs up onto the porch.

BABOOM!!!

Again the muzzleloader went off, and the boys went around to the side to see what was going on. Burl Otis picked up a huge rabbit by the hind legs and held him up. A perfect head shot.

"By the wood pile. Now we got something to put on the fire."

Josh and Eddie were impressed.

Josh walked over and grabbed an armload of firewood as Otis handed Eddie his muzzleloader to carry inside.

"I'm gonna go clean this hare and then skin the cat. You boys go on inside and make yourself at home. We'll start dinner in a bit," he said.

"Alright!" Eddie exclaimed, admiring the huge antique firearm.

Josh and Eddie let themselves into Mr. Otis' log home and Josh laid the firewood down on the large hearth in front of the fireplace. The inside of the cabin was as interesting as the outside. The inside walls of the cabin were log as well and were absolutely covered with antiques either collected or saved by the Otis family through the years. An old hand-cranked apple peeler, wash boards, jars, a wind-up telephone, bamboo fly rods, old tools, old plates. It was a museum unto itself. On and on it went around the room with every log having something nailed to it that was old and representative of the Otis family. The boys studied it all and discussed what some of it was or what it did.

After a few minutes, Burl Otis stepped inside carrying the freshly cleaned and well-washed rabbit. He noticed the boys admiring his collection of family heirlooms.

"Ha. Looking at my junk, huh?" he said jokingly.

"This is some cool stuff, Mr. Otis," Josh replied.

"Every bit of it is Otis family. It was all used at one time or another, except for the phone. We've never had phone service."

"Wow."

"Ya see these tools up here?" Burl Otis pointed to a double-ended bucksaw, some small hand tools used for stripping bark and shaving wood, an axe head minus the handle and a hand-cranked wood-boring drill.

"Those were the only tools used to build this homestead back in the middle 1800s." Burl looked at the tools with fondness, knowing that his great-great-grandfather, Zeke Otis, settled this land and built this very home with only these tools and his bare hands.

"Very cool," Eddie said.

"Yep." He paused, looking around. "Well, let's get this bunny on the fire, whatta ya say."

In just a few minutes Burl Otis had a pleasant fire going and their dinner skewered and roasting over the flame. Nighttime was settling in as the inside of the cabin took on a beautiful glow. Josh sat by the fire with his old Barlow knife, whittling away on a piece of oak about the size of a ruler. The three sat in silence as the fire crackled and popped and Mr. Otis would occasionally reach over and turn the spit, which held the rabbit over the fire. Lying close to the coals were three huge baking potatoes, grown right on the property, and slowly cooking and pulling in the flavors from the wood and smoke.

Eddie and Burl were studying Josh's craftsmanship as he methodically carved away at the chunk of hardwood. They would glance at each other and then back at Josh, each trying to figure out what he might be creating. The fire crackled and spit out a fiery spark onto the limestone hearth in front of the fireplace. Eddie watched it burn out and then looked back at his friend.

Eddie broke the silence after a while.

"What's that gonna be?" he asked, nodding at Josh's' carving job.

Josh kept whittling, thought about it for a moment and looked up at Eddie.

"My toothpick," he said seriously.

There was a brief pause and then an eruption of laughter in the room. Burl Otis was enjoying having some company for a change. Not too many folks came to visit the Otis family.

"It's good to have you guys up here," he said, drying his eyes from laughing.

The fire continued to pop, and hiss as the sun continued to fall. Burl's face got a little more serious.

"So, tell me boys, what brings you up Tater Holler looking for an old man like me?"

The mood became more solemn.

Josh and Eddie shifted their sitting positions so they would all be in a semi-circle around the fire. Josh glanced at Eddie and cleared his throat. He was a bit nervous and his shaky voice showed it.

"Mr. Otis. We came up here to talk to you about something we found that we believe is tied to you and your family from way back," he started.

There was a pause, as the firelight flickered off Burl Otis' weathered face. His face was pointed down at the floor, but his eyes were aiming right at Josh. "You found the red milk can," he said in a low, whispering tone, grinning slightly.

Something hissed in the fire as Josh looked him in the eye.

"We found the can," Josh said, equally as somber, nodding slightly.

Burl Otis didn't move from his position and went into thought for a moment.

"I thought it was you boys," he said, maintaining his whispering tones.

"Whatta ya mean?" Eddie asked.

Burl looked at them both.

"At the sandbar. You boys were fishing. I was scouting for where to set traps that day, where that creek dumps out into the river. Only I was on the other side of that stone trestle."

"It was you who I saw through the tunnel that day!" Josh exclaimed. "I knew I saw something. Remember, Eddie?"

"Yeah… I remember. That was you, Mr. Otis?"

"Most likely… Yep. I couldn't believe my eyes. That old can has been missing for decades. I just knew it had to be the old, red Franklin can. They say it used to sit on the Franklin porch up Blue Creek all the time, years ago. The Franklins lived along the creek, ya know? The Franklin family didn't know 'til years later that the can held the deer hide. 'Course *no one* knew 'til years later. It was just porch decoration—lotta people have 'em. But… Clyde left a note in his bible about the can. That bible was lost and wasn't found again 'til 1958! The note in the bible told of the clues and such."

Josh and Eddie were wide-eyed and trying to absorb all he was saying.

Josh asked, "But if the Franklins found a note in a bible, how did everyone else find out about the red can? Seems like the Franklins would have kept it a secret."

"That's true. But the Franklins didn't find it. Of all people, a newspaperman found the bible with the note still in it."

"Oh, brother," Eddie said. "And how did a news guy find it?"

"Clyde's bible was found in a used bookstore and bought by a man named John Hopes, a junior writer for the Charleston Gazette. And Hopes, being a writer for a newspaper, did what he did best. He wrote a front-page article about everything he could pull out of the note he found. A bunch of information and clues about the legend. And again, being a writer, he took a little artistic liberty and embellished whatever he wanted to hype the story even more. So that spilled the beans to everyone who knew anything about the legend. It also incriminated Clyde Franklin, but he was dead already, so it didn't matter."

"What rotten luck for the Franklins," Josh said.

"Yeah, but good luck for the rest of us!" Burl said.

Josh looked puzzled as he thought.

He said, "But what happened to the can? How did it end up down at the trestle buried in the mud?"

Burl Otis grinned as he looked at him.

"The Great Flash Flood of 1936. It was devastating. The story goes that there was some kind of weather system that moved in and hung around upstream around Hillsburg. It rained for days and the ground soaked up what it could but once it started running off the hills, the creek rose so fast people couldn't do anything but run uphill. It was coming up six or seven feet an hour. They left their homes and belongings and just ran right up into the mountains. It washed away over twenty houses and left behind nothing but devastation, and it took the red can with it, and it hasn't been seen since."

Josh and Eddie were amazed.

"So, everyone found out in 1958, after Hopes discovered the bible, that they needed the red can with the deer-hide? After it had sat there on that porch of the Franklins for so long?" Eddie asked.

"That's right." Burl grinned.

Burl paused as the firelight flickered in his dark eyes.

"I watched you boys from a distance tryin' to pry the lid off of the can and I could hardly stand it. All that history was coming back to me and all the stories told to me by my family about the legend. Man, I was going nuts." He smiled.

"Why didn't you come over and help us?" Eddie asked.

"Well, think about it. A big old burly mountain man like myself running from the trestle tunnel over to you, going on about gold and legends and murder. Woulda' been a little aggressive, huh?"

"I guess so, yeah," Eddie replied.

"And, too, I don't let people see me much. I'd rather see than be seen. It's kind of a family tradition, ya know?"

He looked down and then back up at the boys. Eddie got the quick impression that it was a phobia that Burl Otis was not really proud of. Social insecurity.

"So, I watched you guys. I watched you pull and twist on it and I was hopin' you'd just give up and leave it there."

Josh shook his head and grinned a bit.

"Then you got smart and used leverage. That was good thinkin' by the way. And... when I saw the deer-hide... let me tell ya, my heart was poundin'."

Josh thought for a moment, recalling the events and replaying them in his mind. He grinned and looked back up at Mr. Otis.

"You threw the rock at the garage, didn't you?" Josh asked.

Burl Otis looked at the boys and then looked down at the floor and wobbled his head around like a young boy who had just been caught with his hand in the cookie jar.

"Yeah… I was… what I wanted to do by then was flush you guys outta there and go in and grab the deer-hide… just to see it. I wasn't going to take it with me, but you can imagine how bad I wanted to see it." He paused. "But ya didn't come outta there. Not very far, anyway."

Josh thought. "Where were you when you threw it?"

"By the riverbank," he replied.

The boys looked at him with astonishment.

Eddie said. "Good arm!"

They all enjoyed another laugh.

Josh thought again. "Behind the tree! You were behind that tree."

Burl nodded his head.

"I knew I saw something again there, too. I was blaming Radcliffe." He looked at Eddie.

"That's right."

Burl Otis reached over and cranked the big hare a quarter of a turn and brushed on a sauce made from apple jelly and various seasonings that smelled of pumpkin pie spices. They sat in silence for a moment, once again listening to the fire pop, while the flames flickered off of the dim walls of the cabin, each person staring into the fire as Josh resumed his whittling.

After a minute, Josh said, "Mr. Otis… can you tell us about the legend? Will you tell us the story?"

Burl Otis pulled a deep breath in through his nose, never taking his eyes off the fire. The flames danced in his eyes and the light of the fire gave his face a mix of shadows and a warm, red glow, as he slowly exhaled. There were no lights or candles or lamps to light the room, only the flickering fire to see by. Burl went into deep thought. He slowly nodded his head and then began the story of the *Legend of the Southern Jewel*.

CHAPTER NINETEEN

He stared into the fire and spoke very deliberately as he thought and recalled the legend.

"The year... was 1903. My great-grandfather, Arthur Otis... he was a good man, but sometimes... well, he had an ornery streak about him. He was a mountain man like me. Most people were afraid of him because he came across as being a bit stern or intimidating. Kids especially didn't like him. They thought he was a wild man or a hermit or something. Anyway, he was bellied up to the bar at the Cross Roads Tavern one night, with a guy named Franklin—Clyde Franklin. They really had nothing in common other than the whiskey they were drinkin' but the more they drank, the more they talked, and Franklin had some real interesting things to say, apparently."

"What were they talkin' about?" Josh asked quietly.

Burl Otis turned the rabbit another quarter turn and then took a long drink of cold well water from a metal cup.

"Ya got to remember that everything I tell ya is according to the legend, OK? There were some witnesses to these conversations back then, but they went unnamed. But, according to the legend, they were talking about hard times... and gold. A dangerous combination, I might add. Hard times make people do desperate things."

Burl thought for a moment and then continued.

"Ya see, Clyde Franklin worked in the railroad yard way up at the head of Blue Creek by the coalmines. He knew 'most everybody in town and drank with a lot of them after work occasionally. Ya see, all these railroad guys and mineworkers would go wash down all that coal dust with spirits after their shifts. Laborers and management, it didn't matter. They drank in the same bar and the bar owner would run tabs for these guys that they could pay on payday. Well, it started getting harder and harder for them to pay because of a reduction in hours up at the yard. That was the first sign of hard times back then, when you couldn't pay your bar bill." He grinned slightly. "So anyway, somehow Franklin got wind of a gold shipment that would be passing through Blue Creek on the C&O. Not just any gold shipment, but a huge pile of old Confederate gold. The stuff that came from foreign countries to fund the South during The War. It was on its way to a museum or something over in D.C. for a temporary show. I don't know what they were going to do with it after that."

"Clyde Franklin thought he could get away with stealing something that... high profile?" Josh asked eagerly.

"He didn't think he could. He was *sure* he could. He *did* get away with it. But here's the thing—he couldn't have cared less about the value of it. He didn't want it for the money. No... Clyde Franklin was an old Confederate soldier. He just wanted the gold out of Union hands. He felt it was stolen, and he wanted to steal it back. He was an older man, still bitter over the outcome of the war. He called it *The War of Northern Aggression*. That war had a lot of names, and West Virginia was quite divided on it, too. We were technically a northern state, but there were a lot of men who went down to Richmond to fight for the South. Clyde Franklin was one of them."

Josh and Eddie both sat back in their chairs as Eddie raised his eyebrows and let out a deep breath. "Wow."

"So he and my great-grandfather sat at the bar that night, and the more they drank the bigger the plan got. The bigger the plan got, the more they drank and by the end of the night, they were best friends, or so great-grand dad thought."

"Whatta ya mean?" Josh asked.

Otis put his palm up. "I'll get to it."

Josh and Eddie exchanged glances.

"Over the next few weeks Clyde managed to find out what day and what train that gold shipment would be shipped on. He knew the security guards would be on the train and how many of them there would be." Burl paused and looked up at the wall, collecting his next thought. He went on, "Now… Clyde also had access to railroad supplies, including dynamite and an official signal lantern. It went out right under his coat one evening and was never missed from the yard until after the robbery. During inventory the following weeks, they discovered those things missing from company stores, but it was too late then."

Burl Otis' voice was still low and whispering, as if there may be someone outside his window trying to listen in. The fire dwindled a bit, so he reached for the poker to stir up the coals before adding another log. He brushed their dinner again and flipped the potatoes over.

He continued. "That's how they stopped the train, ya know… with just a signal lantern. That's the legend, anyway. The missing lantern was never found, but in those days, that's the only means they had to signal trains to stop at night—wave the signal lantern. They wouldn't stop otherwise."

"So… how do you know about all this and the law never did?" Eddie asked.

Otis grinned just a little. "Loose lips sink ships."

Josh and Eddie looked at him—waiting for the explanation.

"It's an old saying. The legend says, after the holdup, Franklin hid the gold and just kept enough to live on. He most likely had a guy in Charleston who would buy it and melt it down for a very good price. Franklin could live very well on that. He would go to the Cross Roads and drink the night away and the more he drank the more he talked. *Loose lips.* He was boastful, so he would tell just enough to make people wonder. He would tell one guy that he knew how the robbers stopped the train. And then he would tell another guy, a few nights later, how the robbers managed to kill all five men on the train. Then he would tell another guy something else until people started putting things together and wondering about him and his involvement in the train heist. He quit the railroad job, too, and folks wondered how he had the means to survive with no income. Also, he had no trouble paying his bar tab." Burl was leaned forward with his elbows on his knees, still speaking low and whispering.

"But the law never knew, really. Or they didn't know enough to arrest him. Oh, they say they questioned him a few times but with no hard evidence all he had to do was deny it, right? They had to have some kind of evidence, ya know. Proof. There was no *smoking gun.* The only thing that was left behind at the scene, one single clue, was…" he paused, thought a minute and got up, and walked over to a tall, narrow oak cabinet that held six very old guns. He reached to the bottom of the cabinet, moved one of the gun stocks over just a little and pulled out an old, worn, leather wallet. He walked back over and sat down by the fire with the boys.

"This. This is the only piece of evidence that was ever found at the scene of the train robbery in 1903."

"Arthur Otis' wallet!" Josh said softly. "We read about this at the library. Oh my gosh… it's like a piece of history."

Burl handed the old wallet to Josh. Josh handled it and looked at it as if it were the gold itself. He opened it and, stamped on the inside was the name "ART OTIS" in letters about a half-inch tall and all capitals. Eddie scooted closer to get a better look. Josh looked at Burl as if to get approval to inspect further. Burl Otis nodded and swished his hand to say *go ahead*.

Josh held it to get good light on it and opened up the bill section. Inside the bill area was something oblong and shiny, and Josh repositioned the wallet again to get better light. He squinted a bit and then slowly reached in to pull out what was in there. It was a nickel… flatter than a pancake. Josh looked at it as he held it up in front of his face, giving Eddie a good view of what he was holding.

"No way!" Eddie said.

Burl Otis grinned a bit. "It's the one you boys couldn't find."

Josh smiled and shook his head, putting the coin back in the wallet. He then looked inside the wallet again to further inspect. The wallet was very simple and unlike modern wallets. It was no more than a couple pieces of rectangle leather hand-stitched together to hold paper money, if a man was lucky enough to have any back then.

"Oh, that's all that's in there," Burl said. "Anything else has been stripped out of there over the years. Most of it probably taken by Franklin that night. He scavenged it of anything valuable and left it at the scene to incriminate Art Otis as the sole train robber. Keep the nickel too, it's yours."

"So, where did the story about the southern sympathizers come from? The old newspaper articles that we found said it was a band of old Confederates just trying to get their gold back, or something," Eddie asked.

"Well, it *was* an old Confederate trying to get his gold back, that's for sure. It just wasn't a band of them. That was just fabricated by the press. The law had to have somebody to blame, and the press had to have something to write about," Burl said. "The newspaper guys were more right than they thought, actually." He paused. "But they never really knew. Never had a clue. Art Otis and Clyde Franklin pulled off that train robbery cleaner than a whistle. Everything went their way that night." He paused and looked back over at the fire, the flames flickering in his dark eyes once again. "But it didn't end up well for my great-granddad. He would have never robbed a train and then just disappeared to go live somewhere else. This was his home. This was his cabin. The Otis homestead and the mountain." Burl spread his arms with his palms up when he said it. "He raised a family here. It just gets a little hard to pay the taxes when all you do for money is fur trapping. He put out some ginseng plants late in life, but they take years before you can harvest them. Good money in ginseng, but I don't think he reaped the benefits for too many years. He was just a desperate man trying to keep his family in his family home!"

Josh tilted his head a little and looked at Burl, closing the wallet and handing it back. "What do you think happened after they got the gold off the train?"

"I'll tell ya what happened." He paused and looked up at some old Otis artifacts on the wall. The axe, the bucksaw, and then down at the wallet. "Clyde Franklin killed Arthur Otis in cold blood that night."

A bit of attitude was in his eyes when he said it. It was in his voice, too. He drew a deep breath and walked over to the table and picked up a large, oblong platter. He then stepped over to the fireplace and pulled the skewered rabbit off the fire and placed it on the platter. He carried the platter back over to the table, his heavy footsteps making the boards creak under his feet as he prepared his next words. He lit a lamp that hung on the wall by the table.

"I mean, don't get me wrong, Art and Clyde killed five other men that night and I don't mean to say that was right or anything, but putting that aside, Franklin just absolutely double-crossed Art Otis the worst way you can," he said, "and I am convinced… that was his plan all along. Ever since the first night at the Cross Roads Tavern, Franklin planned to have great-granddad help him steal the gold, and then kill him. Who's gonna miss an old mountain man, anyway? And then he tossed his wallet on the tracks. It wasn't found in the weeds or down by the river. No, they found it right in front of the cowcatcher on the train, right between the rails! And… it instantly made Art Otis a guilty man and the source of their manhunt, like I told you."

The boys were awestruck. There was dead silence in the cabin, except for the crackling of the fire, as they pieced together all the information. It was a solemn moment.

"What do you think he did with him? With the body," Josh asked quietly.

Burl shook his head. "I don't know. These hills are dense. He coulda' taken him anywhere. I have been walkin' 'em for years and have found no clues as to the whereabouts of Art Otis and he was a big man, too. How far could he drag him? And I know these hills like nobody else, ya know." He thought for a moment and shook his head. "There was *so* much gold, too. Easily enough for two people; it was senseless for Franklin to want it all for himself. I just think once he got a taste of it, his greed overtook him and he lost his mind, pulled his gun and killed him."

Burl Otis walked back over to the fire with another plate and pulled the huge potatoes out of the hot coals with his calloused bare hands. Josh glanced at Eddie.

Josh appeared to be in thought for a second and then said, "Mr. Otis, you seem like… well… the Sheriff told us that we should stay away from you and that you were nasty and a…. uh… umm."

"What, a moonshiner?" Otis chuckled a little. "And a nasty old man?"

"Well, that's what he said. He said your family has been running 'shine up here for decades, but I mean, it doesn't matter, I just..."

"Yeah... I know what Collins says about me and my family. He's been saying it for years." Burl Otis spread his hands out wide. "Feel free to look around and..."

"No, no, no, I didn't mean that I believed him. I just can't figure why he would say those kinds of things if they weren't true."

"It's true," Eddie said, thinking. "He's a Sheriff. He has an obligation to the truth. There are laws against spreading lies about people."

Burl Otis went over to a cabinet and pulled out a long loaf of unsliced bread and laid it on the table along with a long, sharp knife. He then pulled three clean plates out of another cabinet and placed them on the table with silverware and clean hand towels for napkins. He walked over to the stove and pulled a medium-sized simmering pan off the fire. Fresh green beans with a big hunk of salt pork meat. He sat it on the table on top of a square piece of wood to protect the table from the heat.

"You're right. He has an obligation to be truthful." He paused. "Come and eat, there's more to the story."

Burl's table was a heavy-duty picnic style table with benches down each side. It had sat in the same exact spot over the years and was an original "Otis" piece. It was stained walnut, from real walnut hulls, and showed the scars of many years of use. Initials of mischievous Otis boys were carved into the seats that dated back a hundred years, including the current owners'.

Burl Otis said a simple man's prayer, poured the remaining glaze over the hare and then dinner was served. Josh pulled off a hindquarter and helped himself to a potato, a scoop of beans, and a hunk of crusty bread. Eddie did the same but opted for the tenderloin—the most succulent portion of the animal.

They dug in.

Both boys were amazed. It was delicious! The apple jelly and spice glaze was exceptional. The real butter that ran over the potato was creamy and perfectly salted. Nothing had ever tasted better to the two hungry adventurers.

They ate the first few bites of the meal in silence. A sign of good cooking. After a bit, Eddie slowed down enough to ask, "So, why would Sheriff Collins spread rumors like that, Mr. Otis?"

Burl Otis thought for a moment and stared deeply into the fire that was burning tall across the room and then spoke in his deep tone once again, slowly and softly.

"He speaks this way about me and my family because… he knows."

Josh and Eddie stopped eating and looked at him as he stared off, as if in a trance.

"He knows what?" Josh asked, equally quiet.

There was a pause and then Burl said, "Sheriff Collins' mother…"

The boys listened harder. He looked over from the fire and right into each boy's eyes. He said it slowly, "Elizabeth… Franklin."

Josh's fork hit his plate.

Burl continued, "Collins' mother was a Franklin. Sheriff Collins knows almost every bit as much as I do about the legend. It has been handed down through his family, too. He knows about the milk can and the deer-hide that was inside. He knows how his great-grandfather and mine conspired and he also knows that Clyde Franklin killed Arthur Otis, although he probably won't admit it. He knows the answers to the whereabouts of the gold are hidden with the document in the milk can and he has been after it for years. Of course, we all have and then, suddenly… it just pops up. Thank goodness you boys have it." Otis took another bite.

Josh and Eddie looked at each other with significant concern. Burl Otis picked up on the fact that something was wrong and his eyebrows dropped and his head cocked slightly to one side.

"We *had* it," Eddie said as he looked at the floor.

"Somebody took it out of the can in the garage," Josh added. "We made a copy, but, yeah… the original is gone. Stolen from the garage."

"Mm." Burl let out a deep breath, blowing it through his pursed lips. "Do you have it with you? The copy?"

"Yeah. In my bag."

"We're gonna have to study it and see what we can decipher." Burl said.

Burl thought for a minute, trying to figure out who would know about the deer hide in the garage. "Who else knows about it?"

Josh replied, counting on his fingers, "Me, Eddie, you, our friend Giselle, and her boss at the library."

"What's his name?"

"Elton Mansfield."

Burl thought for a moment. "Hmm. Never heard of him. How did he see it?"

"I dropped a copy of the map when we were at the library looking stuff up and he found it later."

"He didn't give it back?"

"No, he kept it."

"That's strange. Nobody else? Is that all the people who know about it? Mom? Dad? Sisters… anyone?"

"No, that's all. Just five of us," Josh said, as he went into thought.

"It's a pretty small circle of people. I mean, we can rule out me, Josh and you right off the bat. That only leaves Giselle and Mansfield. I am positive that Giselle wouldn't have taken it and I am sure, also, that she didn't tell anyone." While Eddie was talking, Josh was thinking.

Burl Otis thought for a second and then raised his eyebrows a bit. "Well, that just leaves Mansfield, then. He's the only one who could have broken into the garage and taken it. But the question is, why? Who is he and why would he do it? After all, he already had a copy, right? Josh's copy? It doesn't even make any sense unless he just wanted verification."

Josh was in a straight-ahead stare, his eyes fixed on nothing in particular, and he had a knowing expression. He nodded in disbelief.

"The garage wasn't broken into," he said. "The person who took it walked right through our garage, saw it and walked off with it." Josh paused, still staring, "What nerve he has."

"Who?" Burl asked.

Eddie thought for a second, let out a big sigh, and put his head in his hands, because at that moment, he knew who it was too. The worst-case scenario had occurred. "Oh, man!"

Josh drawled, "Sheriff… Collins."

CHAPTER TWENTY

"Hmm, well, that's not the best thing that could have happened," Burl Otis grumbled. "If that deerskin is in his hands, he will get busy figuring things out right away, you can bet on that. Collins has been *so* obsessed, and now that he has the information, he will be up twenty-four hours a day deciphering it."

"I'm gonna make a quick call," Josh said.

"Who ya calling?" Eddie asked.

"Giselle," he replied. "I think we need to know more about Mansfield. Who is he and why is he holding our copy, knowing that it's ours? Also, she can look up the Collins/Franklin connection and see if there is any past dirt on him—the sheriff."

"Maybe so," Burl said. "He is really, really obsessed with it. The entire story is in his family too, ya gotta remember. I don't know if he has been on the outside of the law, but…"

"He was outside the law when he took the deer hide out of my garage," Josh replied. "And being obsessed is one thing, but spreading lies about someone else's family, that's another. It doesn't make sense. There has to be more to it."

"Well, you're right about that, and your friend can research it, but I really don't think there will be much to find. I have a hunch about that Mansfield guy, though. It seems more than peculiar, him keeping your copy like that." Burl sat up a little straighter in his chair. "What I think we need to do is study the copy that you still have. We need more information on where that gold may be and we need to be the first ones to it, if it exists."

"It's in your pack, Eddie. I'll get my phone and the copy."

Burl looked at Eddie. "How accurately did you boys copy that document?"

"Letter for letter," Eddie said. "There was even a little drawing at the bottom. We traced that line for line. Everything is just like it is on the original."

"What was the drawing?" Burl asked.

"We weren't sure, just a little sketch of some kind. Maybe you will get something out of it, I don't know." Eddie shrugged.

Josh returned to the table with his cell phone and the yellow copy of the deer-hide document.

They quickly cleared the table, cleaned up the dishes, and then began their work.

Eddie opened the paper while Josh tapped out seven numbers on the cell phone. Burl Otis looked down on the cell phone as if it were from Mars. Technology was nothing that interested him. He figured that all these gadgets that were invented to simplify our lives, had done nothing but complicate most peoples and had added a hundred digits to their stress level every time the blasted things failed. You get used to having weather radar on your telephone in your pocket and suddenly you can't do without it. Heaven forbid it fails when you feel a sprinkle outside. No sir. Burl Otis liked things simple. He could feel the weather, anyway. He had a bad knee that could predict a low-pressure system two days away.

Giselle O'Conner's phone sang out a dance mix of the B-52's *Loveshack* and she answered within the first couple of bars.

"Hello."

"Giselle, it's Josh."

"Hey, you guys made it up there?"

"Yeah… long story. I'll tell ya more later. Did you find anything out about Mansfield?"

"Really no, just that they have been in the area for about a hundred and fifty years, but that's all. I did a general search on the Mansfield name in this area and, ya know, nothing weird turned up."

"Ok."

"Yeah… I don't know what's going on with him other than just one thing. Elton Mansfield had a great-great-grandfather by the name of Edmund, who was killed by a gunshot only three months after the date of the train robbery. It was in a newspaper article that I pulled off of the archives. The killer, again, was never found, and they left no clues behind. I thought it was interesting that the dates were so close, but maybe it's just coincidence."

"Hmm…"

"Hey, what did you guys learn?"

"Oh man, a lot. For one thing, Sheriff Collins is directly related to a man named Clyde Franklin, a man who Mr. Otis believes helped his great-grandfather rob the train."

"No way! Are you kidding?"

"Nope."

"Wow, Collins must know a bunch of facts about this, too. No wonder he's acting so weird."

"He *does* know a lot about the legend. In fact, he knows about as much as Mr. Otis. The Franklin family, including Sheriff Collins, has been trying to figure this thing out for generations. The story keeps getting handed down from one generation to the next and I guess we hit the mother-lode of clues when we found the thing in the red can," Josh said.

"What about that document? Did you guys study it yet with Mr. Otis?"

"Just getting to that. But, oh, bad news about the deer hide too. It is missing from my garage and we figured out that it was Collins who took it after visiting me and my parents the other day. He left through the garage and took it."

"He stole it from you? I can't believe that guy!"

"Yeah, it stinks but we still have the good copy that we made. Hey, you should see this cabin!" Josh said, looking around the inside of the beautiful log structure. "It's really cool."

"OK. We have nothing on Mansfield still, other than Edmond Mansfield being shot within a few months of Otis in 1903. Maybe he's just curious about what we are doing and not involved at all." She paused. "But we do now know that the Sheriff is related to one of the suspects in the train robbery. That's the link for him."

"Mr. Otis also believes that Clyde Franklin murdered Arthur Otis, his great-grandfather, that night after the robbery to keep all the gold for himself, and then tossed his wallet in front of the train so it would be found, ya know, on purpose, and then it would look like only Arthur Otis pulled this off by himself and simply dropped his wallet accidentally in all the excitement."

"Wow. Does he have anything to back that up? I mean, the only way to prove that is to find the remains of his body. And that's not likely!"

"No, it's just legend, but he is pretty convinced and it all makes sense, too. He has a lot of other facts, it seems."

"Hmm," Giselle thought, as she processed all the information.

"I just wanted to call and fill you in and see if you had anything on Mansfield. We are gonna dive into this document now with Mr. Otis and see what we can figure out. It's gettin' exciting!"

"Yeah… I guess!" she agreed. "Oh, I got your message, too, about Radcliffe and the raft thing. I can't believe you guys did that. Be careful with him, he could be just using you." She paused. "Listen, I'm sitting here by the computer so if there is anything that I can look up or search, give me a call."

"Yeah, we will." Josh loved hearing this girl say *give me a call.*

"Alright, see ya."

"Bye."

Burl Otis and Eddie had the yellow legal pad copy of the document unfolded on the old Otis table as Burl slipped on a pair of reading glasses.

Burl looked up and down the paper as he began taking it all in, looking first at the broken sentences and then the drawing.

Whe-- -teel --r--s r-n

St--ms f-ow fr-- hil-- -igh

A southern -ewel rest-

Fr-m - -ain- n-gh-

San- -s a -aul-

Key -rom -he doo-

In -n I- -an- -ank

Josh and Eddie were on either side of Otis, looking at the paper and then at each other and then at Otis. His large dark eyes were fixed on the paper and the boys watched them dart back and forth. He stared at the letters for a while and then drew in a deep breath and exhaled it through his nose. "Boys, I don't really think this will be that hard to figure out." He paused. "Some of these words are just missing one or two letters and it's just the process of elimination to figure what the word is. Have you guys tried that?"

"No, not yet," Eddie confessed. "Been so busy with everything else."

"Well, first line: Whe-- -teel --r--s r-n. And the first word is Whe--."

The three simultaneously ran possibilities across their lips quietly; *Whets, When*, no, not enough letters, *Where…*

Eddie said, "Maybe it's *Where*."

Josh agreed. It was the simplest possibility.

Burl took a short, broken pencil and wrote the word *Where* on a separate piece of paper.

"Ok. *Where.* Next word is *–teel.*"

Josh said, "Just run through the alphabet on that one, it's only one letter."

They started doing it again, silent mumbling between them, trying all the possibilities, and then Burl said, "*Steel.* It's the only one that works."

With no hesitation he wrote the word *Steel* on his paper after the word *Where*.

"*Where steel…*"

Josh and Eddie looked at each other.

"We should have had this done already," Josh said, shaking his head.

It's true that what they were doing now was just a game of fill in the blank, but their lives, since finding the document in the can, had been a whirlwind of adventure and one thing after another, such as two long bike rides to the library, a trip to the Town Offices, an intimidating visit by the Sheriff, a new friend who happened to be a gorgeous young girl, another new friend who most kids would rather distance themselves from, and another new friend who owns the coolest log home they had ever seen, a raft project, a near death experience with a cougar, and the best rabbit they had ever sunk their teeth into. All these things had left them with very little time to do any sort of deciphering work on the document, but now they were doing it! They were sitting by lamplight in the presence of a man whose family was history in those parts, in the warmth of the best log cabin ever built in this county, deciphering a map to possibly the greatest treasure ever to be rediscovered east of the Mississippi River, *The Southern Jewel.*

"Next word. This one is going to be harder: *--r--s*"

Burl flipped his piece of paper over and began writing possibilities for each letter. Josh and Eddie leaned in and offered opinions.

Burl said, "Well, we need some vowels somewhere." The three started throwing vowels at the blank spaces here and there to see if something would jump off the page at them. They spoke the possibilities: "Curses, verses, barges, partys."

Burl looked up and down the draft, squinted his eyes and looked puzzled at times. *"Horses,"* he said. *"Where Steel Horses..."*

"Ran, Eddie added.

"Or Run," Josh said. *"Where Steel Horses Run."*

"Boys, I do believe we have the first sentence!" Burl announced.

"What does that mean? *Steel Horses*?" Eddie queried. "Isn't a steel horse a motorcycle?"

Burl shook his head and offered a quick history lesson. "Well, back in the late 1700s, a man by the name of James Watt helped to perfect an invention called the steam engine and right away the world began trying to use it in many different ways to make life a little easier. So soon was born the Steam Locomotive— a huge heavy beast of steel. Of course, up until that point the principal form of transportation was horseback, and it just came natural to nickname this new contraption a *Steel Horse*."

"Ok, so *where steel horses run* means where a train runs, on the track?" Josh reasoned.

"Right," said Burl. "And I do believe that fits right in with what we are trying to figure out. We have a train robbery, and we have train tracks right here close. Oh, and as a matter of fact I can show you the exact location of the robbery sometime. Right down to where the train was stopped. It's just above the old trestle down there where you guys fish, maybe a half mile."

"I would love to know where that is," Josh returned.

Josh and Eddie had walked those railroad tracks many times, never knowing what would later occupy their adventurous spirits. Many times they had walked right over the site of a historic robbery/murder and maybe even picked up a rock from that very scene and chucked it into the Elk River down below. Their lives had surely changed this summer.

"Let's keep working!" Burl advised.

The team worked continuously as time slipped towards midnight and after. Letter by letter they filled in blanks and figured out one word at a time, some words taking much longer than others. *A Southern Jewel Rests* they already knew. They figured out the words *streams, rainy, vault,* and *island* and also *door* and *bank.*

Burl Otis got up from the table more than once to fill up his coffee cup. They were all intent on solving this part of the puzzle tonight! They wanted to know what was so important that it had to be stored away in an old milk can, sealed shut with wax, lost to a flash flood, and then hunted for many years by many parties only to be accidentally found by two young fishermen more than a hundred years later. Tonight they would solve this part of the puzzle as lamplights flickered in their eyes and fatigue gave way to anticipation and excitement.

At around 1:30 in the morning their hard work paid off, and they had the letters filled in. Josh read it aloud:

"Where steel horses run

Streams flow from hills high

A Southern Jewel rests

From a rainy night.

Sand is a vault

Key from the door

In an Island bank"

"And it's dated *September 1st, 1904,*" Eddie finished, "the date this deer hide was written."

CHAPTER TWENTY-ONE

Cross Roads Tavern
1903

The old black bartender poured two more drinks as requested by the two men sitting at the far end of the long wooden bar. Regulars, they were, though he had never seen them drink together before and yet these two men were having an intense yet private conversation. They looked each other in the eye and occasionally would look around to see if anyone was close to them, within earshot. The bartender was somewhat amused and even curious about these men as he continued his job of serving drinks and washing and drying glasses, but he did not give them too much thought—the first night.

The Cross Roads Tavern was situated on a six-acre island in the middle of the Elk River near Blue Creek. It was suitably named because it sat near the crossroads of Blue Creek Road and Elk River road, just north of the island. There was a very old swinging bridge that connected the island to the area across the river just near the old Blue Creek General Store.

Outside the three-story wooden structure that night, it was properly dark, with the only light coming from a half dozen dim light bulbs that were strung down the pathway that led to the landing where the steamboats arrived. Boats would travel upriver through a series of crude locks from Charleston and drop passengers off for the weekend to enjoy *Island Life,* as they advertised it. But this was no family vacation destination. This was a getaway primarily for men in those days, to gamble, drink and fight. And plenty of all three went on there.

The basement was half below ground and half above ground and was mostly for the storage of food, drink and hotel supplies. Its walls were of stone and inside was poorly lit with only lantern lights and small rectangular windows to provide illumination for the service workers.

The main floor was the tavern floor with the bar, a few card tables and a roulette wheel. There were always plenty of locals in the tavern along with the wealthier Charleston men, washing down the dust of their day's work until nighttime called them to their homes. The stone workers, all German immigrants, had their corner every night. These men were the best at what they did and were on the river for two years to construct limestone train trestles over the small creeks and streams that flowed out of the hills along the C & O Railroad. One German gentleman seemed to be the foreman, and he and the others had their corner table every night. These workers had a small labor camp set up on the far north end of the island. The camp was granted by the railroad to house them while they completed their project in that area of the C & O and thus; they had a short walk home in the evenings.

Above the tavern floor were two resort floors with six rooms each. These rooms rented for two dollars a night. Nothing fancy, just a bed with fresh clean linens and a washbasin with a mirror. There was a hat and coat stand in one corner, as the men would dress properly to come up the river. At the end of the hallways on the resort floors were bathrooms with large tubs.

The very next night, the old black bartender observed these same two gentlemen in the very same intense type of discussion.

The two men would stare into each other's eyes, looking for any signs of distrust or treachery as they conversed. This went on for a couple more nights as the bartender served them up nice and strong. The more these men drank the more careless they became and, as they let their volume increase in their conversation each night, the bartender could pick up phrases of conversation from the clean-cut gentleman about *gold shipments* and *access to the tools we need* and *a special train that will be running.* The unkempt-looking woodsman looked him in the eye and offered suggestions of *dynamite* and a *signal lamp.*

As they talked, the bartender became more and more uneasy as this sounded like something that he didn't really want to know about. But his ears stayed trained on the conversation because it was also something that he didn't want to miss a word of.

As days passed, the clean-cut gentleman, whom the bartender came to know as a man named *Franklin*, had infrequent words with the stone foreman over at the corner table, who he later learned was named *Mansfield.* But conversation between these two men was always brief and never happened when the scruffy man was around, which also seemed unusual.

The Cross Roads Tavern was also suitably named due to the fact that two men, Clyde Franklin and Arthur Otis, would enter the crossroads of their lives on these nights of planning, and the old bartender, Washington L. Brooks, would be there, drying glasses and serving drinks, and taking in all the bits and pieces of information that he could hear over the noise of shuffling chairs, high spirited working men and card-playing hustlers.

Brooks would never tell a stranger what he had heard on those nights.

CHAPTER TWENTY-TWO

Late in the evening, after helping Brad through the shoals and returning home, Tiny Brooks sat in a century-old rocking chair with only a small lamp lit in one corner of his modest shack on the banks of the river. The scent of fried catfish and homemade hush puppies could still be detected in the air, but the leftovers had long been put away.

He was slowly sorting through pictures and letters of Brooks family history, looking at each old picture with fondness and pride. Wonderful memories he had of his relatives, aunts, uncles, grandparents who had all gone on before him. Each picture was a memory in time of a family get together, one of the many they had had there on the banks of the river. His Uncle William, always the practical joker. Earl, the serious one, was deeply religious, and was the man whom the family looked to for guidance in hard times. Images of Mama and Papa on this same porch forty years ago. And Aunt Pauline, who made the best fried chicken on the river!

All were gone now, but the pictures and memories remained strong in his heart.

Tiny continued to relax and reminisce after a great day on the water and a fine meal until he came across the one picture that always intrigued him. It was a picture of his great-great-grandfather, Washington L. Brooks. The picture was cracked and faded with time but the image was still clearly visible and showed a man who looked to be in his 50s or 60s standing on a sandbar by the river with a cane fishing pole in his hand and six freshly caught catfish on a stringer. He was dressed in an old white cotton work shirt and black slacks with no socks or shoes but a smile on his dark face as big as the New River Gorge. The contentment of his life on the river was clear. In the background was a newly constructed stone train trestle with a tunnel which provided passage for the small mountain stream to pass through and flow into the Elk River.

Tiny particularly liked this picture and even remembered holding it as a child and looking at it with significant interest. It was a picture that reminded him a lot of himself, still living on the river, still existing with simple means and a heart full of happiness and peace.

But what was written on the back, was like a ghost from the past.

A simple note to the only son of Washington L. Brooks read:

Charlie, we know it's here somewhere!

One day the river will give it up!

Paps

Tiny Brooks had always heard of a legend of some sort here along the Elk River, but as it filtered down through the generations, it had become a yarn and it was hard to separate the fact from the embellishment. The story told in his family came from the man in the picture and told of two men in an island tavern conjuring up a plan to, somehow, hold up a train and make a gold heist, using an old railroad lantern to flag down the train and dynamite to take care of the business of getting rid of the witnesses!

Washington L. Brooks had heard these plans for himself in 1903 and had told no one outside of his family, and close family at that. Tiny had been told this old story many times and the interesting part of it was that it *had happened*. It was more than just a legend—it was factual! Tiny also knew that it had involved the Otis family and that was what concerned him about the boys heading up to Tater Holler. Tater Holler was the location of the old Otis place, the Tater Holler Homestead, one of the oldest homesteads in the county. Tiny Brooks had seen Burl Otis many times up and down the river but had never become acquainted with him. He only knew the rumors of the Otis family being unfriendly and hermit-like and was concerned for Josh and Eddie trekking up through that neck of the woods.

As Tiny thought about the old legend and read again the words on the picture, he couldn't help but wonder what the boys were really up to. He knew them pretty well, and he also knew that Tater Holler was not a much-desired camping location. It was hard to get to, hard to climb, and once you got back up in there, it was nothing special. No good flat areas for setting up a tent and, other than an enjoyable view of the river valley, no reason to exert so much effort for so little reward — unless they were up there for another reason, of course.

As the sun rose the next morning Brad Radcliffe could tell it would be a magnificent day. He got up and had an excellent breakfast prepared by his mom and then headed down to the riverbank, long before his father arose. He prepared to sail downriver to meet Tiny Brooks to do some dredging work on the shoals of the river just below the baby blue bridge. Brad carried a bag with a jar of peanut butter in it and a sleeve of saltine crackers. That would be his lunch. He also toted a gallon jug of fresh drinking water drawn right from the sink.

Brad untied the dock line and stepped aboard his craft, then grabbed the long pole and gave himself a shove off of the bank. Once again life was free and easy as he started his drift on the river. This leg of the journey he would go solo and the sense of freedom was incredible. There was no need for the sail, which would remain furled for the downriver drift. The river's current provided adequate speed and enabled him to relax and enjoy the ride.

Brad once again took in the sights while coasting along: the turtles sliding off the logs and into the river, the bass hitting the top water bugs and the kids in their back yards playing, having been sent outside after breakfast by their mothers. One boy was up on the roof of his dad's shed with a long stick in his hand, sighting down it like a rifle. An obvious game of war! Reconnaissance or maybe sharpshooting.

Tiny's little shack was literally just a few feet up the river bank from the water, high enough to avoid any floodwater but close enough to be one with the river. That's just the way he liked it. His ancestors had built this home with that intention and it had suited every Brooks since then just fine.

Brad rounded a slight bend in the river and the old Brooks home came into view. Brad poled the raft to get closer to shore as he planned his approach to the front of Tiny's home. Tiny was on the front porch having a morning tea when he spotted Brad coming from upriver. That big Brooks smile spread across his face as he swallowed his last drink of honey ginseng and went down the old wooden stairs to catch a rope tossed to shore by Captain Brad.

"Mornin' Capn', "Tiny joked.

"Mornin' Mr. Brooks! Ready to throw some rocks?"

"Ready as I'll ever be! Let me grab my bag."

Tiny returned from his shack with a brown burlap sack containing his daily provisions for working in the river. He also had a five-foot pry bar and a shovel which Brad was staring at as he came down to the raft.

"In case we need to move some big ones," Tiny said.

Tiny stepped onboard, grabbed the long pole as Brad took the tiller and again the beautiful milk jug raft was adrift on the mighty Elk River. Tiny looked around and moved his body to check stability just as he had done the day before when he had helped Brad bring it back through the shoals from the mouth of Tater Holler. Still impressed, he flashed his bright smile at Brad for a job well done.

The team reached the shoals and tied off over by the shoreline. Tiny produced two empty milk jugs from his burlap bag that were painted, one red and one green to be somewhat "marine correct" for buoys.

"We can set these with an iron rod down through them and clear out everything in between. Maybe make a pass about 20 feet wide," Tiny suggested. "Every fisherman on the river will appreciate this."

"That sounds good," Brad replied. "Let's get to it."

Josh Baker's cell phone rang just after 8:00 am that same morning. The boys had spent the night in the old Otis boys' bunkhouse. This was a separate dwelling, wood construction, not attached to the house but built very close to it. The room was rectangular and about 20 feet long and maybe 12 feet wide. Bunk beds were built into the construction, two on each long wall. Right in the middle of the floor stood an old pot belly wood-burning stove. Chucked full of wood at bedtime, this stove kept the Otis boys plenty warm through the winter nights in the hills of West Virginia down through the years. The stove was not needed on this warm summer night, however, and both boys had slept like rocks with the windows open for clean mountain air.

Josh swung his legs around and his feet hit the old wooden floor. He reached for his phone with a sleepy face and checked the caller I.D. It read "Giselle." Josh touched the answer button and with his morning voice said "Hello." Eddie looked down on him from the top bunk on the other side of the room. Josh mouthed the name "Giselle."

"Did I wake you up again?" a sweet voice said on the other end.

"Getting to be a habit, Giselle. What's going on?"

"Well, I was up a little later after I talked to you last night and guess what? The Charleston Gazette, the newspaper?"

"Yeah, Yeah." Josh was rubbing the sleep out of his eyes and shaking the cobwebs out of his brain.

"Well, it was founded in 1873 and at that time it was called the Kanawha Chronicle and was a weekly paper. By 1902 it was well established and, lucky for us, kept excellent records even despite a fire in 1918."

"OK, wonderful history lesson."

"No, wait. What I found online was one last article about this robbery."

"Oh, really?" Josh's eyes widened a little, and he sat up a little straighter. With this reaction, Eddie rolled up to attention, too. Josh hit the speaker button on his phone. "Another article," he told his friend.

"You won't believe it," she spoke slowly and deliberately, "There was a reward for the recovery of that gold and for solid information about who took it!"

"Well, that's cool, I hadn't thought about that but it doesn't seem real unusual for a heist this big and high profile," Josh said while stretching out his sleep-deprived body. Eddie shrugged in agreement.

"True, but here's the thing; I did some legal research, too, and if the reward was never officially rescinded, then it is still valid. You get what I'm saying?"

"Oh wow, OK then." Josh looked at Eddie. "The incentive program. I like it." They smiled.

Giselle went on, "And that could explain why anyone who knows anything about this on the river would practically devote their life to finding it."

"Including Collins and Billingsworth," Josh replied.

"That's right."

Eddie jumped down from the top bunk. "Giselle, what does the article say exactly. Who offered the reward?"

"Ok, I'll read it. It's short."

Reward Offered for Missing Gold from C & O
Railway Heist

Officials in Washington D.C. are offering a reward for the missing gold stolen from a train in Kanawha County, West

Virginia. Officials say they will pay an undisclosed but generous amount for the return of the gold or information leading to the return of the gold that was stolen from a train a year ago in central Kanawha County. Anyone with information as to the whereabouts of the gold may contact their local town officials and your information will be officially documented and forwarded to the proper authorities in Washington.

"Well, I don't think I would want to go to our local officials with the information we have," Eddie said.

"No," Josh agreed. "And you know what I want? Think about this, Ed."

Eddie looked at his friend.

"I want our original copy back. The one we found. The deer skin."

Giselle said, "Yeah, just walk into Town Office and take it."

Josh shook his head. "Town Office? I don't think it's there. I'm thinking it's at Collins' house."

"Ah, ok. That's easier. Walk into the sheriff's house and take it."

"Well, maybe there is something that we missed, another clue."

Eddie said, "He lives alone, and his house would be empty during his shift hours at the office."

"No way guys. The risk is not worth the reward. And it's an enormous risk. You know he has security in that house. And what do you need it for, really? You copied it well. You have all you need."

Giselle made sense. It would be tough, and if they were caught, the party would be over. No more adventuring for these two.

"She's right!" A big voice boomed from outside.

The door to the bunkhouse was knocked open with a size 12 work boot as Burl Otis came walking in with a tray of biscuits, butter, blackberry jam and thick-cut fried bacon.

"Morning Boys! Old-fashioned Otis breakfast is ready!"

"We'll let you go now, Giselle," Josh said.

"Alright, let me know if you learn anything else."

"Ok, you too!"

"Bye."

"Hope this is OK for you boys. Just whipped it up kind of quick."

Burl sat the old wooden tray down on the table. The tray itself looked like an Otis relic and each biscuit was as big as a coffee saucer.

"Oh man, it looks and smells great!" Eddie exclaimed, jumping from his bed to grab a sample.

"I couldn't help overhearing when I was at the door, but I think your friend is right. We now have all the information we need to interpret the meaning of the document."

"Just aggravates me that he can do that and get away with it. Come into my garage and walk out with it like that. And he's the sheriff! That just makes me suspicious of him and Billingsworth. Those guys are up to some kind of no good. I know it!" Josh said.

"Well boys, what I would suggest is don't try to get back the original unless it becomes necessary. And maybe it won't be necessary at all. We have a lot of good information for now so I would say move on with that and I'm here to help you if you need it."

"Really?" Eddie exclaimed. "You'll help us out?"

"Of course. I just need a day to get some things done around here and then I'm free. I can go upriver with you guys and stay in my old trapping shack for a few days. I have some repairs to do on some traps down there. That way if you need me, I'm there."

"Trapping shack? Where is that?"

Burl Otis grinned a mountain man's grin that said *my secret*.

Josh and Eddie looked at each other, both thinking the same thing. They had been all over the hills within a three-mile radius of their home and never saw a trapping cabin in the woods. But they were thrilled at having the help and local knowledge of Mr. Otis. He could be a significant asset in their adventure!

After eating and cleaning up, Josh and Eddie emerged from the bunkhouse to a beautiful summer morning up on the mountain. The warm rays of a sun rising through the trees and hitting their faces felt like heaven. Josh noticed a newly stretched cougar hide tacked to the wall beside the rabbit hide Otis had tanned previously. Burl Otis got up really early. The cougar dominated the side of the shed.

Josh stared at it and shook his head as the recollection of the terror stirred him once again. *That was so close*, he thought to himself.

"It'll make a nice jacket," Eddie commented.

The three guys spent the rest of the morning splitting firewood, feeding the various farm animals around the homestead and moving some goats from the hill below the house to the area over behind the barn. Nature's weed-eaters! In a week that brush would be clear!

In the afternoon they took turns shooting an antique re-curve bow hand made by a previous Otis boy. The arrows flew true, and the boys were impressed. In the evening they all sat around the table by lamplight and discussed the meaning behind the riddle on the map. They kicked around a few ideas about the reference to *sand* and an *island bank* and also decided that it may benefit them to stop and talk to a river legend, a man who knows everything about the river, a man who knows every catfish for ten miles— Tiny Brooks.

Once again, the night was spent in the bunkhouse, and the next morning as the sun rose, so did the boys. It was the day that they were to meet Captain Brad at the river's edge for their trip back upstream. This time Burl Otis would join the ride—a genuine test of the raft's buoyancy.

CHAPTER TWENTY-THREE

The trio set out from the Otis homestead and entered the pathway at the end of the property that led into the woods. Daytime let them see where they were going now, and they could observe nature and the surrounding sights. The main path was well trodden and had many smaller paths that led off of it to unique parts of the hills and valleys that surrounded the Otis house and the woods where Josh and Eddie so often frequented a few miles away. Morning dew still lay on the leaves and two squirrels stirred a few yards ahead of them, gathering nuts and playfully chasing each other around a tree as they spiraled their way to the top.

They worked their way up to the ridge and to the point where Burl Otis had made an expert shot on a cougar. They paused and both Josh and Eddie walked over to the spot and silently replayed the event in their minds. They looked at each other, both thinking the same thing. They were lucky to be alive and had Mr. Otis to thank for it.

As they started down the other side, which was the rugged portion of their hike just a couple days earlier, Mr. Otis redirected them to a different route that was a little longer but much easier to descend. The almost undetectable path wound around the sides of the holler and snaked its way to the bottom. The beautiful scents of the forest helped to make this lengthy walk a pleasure, and Josh would periodically inhale deeply to take in the bouquet of the hickory nuts lying on the ground and the wild lilacs that grew along the hills and in the coves. About half way down the hill towards the river, Josh stopped and carefully took up a rhododendron by its roots to take home to his mom. He was careful to dig his hands deep and wide around the plant to gather the wet soil that would keep it alive until he got home. Josh knew Mrs. Baker would transplant the state flower into their yard. It was a nice, healthy young plant and was his mother's favorite. Josh placed the gift in a gallon plastic bag from his backpack, then they carried on with their hike.

The three hikers made their way down the mountain by about noon and, sure enough, Brad was there with his raft, waiting for the boys to return. He was sitting on his vessel with a fishing pole stuck in a makeshift rod holder, just killing time as they approached and stepped onto the small rock bar. The boys and Mr. Otis noticed the heat of the day building for the first time as they stepped from the shade of the forest.

Brad heard their steps and casually turned around to see his two passengers and a surprise guest. He said nothing at first as he sized up Burl Otis and looked at him as if he were trying to remember if he had seen him before.

"What's going on, guys? How was camping?" He broke the ice.

"Hey Brad, camping was great. We never took the tents out of the backpack!" Josh joked.

Brad and Burl were still eying one another—neither were too comfortable meeting strangers.

Finally Eddie said, "Uh, Mr. Otis, I'd like you to meet our friend Brad. Brad, this is Burl Otis."

Brad stepped off his raft and onto the riverbank as Burl Otis moved a little closer to him. The two stuck out their hands in a gentleman's handshake, Burl's hand all but enveloping Brad's. They exchanged greetings as Burl studied the craft in the water before him.

"Interesting looking boat you have here," Burl commented as he looked it over well, pondering if he should keep walking or take the ride with the boys.

"Thank you, sir. Eddie and Josh helped me put her together." He gestured towards his new friends.

Eddie shrugged, "Yeah, it's pretty stable and handles really well on the river."

The boys had already given Burl the story of the raft and had told him about Brad and his situation. The two friends stepped onto the raft and placed their gear aboard as Brad turned around and reached for his fishing pole to reel in and get ready to launch. Burl nodded his head as if agreeing with himself to go aboard and stepped towards the raft. He gave Eddie a look and then pointedly looked toward Brad. Eddie shook his head slightly. Burl wasn't sure if Brad knew anything about the document or the legend but wanted to be certain, so he didn't say anything he shouldn't. Brad's mind was working a little overtime, too, because he had had a little talk with Tiny Brooks the evening after they had made a passage through the shoals for the raft. Their discussion included Josh and Eddie and a place called Tater Holler, which concerned Tiny Brooks. He had always heard that nothing good ever came out of Tater Holler. Their discussion also included what possible intentions these kids could have in going up into those hills.

"Well Mr. Otis, welcome aboard!" Brad said with a grin.

Burl smiled and put one foot and then the other on board the raft and, to his surprise, it hardly wobbled with his 270 pounds. He nodded in approval. There was plenty of room for all four onboard including their gear.

"Well, let's make our way upriver guys, what do ya say?" Josh said.

Burl looked toward the baby blue bridge and the shoals in the distance. "Anchors aweigh!" he grinned.

Brad grabbed the long pole to shove off from shore as Eddie untied the line and coiled it up on deck, ship shape. With one hard push they were away from the bank and on their way to the middle of the river. Once there, they could line up for their approach through the new shoal passage. Burl stood in the center of the raft near the mast and watched the team execute the maneuver as if they had been doing it all their lives. He was quite impressed and thought the raft was a clever contraption and a cheap way for a few teenagers to have a way to get up and down the river.

The raft poled nicely today and, as the boys neared the middle of the river, they felt a perfect breeze from the southwest. Perfect for sailing!

Eddie untied the sail as Josh readied the lines for hoisting.

"Make sail!" Brad called out as Josh pulled smoothly on the mainsheet.

The sail climbed the mast and as soon as it topped out, the wind snapped it tight and Burl felt noticeable acceleration. He repositioned his feet for balance. The colorful paint-tarp sail stretched full and pulled them along impressively. Poling was unnecessary today even though they were sailing against a slight current, upriver and with a full crew!

They cruised along for about a mile. Josh was forward, cross-legged, looking off the bow with his rhododendron beside him as he splashed water into the bag and onto the roots. He spotted the shoals about two hundred yards ahead and then noticed two brightly colored milk jugs, one red and one green, sitting on top of the water. As they got closer Josh pointed them out to Eddie and they saw the jugs were connected to two steel rods driven into the river bed.

"That's very cool," Josh commented.

"And they rise and fall with the water level, too. If the river is up the markers will go up with it. Smooth like butter."

"That's brilliant," Burl Otis commented. "Who helped you with that?"

"Tiny Brooks," Brad said, "just a couple days ago. Not sure if you know him or not. We must have moved three tons of rock just so we'd never have to do it again."

Tiny Brooks. Burl rolled that name around in his head. It sounded familiar to him and he remembered there were some Brooks who had lived along the river for many, many years here, but he had somehow never become acquainted with them.

"You guys did a nice job. How deep is it now?" Eddie asked, wiping sweat from his forehead.

They closed in to within about 20 yards of the passage.

"We have about two and a half to three feet now. Plenty for any small V-bottom on this river and way more than I need for the raft."

The wind was still strong, and the raft was lined up straight. The passage was about twenty feet wide and the water rushed through it swiftly but without a ripple. Brad dug the pole in and gave a little push to overcome the increased velocity of the water through the gap. In just a couple of seconds they popped out the other side to the tranquil, deeper waters upstream of the rapids and just underneath the old baby blue bridge that was a landmark of their little town.

Burl Otis clapped his hands and laughed. "Wow. Nicely done gentleman. Nicely done! I'm very impressed."

They all enjoyed a laugh and some back slapping for Brad and then set their sights ahead for the continued ride. They made their way along as the shade eluded them. The summer sun was directly overhead now, burning the tops of their heads. It was hot and getting much hotter, with no drinking water on board. Josh and Eddie had consumed their water supply on the hike from the woods to the river, and Burl Otis was wiping sweat from his brow. All four were occasionally throwing river water on their faces and necks to cool off. Brad had an idea.

Tiny Brooks' house was just a quarter mile away, and he had told Brad to drop in anytime he was on the river. Brad would take him up on his hospitality for a drink of cold water. Of course, Josh and Eddie were good friends with Tiny also, and agreed it was a splendid idea.

As was the case most of the time, Tiny Brooks was sitting on his shady boat dock in a chair with a line in the water. He noticed the raft making its way up the river with the three boys and a large man on board. He was wearing his signature "river wear" of old knee—length black work pants and white cotton button-up shirt. Long-sleeved, but with the sleeves rolled up just below his elbows. No socks. No shoes. Big smile.

The raft drifted up to the dock as Burl, Josh, Eddie and Brad stood tall on the stable craft waiting to step off after a smiling, but curious dock hand tied them off.

"What's going on fellas?" Tiny asked.

"Just seeing if we could bum a drink of water," Eddie said.

"Can't bum from a friend!" Tiny smiled. "Come on off there. Let's go up to the house."

Josh said, "Tiny, this is Burl Otis, a friend of ours. We're giving him a ride upriver too. Burl, Tiny Brooks."

The two gripped each other's hands tightly and looked into each other's eyes, Burl still looking for any recollection.

"It's good to meet you Mr. Otis, come on up and welcome to my place."

"Thank you very much, Mr. Brooks. It's a pleasure! Are you of the Brooks family that has been here on the river a while?"

"Oh yes, sir. As a matter of fact, this house was my grand-pappy's. Of course, I've had to do some work on it through the years, but yes, we have been here since the early days of this area."

"It's always nice to meet a local!" Both men laughed.

The three boys shook their heads as they all stepped onto the dock and proceeded up the stairs to Tiny's humble house on the river.

As they stepped onto his front porch, Tiny asked, "How about you, Mr. Otis, are you from a river family?" Tiny halfway knew the answer to that.

"Well, not right on the river like you are, but up Tater Holler. My family settled that area back in the mid-1800s when there was nothing anywhere around here except a few Native Americans and a lot of wildlife to trap and hunt."

Standing on the boat dock by the Elk River, the two old men got to know each other a bit. Tiny had let go of the rumors he had heard about the Otis family and decided to make his own character judgment.

"Yeah, same here. My folks have been here for ages! This old river just gets in your veins, ya know?" He smiled and paused. "Tater Holler, ya say? That's really hard to get to from here, right?"

"Yeah, from this side it is. But from the back side of Tater Holler, it's not. There are roads that run into there from Hickory

Holler. It's far easier than climbing the hills from this side," Burl said. "I use a bunch of old trails when I need to go somewhere. Pretty self-sufficient on the mountain up there with a garden and livestock, but occasionally I'll wander down to the market and get a few things. What money I need, I make trappin'. I just like the lifestyle of not having to depend on anyone for anything."

"I have the same passion, Mr. Otis. The simpler the better. Come on in, guys, let's get something cold to drink."

The three thirsty adventurers stepped into the house, a small river shack with a front room that went across the full width of the front and then a hallway down the middle with a kitchen to the right that looked across a small bar into the front room and two bedrooms to the left, off the hallway. The bathroom was at the very end of the hallway on the right.

The home was simple and clean on the inside, with framed family pictures on the walls and end tables. An antique steel fishing rod and reel hung over the front door, an obvious relic of a previous Brooks man. A large, oval throw rug covered hardwood floors and a modest couch and two chairs made up the furniture of the front room, along with a coffee table and two small end tables by the couch.

"Make yourselves at home, guys. You're in luck; I have a fresh pitcher of sweet tea made up for ya," Tiny said as he stepped into the kitchen.

"That sounds perfect," Eddie responded.

The three were looking at the pictures and the Brooks memorabilia hanging on the walls from many years ago. An old fishing creel hung by a front window, a very old and rusty oil lamp was on a small shelf, some antique fishing lures were mounted to a board and hung by the front door, along with an antique South Bend octagon fly-rod. Josh then noticed a small box of loose pictures on one of the end tables.

Josh said, "Ya know, if you took your house, Tiny, and Mr. Otis' house and put them in a museum, you would have the history of our area of the state for the last one hundred and fifty years all in one spot."

Burl Otis laughed along with Brooks, "No museum would want my old junk," he said.

"Mine either!" Tiny laughed, looking through the rectangular opening that separated his kitchen from his front room, not believing that anything valuable was being displayed there. "No, when I die they will just push this whole house down into the river," he continued jokingly.

Burl said, "It's a nice place you have here, Mr. Brooks. And the location is perfect."

"Yeah, for an old river man like me it is. I never get tired of waking up and hearing that water running past outside my windows, getting out of bed and having that morning coffee on the porch or down at the dock. Starts my day off just the way I like! I got an old muskrat that comes up here in the evening begging for apples! Every evening."

"Like a pet," Brad commented.

"Like a pet," Tiny repeated, smiling big.

Tiny returned from the kitchen with a tray of glasses filled with ice and then returned to get the pitcher of tea. As he started filling the first glass, he noticed the boys still looking around at his displays of Brooks possessions that had surrounded him for so many years, surprised at their continued curiosity. He filled all the glasses and joined his guests in a refreshing glass of ice-cold sweet tea. He began thinking again about the boys' trip up Tater Holler and their return with Burl Otis. He couldn't help wondering what with what was up, especially with what he had always heard about Tater Holler. He decided to throw a line out and see if anybody bit on it.

"But I do agree there is a lot of history around here. Interesting stuff, too," he said, and then paused to let it sink in. "My people moved into this area in the middle 1800s from Georgia. Underground Railroad, ya know? Escaped the slave trade and found a place to hide up here until the war ended. And then my great grandfather did what he could for work; helped on farms, worked on a riverboat for a while, worked as a bartender up there on the island. Whatever he could do to make money, he did it. He established a home for the Brooks family and here we stayed." Tiny smiled again. Proud.

Everyone liked the story and commented on it. Eddie and Josh knew that would put Tiny's family in the area solidly during the time of the train robbery, and they couldn't help but wonder if he had any clue at all as to the whereabouts of the missing gold. The only problem with bringing Tiny in on the secret was Brad. At this point Brad knew nothing about what was going on, and the boys weren't sure if they knew him well enough to let him in on the secret. He had a good means of transportation which could become valuable in the search. But it had only been a few days. Could they trust Brad? It crossed Josh's mind again that Brad's problem was with his dad and not with them or even himself. Josh redirected the conversation for the time being.

"Tiny, Mr. Otis saved our lives up there on the mountain. Mountain lion." Josh nodded his head. "It was close."

A look of significant concern appeared on Tiny's face. He knew what prowled these hills at night. He had seen them before, too. He also knew they had all avoided his comment about local history.

"Ya don't say. Seems to be more of them these days than there used to be. Bear, too. You guys need to be careful. I see a lot of tracks by the water in the dry season," he said, pointing his finger their way as to drive his point home like a father.

"I was just lucky to have a good clean shot on that one," Burl said, "otherwise…"

They paused, thinking of what could have happened.

Tiny recalled hearing the unmistakable thunder of a muzzleloader a few evenings ago.

"So, Tater Holler, what brings you down our way?" Tiny asked, smiling. Curiosity was killing him.

"Well, I thought I would escort the kids out of Tater Holler and while I was at it spend a couple days at my trapping cabin. Do some repairs before season this fall."

Ah, good idea. And get a raft ride before Brad starts charging a fee, right? Tiny smiled.

"Excellent idea!" Brad jumped in, smiling.

Josh and Eddie laughed and glanced at each other. This was nice camaraderie, but what was on their minds was the treasure. The gold. They wanted to move forward and see what else they could uncover—what facts, what clues—and sort this out, myth or mystery. Whatever the outcome. It had become their passion since that day on the sandbar by the trestle.

Shade flowed quickly through the living room as only a rain cloud can do and darkened the room slightly. The men sipped their tea.

"Looks like a summer shower?" Burl commented.

Tiny looked out the window and nodded his head in agreement. He was an authority on the river and its climate.

"A quick one, I think, but yeah, looks like you guys might have a delay."

No sooner had he said it when a faraway rumble echoed down the river valley. The room lightened again and then darkened, this time even more as the wind moved the thin curtains in the front room.

"We better get our packs off the raft," Eddie said, "and your plant, Josh,"

The three boys moved quickly to get their equipment and Josh's rhododendron off the raft, and Brad secured the vessel a little better with an additional line. The two older men had come outside with their drinks to supervise and to offer help if needed, but the boys had everything handled well. They bounded up the stairs with their gear and, when reaching the top, Josh and Eddie peeled off their backpacks and tossed them up against the front of the house on the wide front porch. Eddies landed with a *clank*!

Josh and Eddie had spent a little time on Tiny's front porch before but had never noticed until just then that right there on his porch lay the perfect twin. A perfect match to the old red milk can that they had found stuck in the mud down by the sandbar a few days ago. This one was painted white and blended with the house somewhat, but it otherwise matched theirs perfectly.

Eddie reacted, and Josh's head turned his way. A look of curious astonishment covered his face.

Burl looked at them both and a slow smile came to Tiny's face. His eyes went back and forth from the boys to the old milk can as he wondered. *Could it be?*

They paused.

"You like the old can?" he asked.

Burl looked back and forth between the boys, and Brad stuck his head in as he reached the top of the stairs. The boys said nothing. Josh raised his eyebrows and nodded his head. Tiny looked at them both and then at Otis.

"It's a milk can. They used to haul milk in these. There might be fifty of them on a wagon or in later years on the back of a truck, and they would go around and deliver them. I found this one about twenty-five years ago."

Josh and Eddie looked curious but uncomfortable.

Eddie said slowly, "Yeah, we found one. We found one down by the sandbar in the mud. Filthy. Had to pull it out and clean it up."

Eddie looked at Josh. Had he said too much? Josh didn't know and didn't react.

Burl looked between the boys again and then to Brooks. Thunder rumbled a little closer now, and it got a little darker once again. Tiny removed his hat to scratch his head and then sat down on a metal chair on the front porch. There were three more chairs and all except Josh took one. Josh sat directly on the porch floor.

Tiny went into thought for a little bit as everyone surveyed the clouds and coming storm.

"Did it have a lid on it?" Tiny asked looking at Eddie then Josh.

"It did." Eddie replied softly.

There was a lengthy pause as rain could be heard starting to fall in the distance, large drops cracking the leaves as they came down. The boys and Burl knew that Tiny was going somewhere with this, and all three wondered why. Brad was oblivious at this point, looking down at his raft which had begun to move around as the wind picked up.

"Ya know," Tiny paused and leaned forward in his chair. Once again thunder rumbled, following a distant crack of lightning, "I guess there is one of these things still floating around the river here somewhere that is kind of… important." He took another sip of iced tea as he never broke eye contact with Eddie.

Josh and Eddie realised that Tiny knew. It amazed them that there was another person who knew the legend and knew about a document hidden in a milk can. Now, what to do? Should they take the conversation and go with it? See what they could learn? If so, they would have to be confident in Brad. They knew Tiny well enough to know he could be a genuine asset in finding something missing on the river. He knew every drop of it. Tiny could have a piece of the missing puzzle that could be very important to locating the treasure. But what about Brad? Josh and Eddie were thinking the same thing about the dilemma as Eddie looked at Brad, who was still looking at his raft. They wanted to trust Brad. They knew the challenges he had to deal with every day of his life. And it was not about being greedy and having to share money, because the boys weren't even that caught up in a reward for finding it. It was just the search, the hunt that had captivated them so much the past few days. But a little reward money could change Brad's life, his future. At this point in his life he had no hope of going to college or even learning a good trade. He would most likely be a prisoner of cheap labor.

Brad turned around and looked straight over at Josh and then Eddie and grinned proudly at his raft. Something so simple and Brad was a different person. The boys saw it in his eyes. There was good in his heart, and he was a victim of his fathers' dreadful habits. If fate was on their side, they would trust him and help to change his life. Brad would become a member of the team.

CHAPTER TWENTY-FOUR

The five guys sat on the front porch as the rain intensified and the skies grew even darker. Intermittent flashes of lightning and claps of thunder flashed and boomed all around them. Josh received a text message from his mom and he responded promptly. Burl was looking at the boys. It was their call. It was their discovery. He would just wait and see what they decided. It wouldn't take long.

Josh said solemnly, "Tiny, you know about the legend?"

Tiny smiled slowly, not the big iconic smile of his but more of a smile of trust and security.

"Oh, yes sir, I do," he said softly, never breaking eye contact. "That story goes way back with my folks and I know it's true. I am certain of it."

Burl Otis was slowly nodding in agreement, and Tiny acknowledged him. Two old timers on the river whose families both had ties to the legend.

Eddie said, "Can you tell us what you know?"

Tiny inhaled hard through his nose and sat up tall in his chair. The trusting smile came back to his face, and he took just a second to think about it.

"Oh yes, I can." He paused briefly, "But why don't you tell me first what you have found and then we can go from there."

Josh began. He told Tiny about fishing down at the sandbar by the trestle and finding the can in the mud over on the bank. He went on to tell him of the document that was in the can and their attempt to decipher it in the garage. He told him of their trips to the library to uncover local information and about the train robbery article and about Giselle and Mansfield and how he scooped up their copy of the legal pad document.

Tiny thought for a minute when they mentioned Mansfield.

Eddie picked up the story about the internet search for the *"Southern Jewel"* and what they had found. They told him about the article Giselle found about the wallet being the only clue ever found at the scene or anywhere else. Josh then explained how they went to the Town Office to get information on a man named Art Otis, the guy whose name was on the wallet, and how that had led them to Burl Otis, the man on Tiny's front porch right now. Between the two of them they explained how they bumped into Brad at "Brads Landing" while he was building the now-famous milk jug river raft.

Tiny cringed when Josh told him about Collins coming to the house and stealing the deer-hide document out of his garage so blatantly, and then went on to tell the details of going down river, almost getting eaten by a cougar, meeting Burl and having the best wild rabbit they could imagine. Tiny smiled big about that.

And then Burl chimed in with his details on the legend. Tiny listened intently as the ominous clouds continued to roll overhead. Occasionally they would make comments back and forth to each other about something that was said, but mostly Tiny just sat quietly and let Burl and the boys do the talking. Burl told what he knew of the meetings that Clyde Franklin and Art Otis had on the island on those nights so long ago. None of this surprised Tiny because he knew that story well. They explained about the red can that was on the Franklin's front porch for years after Franklin died, with nobody knowing the valuable contents within, and then the flood of 1936 that took it away. Burl told of the man named John Hopes who found Clyde Franklin's Bible and the note that told about the red can and its contents. They talked about Franklin's "loose lips" after the robbery and how people began to suspect him, and how the gun, the lantern, the gold and Art's body were never found. And then Josh told Burl's side of the story about Franklin killing Burl's great grandfather and moving the body, and how that wallet was placed on the tracks to make it look like Art Otis was the only criminal and that he had worked alone.

Tiny took it all in slowly, shaking his head at times at the depth and breadth of this legend, which was a part of the history of their small town.

Burl told Tiny how Sheriff Collins was related to the Franklins and of his obsession with the hunt to the point of thievery. And that Mayor Billingsworth had an interest in it, as had most mayors before him.

Josh went to his backpack and pulled out the copy of the document that was written on the legal pad, and they all showed Tiny what they collectively had deciphered:

"Where steel horses run

Streams flow from hills high

A Southern Jewel rests

From a rainy night

Sand is a vault

Key from the door

In an Island bank"

"And that's about it. Now we are to the point where we have to decode this riddle one line at a time and we think it will lead us to the gold. And we figure the way you know the river and the way Burl knows the hills, you guys might help us out," Josh finished.

Tiny sat back in his chair and lifted his eyebrows, processing all this information.

"Well, one thing is for sure guys... what you told me certainly fills in a lot of blank spaces of what I have been told. And they all fit, too!"

At that point everyone looked over at forgotten Brad. He was the deer in the headlights. With eyes as big as Burl's biscuits, he was in a blank stare and had been for quite a few minutes. He couldn't believe what he was hearing.

"Are you guys serious about this?" he asked slowly. "There is a pile of gold somewhere around here that was stolen and buried in our town?" He simplified it.

Eddie responded, "Well, it looks like it could be true, Brad. We're still a long way from knowing where it is, but we have a key to the bank if we can find the bank."

"Problem is there are two other keys out there in the hands of people who know what they are. They know what they have in their hands," Tiny said.

"Well, here's what I know, you guys covered a lot of it already. Some of the same things that you said were told to me by my own family through the years. I knew about the red can and the Franklin family and Mr. Otis, why your name rang a bell, and the flood and all that. I had heard all that, but what comes firsthand from my family are the meetings between Art Otis and Clyde Franklin."

The lightning had subsided but the inky clouds continued to hang over and rain fell steadily, pelting the forest around them and staining the river to a slight mud color.

Tiny spoke slowly. "Ya see, my great-grandpappy was Washington L. Brooks, bartender at the Crossroads Tavern, and he served drinks to Franklin and to Otis on those very nights when they planned the greatest train robbery in West Virginia and maybe the whole eastern U.S."

"Wow," Josh gasped.

"And he heard every word of it because those two drank and drank and got louder and louder. The other guys in the bar didn't pay any attention to them, but Washington Brooks heard it all."

Eddie asked, "He heard it all and didn't report it to anybody before it happened?"

"Eddie, here's the reality of it. Washington was a former slave who escaped the south on the Underground Railroad forty years prior to that time and found a sweet place to call home and to work and to raise his family. In those days a black man didn't make waves, didn't make trouble, not when he had all that refuge for his family going for him. At that time, he was fifty-two years old and everything was going well for him. So if he told a story like that and nobody believed him, the rumor would get out and his life would be over very soon. There were still a lot of haters around in those days. Black men didn't go around telling stories on white men."

"I can see why he kept his mouth shut," Burl said.

"Yeah, he had no choice, really." Tiny turned his palms up and shrugged. "But here's the thing." Tiny smiled a little because he knew he had some information they had not heard that could be a vital clue. "There was another man in the tavern on those nights. A stone mason, and not just a mason but the foreman of the crew of masons who were hired by the railroad to build the stone trestles all down the train line on the Elk River. Now, do you remember the name of the guy who was killed about three months after the train robbery, who is related to your librarian?"

Eddie thought and said, "Well, it was Mansfield—Edmond Mansfield."

Tiny leaned forward and put his elbows on his knees while sitting in the chair. "Edmond Mansfield, the great grandfather of your librarian, was the foreman on that project. He built the trestle you guys fish in front of nearly every day of your lives up at the sandbar."

"No way!" Eddie exclaimed.

"Yep, and that's not all. Clyde Franklin, on those nights, would wait until Art Otis had left, and then he would have little talks with Edmond Mansfield. Little chats over in the corner, away from the bar and away from the other masons." He smiled, happy to deliver fresh clues.

"Did Washington Brooks hear those conversations too?" Josh asked.

"No, no, unfortunately he could not hear the words between those two guys. But just the nature of their behavior was enough to tell him they were up to no good. Ya' know… body language. This is what I've been told."

Josh asked, "Well, I wonder what happened to Mansfield? Who shot him three months after the robbery, and why? And I think the article said they found no gun or evidence at that scene either."

Burl was thinking out loud, "My first suspect will be Clyde Franklin. Just a gut feeling, but if he used Art Otis and killed him, then maybe he used Mansfield too. And then killed him."

"Man! No wonder the librarian Mansfield grabbed our paper when he saw *The Southern Jewel* on it. His family knows all about it too!" Eddie said.

"You can bet they do. And you know when a good dog smells blood, he hunts harder. You can bet that if he knows some new clues have surfaced, that he will be digging. And so will Collins and Billingsworth."

Tiny paused in thought for a moment.

"It's going to be a race to the gold!" Josh exclaimed.

"Burl, you have a lot of information about the legend. Has Collins ever approached you about it, knowing the family history?" Tiny asked.

"Oh yes, a few times. Many years ago he caught me down at the general store several times at fur selling time and swaggered over and tried to make conversation that would eventually lead to the legend. I always told him I had nothing for him and I didn't know much about it. Of course, I knew he wasn't just making conversation, he was digging. Gold digging. And so, eventually, he just quit talking to me and so did a lot of other folks."

"And that would explain the rumors he started about you then. I'd bet my house he started telling the lies to keep other people away from you so you wouldn't tell them either!" Tiny said.

"Makes sense. He's corrupt, I know it. And it's been years. People haven't talked to me for years!"

"So, going back to Franklin and Mansfield, was it just one night or was it more nights that they had their talks?" Eddie asked Tiny.

"Oh no, it was a few conversations that they had over a couple week's time is what I was told. Franklin was buying him drinks." Tiny grinned.

"Butterin' that turkey to cook, ya think?" Burl said.

"You could be right about that," Tiny said, looking straight at him and nodding.

"But what in the world could Clyde Franklin need from Edmond Mansfield, a stone foreman?" Josh wondered aloud.

"Can I see that yellow paper, Josh?" Tiny asked. Tiny remembered something and wanted to confirm it.

Josh handed him the paper and Tiny unfolded it and looked at what they had deciphered. Tiny studied it for a moment, and his head once again nodded in discovery.

"It's right here on paper, Josh. The fifth line down is the reason that Clyde Franklin needed Edmond Mansfield," Tiny revealed.

Everyone including Brad gathered around the paper and counted down to the fifth line.

Tiny said, "He needed a place to hide the gold. He needed… a vault!"

Sand is a vault

Josh asked, "Wow. You think Edmond Mansfield built a vault somewhere in the hills to hide the gold? Gosh, makes perfect sense though," he said, looking down and thinking while chewing on his thumbnail. "I have seen documentaries about the Masons building many, many ceremonial vaults in the Appalachian Mountains. There are hundreds of them. So he would sure know how to do it."

"Sure would. Franklin had a need, and he had an opportunity to fulfill that need. It's a perfect situation for him and right at his fingertips. Both of the men he needed were right there in the same tavern," Tiny said.

Burl said, "And after the vault was complete and the gold placed in it and things settled down a bit, Franklin went back and shot Mansfield."

Josh added, "And that would eliminate the only other person who knew the truth about the robbery and where the gold was hidden, and once again only one man would know where it was."

"I'd be willing to bet that Franklin promised Mansfield partnership in the gold to get him to do it. I mean, a stone foreman made decent money, but with the promise of that kind of cash, he never has to cut another rock in his life," Tiny figured.

"It all fits. It's a real good case against Franklin."

"But the thing is, where? Where in Kanawha County could he have built a vault?" Eddie asked.

Tiny responded, "I think it's close. Think about it. Can you imagine how hard it would be to move 162 pounds of gold bars around as fast as you can with nobody seein' you do it? I mean, a horse or mule could do it. He could have packed it into saddlebags and walked it far, far away, but it makes more sense to me to think he hid it close so he could be real fast in and out. He would have had to hide it on the same night they stole it. That vault had to be ready that night!"

Tiny looked back over at Brad and smiled as if it were kind of funny how overwhelming all this must be for him all at one time. Brad was still in a daze, but soaking up every word.

Tiny said, "Josh, hand me that paper again."

Josh had it in his hand and passed it over to Tiny Brooks.

Tiny reread it and then went into thought. Burl Otis was noticing what a river-wise man that Tiny Brooks was, and he liked that. So did Josh and Eddie.

"The very first time you read this out loud to us, Josh, something caught my ear. And it's here at the bottom, the very last line."

In an island bank

"Now when I first heard that and was processing all that information, my first thought was… this stolen treasure is in the same place that almost all large amounts of stolen money is, or at least finds its way to at some point… The Caribbean."

"WHAT???" they collectively exclaimed.

Tiny chuckled and then explained, "Well, I happen to know that for centuries, pirated gold and stolen money has been taken to Caribbean islands to 'clean it up'. The Cayman Islands are notorious for doing that even still today. They are nearby and easy to get to. Also the Bahamas, who are even closer."

"Oh my gosh!" Josh said in disgust, thinking the adventure had just gotten too big for their means. "That could not have been an option for Clyde Franklin."

"Hold on now guys, Don't throw me off the porch just yet!" He smiled and laughed. "The words *Island* and *Bank* are what took me in that direction just for a moment. It was just my first thought. But now think about this instead." Tiny leaned forward on his elbows again. "Don't we have our own little island just up the river? And isn't that the island that still has what's left of the old Cross Roads Tavern? Didn't Clyde Franklin have easy and frequent access to that island?" He paused and looked around at the boys. "I think we have two lines of this riddle figured out already!" He smiled a little.

Burl said, "Well, you're right about that, Tiny. But the part that doesn't make sense is where it says; *In an Island Bank.* There was never a bank on that island. A hotel and casino, yes, but never a bank."

Burl knew his history.

Tiny leaned back in his chair again. The skies had begun to clear, and the rain had stopped. The air was clean after a refreshing summer downpour. He drew a deep breath in through his nose and now smiled big while crossing his arms. Once again he knew something that everyone else didn't.

He began, "See, back around the turn of the century that old house up there on the island was a resort type place. It billed itself as 'Celebrating the Island Life' but really what it was, was a casino with a dozen or so hotel rooms on top of it. It was a place to come and gamble and then spend the night. Men from Charleston, and some women too, but mostly men, would travel up the river either on a boat or on the train and spend the weekend here. They would gamble and have a pleasant time and then go home on Sundays. The place had a kitchen that put out good food and the rooms were clean, so it was a popular thing to do!"

Once again Tiny leaned forward on his elbows.

"Here's the point I'm gettin' to, and I've heard this from the old-timers. The common thing back in the day when these guys would leave home to come up here was to say 'I'm going to the bank this weekend.' It was like a socialite inside joke."

"Hmmm," Eddie said.

"Yeah, so 'Going to the bank' really meant going to the Island Casino at the Crossroads Tavern right here in Blue Creek, West Virginia. And ya know what?" Tiny lowered to a whisper, "The author of that deer hide document would have known that. Clyde Franklin… would have known that!"

The rain had completely stopped, and the sun shone through between the trees and beamed a ray of light straight onto Josh's face. It helped everyone to see how big he was smiling! He was thinking what everyone else was thinking—the treasure could be right there on their little island in Blue Creek, West Virginia!

CHAPTER TWENTY-FIVE

The doors had long been closed and locked that evening and only a single light was on downstairs, back in the corner. Elton Mansfield was scrolling through microfiche and doing internet searches until late in the evening and wishing so much that he could get that grant from the state to modernize his library. He had a yellow piece of legal pad paper beside his keyboard and a notebook for jotting down his ideas. His helper had some notes and old photos in a folder that was almost as old as the helper himself.

The two men had been friends for many years. Elton had provided the man with some local information back in the 70s to assist in a search that the other man was conducting, or trying to conduct. As it turned out, the two men had a common interest. It was this gentleman who had discovered the note in Clyde Franklin's Bible after he purchased it at an old bookstore in Charleston.

John Hopes was quite elderly now, but still had a very sharp mind. He was a small man, maybe one hundred and forty pounds, fully gray but still quite nimble. He had been a brilliant investigative reporter back in his time, divulging many of the atrocities of the West Virginia coal mines and the harsh conditions that the workers had to endure. He could remember everything from his days at the newspaper, including the day he bought the used bible from the late 1800s in a used bookstore.

"Elton, do you suppose this word in line five could be vault?"

Mansfield studied the word and agreed excitedly that it was the most probable. Just a couple more words to go and they too would have the document completely filled in. Then it would be a matter of decoding its meaning.

Elton Mansfield had solid information regarding the *Southern Jewel*. He didn't have the family information that Burl Otis had or that Tiny Brooks had, other than one little item up his sleeve, but he had access to many resources of information at his fingertips and what he didn't have, maybe another library in the county *did* have. Gathering information was no problem for Elton Mansfield. If he wanted to find something, he would.

His great grandfather left his family nearly nothing. Edmond was killed so suddenly and his family had little to no clues why. He had never received one ounce of gold from Clyde Franklin for building the vault, but what his family did have was three words that he muttered to his wife with his last breath as he lay on his front yard dying. Those words would be kept as a family secret and would prove very significant over a hundred years later.

John Hopes was using an old wheel-type decoder he had brought along from a long-forgotten board game that he had picked up somewhere along the way as a novelty. It was about the size of a greeting card and had five spinning wheels on it. The user would line up the wheels with the letters that were available and the decoder, when turned over, would give you the most likely letters to the word that you were looking for down at the bottom. That 25-cent flea market item was paying for itself over and over tonight. They had filled in the blank spaces in less than two hours and were now nearly ready to decipher the meaning of this century-old riddle. Two words to go.

Boom, boom, boom! A thunderous pound on the door upstairs caused both of them to jump. A look of fear washed over Elton Mansfield's face as he looked at Hopes, hoping *he* would know what to do. Hopes looked up at him from his chair with an expression of anxiety. They both froze.

"Who could it be?" Hopes whispered.

"I have no idea. No one should be here!"

Boom, Boom, Boom! Again.

Mansfield slowly stepped from beside the desk to ease over to the bottom of the stairs. The small corner light that was on downstairs, was enough to shoot a beam of light up the stairway and he could see that beam of light hit the front wall upstairs. Thinking—Mansfield knew the door was locked and that he could safely see who it was by peeking through the front blinds.

Boom, Boom, Boom! Persistence.

John Hopes still looked concerned as Mansfield slowly ascended the fourteen steps to the main floor. He could see a figure through the frosted glass of the front door as he approached it. The blinds were drawn tight on the windows. Mansfield slowly approached the window and ever so slightly parted two blinds to see outside. A flashing blue light hit him square in the eye. Police! But why?

His instinct was to turn and ease back down stairs but again, why, really? He was doing nothing illegal. Private, yes, and confidential, yes, but illegal? No.

Mansfield took a deep breath and put his hand toward the locks to see what this was all about.

As he opened the deadbolt and then the knob lock, the man on the outside did the rest. The door opened swiftly, and, to his surprise, there stood the leathered face of Blue Creek's finest.

Elton Mansfield had a look of astonishment on his face as Sheriff Collins invited himself in. He smelled like eight hours of driving around with your windows open. End of his shift.

Collins looked at Mansfield and then looked around the room.

Mansfield stuttered, "Sheriff, is there something I can help you with? Uh... we, we have been closed for a few hours."

Collins looked at him and then looked around some more.

"Well, Mr. Mansfield, that's exactly why I stopped." He paused. "I know what time you close and on my way home I saw a light on here."

Collins eyes floated around the room some more.

"Everything okay here?" he asked, somewhat suspiciously.

A cop can read when someone is up to something that they don't want to share. Legal or not. It's in their blood to feel it. It's also in their training.

"Oh yes, we are fine" Mansfield responded quickly.

"You said 'we', you have company?" Collins asked firmly again.

Mansfield was a little bewildered and was getting a little dry in the mouth.

John Hopes slowly emerged from the shadows and stepped up behind Mansfield. Collins could only see half of his face. Neither man had heard him come up the stairs. Years of investigative reporting had taught him to move around quietly.

"Good evening, Officer," Hopes said with a grin.

Mansfield improvised an excuse. "We are just doing some organizing downstairs and stocking new books. Everything must be card catalogued. I don't get paid for this stuff, either!" He forced a smile and Collins knew it. "My friend John is helping me. Someday we will be computerized and won't have to do all this work by hand."

Sheriff Collins nodded ever so slightly to make Mansfield think he believed him.

"Mr. Mansfield, do you always work in such dark conditions?" He asked.

Mansfield thought quickly. "Well, we are working downstairs this evening and it was daylight when we went down there." Mansfield could feel himself starting to get a little perturbed. This was none of Collins' business anyway, other than being on county property.

"But... well, thank you for stopping to check on us, Sheriff Collins. I assure you everything is fine here at the library."

Collins put his thumb in his gun belt and took a deep breath as he looked around once again. He grinned and drew a deep breath through his nose.

"Well okay, I'll be on my way. Just wanted to make sure everything was okay."

John Hopes smiled.

Mansfield said, "Thank you very much. We greatly appreciate it, Sheriff, and have a nice evening."

Collins paused just a bit and let his eyes roam once more. He walked to the door slowly, took the doorknob in his hand and then turned around. John Hopes had already started down the stairs, and Mansfield had his hand on the handrail to do the same.

Collins said, "Oh, Mansfield."

Mansfield's head swiveled around to look at Collins and his eyes acknowledged him.

Collins looked at him with cop eyes. "Your card catalogue… It's upstairs."

Mansfield said nothing but slowly nodded, knowing that Collins knew he wasn't telling him the truth.

Collins closed the door and Mansfield eased back downstairs, a little sick to his stomach. *What was that all about?* Mansfield walked over and placed both hands on the rack that held the daily newspapers. He leaned on it and contemplated what had just happened.

Because their families had lived in the area for generations, both Mansfield and Collins knew of each other's connection to the legend, but what each of them didn't know is that both of them now had the biggest clue to come along in decades, thanks to Josh and Eddie. There were now three defined teams who were hot on the trail of the missing Confederate gold, and only Josh and Eddie's team knew that! Mansfield knew that Josh and Eddie had found something big, but he didn't know it was the missing red can. Collins and Mayor Billingsworth knew that the boys found the can and were looking for Otis, but the two town officials didn't know about Mansfield and the yellow legal pad paper copy of the document.

Mansfield now realized that he must work fast.

Hopes looked at him while he bit his cheek.

"John, we have to get busy. We have to decipher this riddle as soon as possible. I know Collins knows something. He just wouldn't have done that for no reason. He's too lazy for one thing! But I could see it in his eyes. Something has happened that we don't know about, and heaven only knows how many people have this same clue that we do."

"Yes, it's amazing how two kids can come strolling in here with information of such high importance." Hopes paused and thought for a moment. "Could they have found the can, do you suppose? The one mentioned on the note in Clyde Franklin's old Bible?"

"That can washed off of Clyde Franklins porch in the flood. People just assume it's in the swamps of Louisiana by now. But I don't know," Mansfield said, washing his hand back over his forehead, raking his hair back. "Any kid who spends a lot of time running up and down the riverbanks will certainly find things. It's possible," he sighed resignedly, "because I don't know where else this could have come from. I'm just concerned that Collins has the same information that we do. If he does, we are in a race for sure!"

John Hopes sat back down at the desk he was working at and put his bifocal glasses back on the end of his nose. "Well… we'd best get busy then."

Mansfield took the work that they had done, with all the letters filled in, and made some copies of it. He gave Hopes one to take home, kept one for himself, and put three more in a file folder to lock up later in the safe upstairs. For now, he placed them by the computer screen on an adjacent desk and stood up.

Hopes said, "How much do you think the kids know?"

"They're kids. There's no way they could know much without help. It's Collins I'm worried about because not only is he lazy, he's greedy and he's devious. He will do whatever it takes to find out whatever he needs, despite his laziness. And he has that badge to help him do it."

Hopes was already scanning the lines of the riddle.

Steel horses… rainy night… sand is a vault… an island.

"Hmm…," he thought.

The two men worked late into the night with strong will and strong black coffee. Elton Mansfield would jump from the computer to the microfiche, and then he would go grab a book or two that he thought would help him. They discussed the possibilities of each line and used all the resources they had at their fingertips in the library to their advantage and, by 2:15 a.m. they were confident that they had each line figured out the way the author had intended. They, too, were very sure that the little island just five miles north of them held the secret to the gold, if not the gold itself. They just had one problem—and so did the other two teams. That island was privately owned now and off limits to just about everyone. A gate and padlock blocked the swinging bridge that led to it, and also a sign that warned of prosecution. It had been purchased a few years earlier by an investment group that wanted to develop it into a youth camp. So far nothing had been done, and it sat just as it had when it was purchased, with overgrown weeds all around and an old three-story structure desperately in need of attention.

Of course, boys being boys, Josh and Eddie had explored the island a few times using their boat. Many times, actually. Rumor was that there was a caretaker who stayed there in the old structure to monitor things and to run off anyone who came to vandalize. It was said that he would shoot at you with "salt shot" if he caught you on the island snooping around. Josh and Eddie had never seen him any of the times they had been there, and there was not much evidence that anyone was taking care of anything on that island.

Mansfield and Hopes didn't know that.

Mansfield hit the power switch on the copier to shut it down and Hopes flicked off the basement lights. They were done for the night.

CHAPTER TWENTY-SIX

Mrs. Anderson looked over the top of her glasses as the little bell jingled and Mayor Billingsworth walked into the Town Office wearing his trademark lizard-skin cowboy boots and white Stetson hat and smoking his morning cigar.

"Good morning Mayor," she said in a strong Appalachian accent.

He took the cigar out of the corner of his mouth and nodded his head to her. "Good morning, Kate. How are you?"

"Fine, and you, sir?"

"Good, good. Any letters or memos for me?"

"No, nothing yet today." She looked back down at her stack of work on her desk. "Always a pile."

Billingsworth smelled the coffee and stepped towards the little room where Kate Anderson kept it fresh.

From two offices down Sheriff Collins heard the mayor arrive, rolled his chair away from his desk and met the mayor at the coffeepot. Collins stepped into the little room towards the back, away from Mrs. Anderson, as the mayor was pouring himself his first cup of the day. Collins brought a strange mood with him and looked worn down, and even unshaven. The two looked at each other and then glanced around. Billingsworth still had the cigar in his mouth as he poured his coffee. Collins stepped close to him and kept his voice down as his eyes darted back and forth nervously. He checked again to see no one was close.

"We have to hurry!" Collins said straightforwardly. "Those kids know too much, and now I have a feeling that Elton Mansfield knows something!"

"Mansfield?" The mayor thought for a moment, cigar still in his mouth. "The librarian?"

"He's not only a librarian. You know his connection. He was in there late last night, at the library, way past hours of operation with some old guy. I knocked on the door to see if everything was good and he was up to something and it wasn't book returns."

"Oh. Collins, you're paranoid! He could have been doing anything!" the mayor said, taking the cigar out of his mouth. "How do you know they weren't researching something or the old guy was not just there using the computers? Could be his father! And I wouldn't worry about those kids either. They're kids... how much could they know?"

The mayor was doing his best to shrug it off, but Collins was certain.

"I know when someone is lying to me, Mayor. Now listen, Mansfield knows of my connection to that legend and I know of his connection." Collins then pointed his finger to drive his point home. "He has never acted so nervous in all the years I have known him."

"All the years? How well do you know him?"

"Well, we know of each other. We are not friends, but we know of each other. It's a small community here on the river, Mayor. You know that. I have spoken to him a few times and he just acts like… well… a librarian! But this time he acted more like a… like a first-time offender, like a kid who had stolen a candy bar for the first time and then was accused of doing it! I could read it in his eyes." Collins smoothed his hair back nervously with his right hand and looked Mayor Billingsworth right in the eye. "He didn't want me to know what he was doing!"

The Mayor broke eye contact with Collins and took a sip of coffee as he went into thought, shaking his head. *His* demeanor became uneasy.

"Mayor," Collins continued slowly, "Listen. I know that Mansfield is absolutely obsessed with this legend just as I am. He is a living descendant, I am a living descendant, and oh by the way, that big Otis guy is a living descendant. We all know of each other! And I do not want any of them finding this before we do!" he said sternly.

Now it was Billingsworth's eyes that were darting around. He didn't want to look Collins in the eye. He returned the cigar to his mouth and walked around the small room apprehensively. His mood changed every few seconds as he thought his way through it and he appeared angry as he stopped pacing and looked back at Collins, taking the cigar out once again and pointing the wet end at him. "You should not have taken that document from that kid's garage! Eventually we will have to explain that, especially if we find the gold," he said scornfully but quietly.

"It was the red can! The missing red can that has been missing for decades! It was right there. Those kids didn't know what they had. They could have ruined it! It is a historic document and had to be preserved!" Collins said with pleading hands. "I was doing a service, Mayor!"

Billingsworth moved closer to Collins.

"You stole it. And if I'm with you in this, then I am an accessory to the crime. Do you know what that is? I'll tell you what that is. It's political suicide! That's what it is!" The mayor now drove his point home. "Absolutely I would like to solve this legend and get that gold. But it's not even ours to keep. Sure, there is a hefty ongoing reward for finding it, not to mention all the bragging rights and political leverage. It could be a political springboard, if played right. But it won't do me one bit of good if I'm sitting in jail for stealing something out of a kid's garage!"

Collins put a finger to his lips as he looked around. They were getting a bit loud.

The Mayor continued, "And I still say that you are paranoid. So what, that you were driving home and saw the light on in the library past hours and knocked on the door and two old guys were acting weird. Could be a million reasons! They could be making moonshine in that basement, they could be printing money, they, they could be doing anything down there, but it's astronomical to think they were working on finding that missing gold. Astronomical!"

Collins was not getting his point across and was looking desperate. Sweat beaded on his forehead on this warm summer morning and he began to pace once again inside the compact room. He looked back at Billingsworth and reached for his pocket.

"Really? Really? Astronomical, huh? Well, take a look at this!"

Collins jerked a piece of copy paper from his back pocket, unfolded it and whacked it down on the table beside coffee maker.

"What is this?" the Mayor asked. He slowly picked it up and scanned it. His eyes widened. "Collins… what is this? What have you done?"

"This is what they were doing last night!"

"How did you get this?"

"I staked them out."

"You what?"

"Mayor, you've got to listen to me! I knew he was up to something! I knew it! So when I let myself out, I closed the door and let them go downstairs. I waited for a few minutes and then opened the door again and put a piece of clear tape over the strike plate on the door casing. It was dark, so Mansfield wouldn't see it when he left. He locked the knob lock, but not the deadbolt—lucky for me. I had to wait until 2:30 in the morning, but they finally left and all I had to do was give the door a good push and I was in."

Mayor Billingsworth's eyes were as big as Frisbees. Collins had once again let himself in to a place and helped himself to what he needed. He was working beyond the boundaries of his badge for personal gain.

The Mayor looked back down at the paper.

"Do you know what this is?" Collins asked and then resumed slowly, looking Billingsworth square in the eye, "This is the document... completely solved. Every letter filled in and underneath it they have written what they believe it means. Little notes all over the place. Mayor, this... is... the... golden... ticket! We can almost just literally go get the gold now. We don't even have to decode it. It's all done for us!"

Once again, the Mayor's eyes floated down to the paper. He read words like: *steel horses, storms flow from hills high, southern jewel,* and *island bank.*

Billingsworth was frozen for a few seconds and then looked up from the paper but didn't focus on anything. He was deep in thought—almost meditation-like, recounting the legend in his head that he knew so well. He muttered, *"Storms from hills high…."* It poured rain that night."

"Yes, yes, it was a deluge!" Collins replied, finally making some progress with the Mayor.

The Mayor went on muttering and staring straight ahead, trance-like, deep in thought. "*Island*... our island," he reasoned.

"It's right here!" Collins said.

Greed had found its way into the veins of the town Mayor as he absorbed the words on the paper and allowed his mind to accept the fact that it could be so close and so easy. Would it be worth gambling all of his future political aspirations to carry on and find this missing treasure? He was right that eventually they had to explain how they had gotten their hands on all the new clues they were in possession of. If they found this, it would not just be a local story. No—it would be regional, statewide, and even national news! There would be inquiries forever, and so many questions to answer. A rush of emotions raced through him and he thought the best decision was no decision for now. He took a few deep breaths and looked down at the paper again. "How did you come up with this?" he wanted to know.

Collins looked at him for a second and then thought back to last night after he had let himself into the library.

"Well, I just closed the door behind me of course and I knew they had been working downstairs, so I slipped down there and started looking around. Mansfield is a neat freak so everything looked in order, really nice and tidy as I looked around with just a flashlight. That guy... I mean every book is in place and every magazine is faced out so you can see what it is and nothing is out of place." Collins paused, thinking deeply and rubbing his chin, "And that's what made this so easy to spot. There was a folder stuck between the computer screen and the computer desk that was just sloppy. It was out of place and wasn't supposed to be there long term. I opened the folder and looked in and there they were."

"They?"

"Yeah… there were three copies of this! I'm sure their intention was to put these away somewhere, but probably in their exhaustion, someone dropped the ball and forgot." Collins' detective mind at work.

"So you just took one?" the Mayor asked, raising his eyebrows. "You do know they will remember how many copies of it they made!"

"Of course! I made one more copy and put the folder back right where it was," Collins said, once again behaving like a detective. "When I finished there, I pulled the tape off the doorway, which locked the door, and left."

Billingsworth, noticeably concerned, turned away from Collins and chewed his cigar a little more and thought. He wanted to move on to Charleston. He wanted to advance his political career and have a nice office in that beautiful gold-domed capitol building. But goodness, if a man can find a pile of gold, wouldn't that be better? Wouldn't that be enough? Who needs politics? Who needs *any* job? But then again, if a man can find a pile of gold, an artifact from our country's past, and use it as a springboard to advance his political career, then he is thinking right! Yes, that would be the ticket!

But… it can't be done that way. Not with Collins as a partner. Collins is too dirty already. And Collins doesn't want the reward. That's small-change. If the truth is known, Collins wants the 162 pounds of Confederate gold. Of course, he would have to launder it. He would have to run it through a bank somewhere foreign just as dirty as he is and then have it wire transferred to another foreign account, the first bank holding the gold as security. Then he will have all that cash to play with and not a worry in the world. The Mayor knew this was true, even as crazy as it sounded. There was no way that a guy like Collins could ever pull that off by himself, but he is crazy enough and he is greedy enough and he is obsessed enough to think he could. And if he gets the gold first, he will try! Collins would need a partner; someone who knows the system better than he.

The Mayor weighed it both ways in his mind, trying to determine what was really best. Another crossroads in two men's lives. A man will have many crossroads in his life and will sometimes make wrong turns but if one can learn from each wrong turn and direct himself back to the right path, then his journey will not be a failure and his original goal can still be his destination. So, what is better? Instant gratification on a huge scale or the road less traveled? The Mayor was eaten up with indecision and would have loved to just think about it for a week, but there was not time. Too many people had too much information and time was running short. A decision had to be made immediately, and then they must hasten. This legend would come to life and the gold would be discovered very soon, with or without him.

Billingsworth turned back to Collins and looked at him; taking the cigar out of his mouth he paused briefly then said calmly, "So what's next? What do we do?"

Collins grinned and together they looked at the paper with all the information they needed.

Elton Mansfield closed his car door and hit the lock button on his keys. His arms and hands were occupied beyond capacity with a briefcase, a lunch bag and three newspapers that he picked up from in front of the library door before inserting his key to begin another day of work. He awkwardly managed to unlock the front door and step across the threshold of the doorway into the little library that he started up on a small grant quite a few years ago. This place was his pride and joy and he knew every book, every magazine, every newspaper, and every square inch of this building and what belonged and what didn't.

That's why he did a double-take when he saw the small piece of tape on the doorway. A triangle of clear packaging tape clung loosely to the strike plate on the doorjamb. He put his briefcase down and placed the newspapers on a table nearby. He knelt to get a better look and analyzed it like a forensics agent. He didn't have packaging tape at the library. It hadn't been there yesterday when he opened. He remembered because he had to jiggle the key a little yesterday to get the tumblers in the aging lock to turn. He recalled glancing at the doorway the day before and making a mental note to have new locks installed soon.

The tape was stuck to the strike plate on just one corner of the triangle and the rest of it was folded back a little and stuck to itself. It didn't inhibit the lock from working, but it was close. Maybe someone had brushed up against the doorway on the way in or out yesterday with a backpack or an armful of work and a piece of tape had clung on the way out. Must be the reason. He turned, disregarding it, and flipped on the lights to his workplace and moved the newspapers from the table beside the door to the rack where they would hang for the day. Mansfield then descended the stairs to the still dark basement, and at the bottom he put his briefcase on one of the tables and reached for the light switch. His eyes then froze, as did his entire body. The light for the power switch on the copier was illuminated.

He ran upstairs to the phone, leaving everything just as it was in the basement. When he was done on the phone, he took a pair of tweezers from a desk drawer and peeled the remaining piece of tape from the doorway. He carefully examined it and noticed a fingerprint on the sticky part of the tape. He then located a small Tupperware container and gently placed the tape fragment inside and snapped on the small lid.

Mansfield heard the unmistakable rumble of Giselle O'Conner's Pontiac pulling up to park outside. She, too, was starting her workday at the library.

Mansfield hurried to put away the small container and greeted Giselle as always as she entered the door. She smiled, returned the greeting and started her day. Giselle was a great helper at the library and had a very good work ethic. She, too, knew what was in order and what was out of place.

CHAPTER TWENTY-SEVEN

Josh Baker woke late that morning after a good night's rest, curled up and comfortable in his bed. He turned off his old two-dollar Hallicrafters short-wave radio receiver that had played on the AM band all night, long after Mystery Theater had ended and he was deep in sleep. His eyes fluttered open, then he gathered his thoughts a little, and rolled out of bed.

For an instant upon waking he thought it was all a dream, but as he came to life, he realized otherwise and the adrenalin immediately moved him. He, Eddie, Mr. Otis and Tiny Brooks had unraveled the code of the document, and now the old article had been transformed into a treasure map.

The arrangement was to meet that morning around noon on the sandbar and formulate their plan to discretely locate 162 pounds of Confederate gold that was stolen from that train in 1903, right across the river from where Josh Baker's house now stands. Not your average summertime, school's-out, adventure!

Josh jumped out of bed, washed his face, brushed his teeth, got dressed and scurried down the stairs to eat some breakfast. At the table his family hit him with a barrage of questions about his two-night "camping trip" and he did his best to dodge questions that might give away their objective of going to Tater Holler. He did not mention the cougar encounter and Mr. Otis. He didn't want to jeopardize any future camping trips. And of course, the treasure map was still confidential, too. The boys would not share this with their families. Not yet.

At 11:00 a.m. Eddie slid his bike to a stop inside Josh's open garage, and Josh came outside to greet him.

"How'd ya sleep?" quipped Eddie.

"Like Indiana Jones," Josh replied, smiling.

Eddie grinned, scratched his head and repositioned his ball cap and looked around the garage. "I'm thinking we should take a couple of fishing poles to the sandbar, just so it doesn't look so much like a meeting. Four guys standing around on the sandbar talking doesn't make sense to someone looking or someone drifting by on a boat. It's my thinking we have to be as low profile as possible."

"It's a good idea," Josh replied, looking at the options hanging on the rod rack on the wall. "Might as well make it real! Let's dig some worms." The boys never missed an opportunity to fish. Why "fake fish" when you can fish for real?

Josh had a favorite spot for gathering large Canadian night crawlers for fishing. Just across the street from his driveway there was a shallow depression that ran parallel to the street. Not really a ditch, just a low depression, and it was in that depression that leaves gathered and stayed nearly all year long. Under those leaves the ground was moist and warm and perfect for a worm farm. Three years ago Josh threw a dozen night crawlers under those leaves and he hadn't had to buy any since.

Eddie grabbed an old coffee can from the garage and he and his friend headed over to the leaf pile to gather some bait. On their hands and knees, they pulled the leaves back and began their selection. About a dozen would do.

Eddie felt something. He sensed an eerie feeling and looked around. Josh looked at him then said, "What, what is it?" still pulling worms.

Eddie lifted up off his hands, but still on his knees, and looked across Josh's left shoulder and up the street to the corner. Parked just beyond the intersection was a dark gray late-model Ford Crown Victoria. The windows were tinted dark, and the engine was running. Josh spun around to see what had caught Eddie's eye.

The boys lived in a small, three-block community along the Elk River where everyone knew everyone and they were sure they had never seen this car in their neighborhood before.

"What do you think they're doing?" Josh asked quietly, turning back around so as not to stare.

Eddie, still looking, turned down both corners of his mouth and shrugged slightly. "Could be just picking up somebody or whatever…"

Eddie put his head back down and resumed worm collecting, but looked up at the car. He saw a large figure in the driver seat and no one else. The passenger side was empty and there seemed to be no movement in the back seat, as best as he could see. They tuned their ears toward the vehicle and heard the electric cooling fans kicking on and off to cool the engine and also the air conditioner compressor keeping the observer comfortable as he sat there.

Confident that they had enough bait for "the meeting" they brushed the leaves back over the worm farm and stood up. Josh grabbed the can, and they proceeded to cross the street to his garage. With heads down, ignoring the car, Josh rolled his eyes toward the car once more. The headlights on the Crown Vic flashed! A shock ran through Josh's body.

"My gosh, Eddie! He just flashed his lights!"

Eddie paused, not knowing what to think.

"You serious?" he whispered.

Eddie, head still down, rolled his eyes toward the vehicle. The lights flashed again!

"Oh Man! Josh, that's for us! I don't know who that could be, but they want us!"

A bit of fear gripped both boys. If it were just a normal summer, they would not have been concerned. But this was not a normal summer. They were involved in the adventure of a lifetime. They had kept secrets from everyone including friends, family and law enforcement, and to say that they were paranoid was an understatement. Nervousness and fear ran through their veins as they took a few more steps toward the driveway and the safety of home, and simultaneously they glanced toward the car one more time. The dark gray Ford then flashed his lights repeatedly at the boys and Josh gasped, knowing that they had seen the lights and the driver had seen them. They stopped and stared at the car. They could not ignore the fact that the lights were flashed at them and someone wanted to talk to them. At that moment a big arm came out the window and, with the slightest hand movement, gestured at the boys to come to the car. Fear ran deeper now. Who could this be and what could he want? Everything they had been taught all their lives went against approaching that car. But Josh and Eddie had the advantage of space between them and the vehicle, and geographical knowledge of the area if they had to run.

"I'm a little scared of this," Josh said, only half joking.

Eddie paused to give it some more thought.

"Josh, let's go see who that is and what he wants. But… if we have to run, split up, stay off the streets, and I will meet you at the bulldozer under the shade tree over where they are building the church."

Now Josh paused and thought. The lights flashed again. Another shock to his body.

"Okay, Okay, let's go."

The boys did a slow and cautious walk to the official-looking vehicle. Josh noticed how clean it was and that the grooves of the tires were deep and new and there were no dings on the front end of the car from gravel or bugs or poor drivers. Eddie inhaled deeply as they approached the car. The air conditioner compressor clicked on again. Josh and Eddie rounded the front of the car and walked to the side but stayed about ten feet out from the driver's window, prepared to run at a second's notice. At that second, the driver's window rolled down about halfway, and Josh and Eddie gasped collectively as they both recognized the driver.

Mayor Billingsworth sat as low as he could in the big sedan, failing miserably to be inconspicuous, his sizeable frame using up every inch of the driver's seat. Josh and Eddie stepped a little closer now, completely bewildered. The Mayor was sitting stiff and still, facing forward in the car, but allowed his eyes to roll left to look at the boys. The kids could then easily see the nervousness in his eyes. He was just as uneasy as they were, and Josh noticed a few beads of sweat on the forehead of the top man in Blue Creek. Before them was not the big-talking, confident, outspoken politician they knew, but a man who was in a situation as uncomfortable for him as a chicken in a fox den.

"Umm… how's it going today, fellas?" The Mayor broke the ice.

The boys both shrugged, with Josh replying, "Good… everything's good, sir. How are you?"

The Mayor nodded, looking down and then around the neighborhood, scanning for observers. His forehead grew a few more beads of sweat.

"Hey uh,… I was wondering… do you think you guys could meet me over at Ryder's in about five minutes? I'll… buy us a plate of fries." He smiled a little as if to sweeten the arrangement.

Josh and Eddie were no less uneasy but agreed, figuring that a town official has to be about as safe a person as they could know, and to meet with him in a public place should not violate any of the rules of *Stranger Danger*.

The boys made a little small talk with the Mayor but he didn't divulge the purpose of the meeting, just reassured the two friends that there was nothing to worry about and he just needed to talk to a couple of upstanding local youths about an issue. Of course, Josh and Eddie knew it had to be something concerning their adventure but played along and, after returning their can of Canadian night crawlers to the coolness of their garage for the time being, they grabbed their bikes and started on their way to the best little diner on the river. They still had time to meet the Mayor and not be late for their "meeting" at the sandbar.

Carefully crossing highway 119, the boys screeched their bikes to a halt at the steps of the little diner, noticing the gray sedan parked at the south end of the small building where some trees concealed it pretty well. At mid-morning they were between breakfast and lunch and upon entering the near-empty diner they saw Billingsworth sitting in the corner booth scrolling his phone, then looking out the window, still appearing a bit uneasy. The two friends approached him slowly and sat down across from the big man. Their eyes went to him and they waited for the Mayor to initiate the conversation.

A small, anxious chuckle escaped the Mayor's lips, and he began in what was almost a murmur, "Hey guys, thanks for meeting me here. I already ordered the fries." He smiled again, still uneasy. He opened his mouth to speak but said nothing right away, still thinking of how to word things. Then he resumed, "Listen, I apologize for the stalking and the flashing lights, but I had to. I had to find you. I have to tell you something. It's for your safety, it really is." He paused a second and glanced out the window one more time. "So... a few days ago you guys came in to the Town Office and were looking around at some documents and things and you probably noticed the Sheriff and me taking notice of it. Well... it was the subject of the documents you searched that aroused our curiosity." A nervous smile appeared again, and he was using his hands a lot.

Josh held up one finger respectfully, and the Mayor paused.

Josh said softly, looking him in the eye, "Mayor, we know what this is about and we know about your connection to the *Southern Jewel*. And we also know about Sheriff Collins' connection." Josh shrugged one shoulder. "Just to save some time."

Billingsworth looked straight at the boys and nodded, realizing that there was no reason to play games. Everybody here knew everything. Talking to kids can be tough!

One more glance out the window and then he looked back at them. But he now looked at the boys with a different face, a face of genuine concern and a hint of worry. The face of a father about to give his sons a very serious talk. He drew a deep breath and looked at each one of them, "Do you boys know how big this is? How dangerous this could be? We are talking about 162 pounds of gold that could be hidden around here somewhere."

The boys glanced at each other. They knew all the numbers. So far there were no revelations here.

"I've got to tell you that there are people involved with this who have been searching nearly all their lives just for a clue! Just one clue! And you guys come along and apparently find the mother of all clues, the document, right?"

The boys nodded. Still no revelations.

"Guys, listen." The Mayor thought of the best way to say this. "There are some involved who may stop at nothing to take you out of the picture in order to find this gold. You may want to think real hard about going any further."

Eddie's eyes squinted and his index finger came up with a little less respect than Josh's, "You're just saying that so you and Collins can go get it! I know what this is about."

"Yeah. Collins came to my house, too. Scared my mom to death. No, we will be just fine. Don't worry about us!" Josh added, a little perturbed.

A red-haired waitress named Katy delivered two plates of French fries and two bottles of ketchup, along with three sodas.

Billingsworth thanked her and smiled nervously, hoping that she had not heard the exchange.

"Fellas, things have changed in the last few days. Intensified. Heated to the point that I am concerned for your safety."

"We're talking about Collins, right?" Josh asked. "You are telling us he would put it all on the line or risk everything that he has or push people around to collect some gold that he can't even keep? And you're in it with him?"

Billingsworth didn't want to mention the Sheriff's name. There was something unethical about it—unprofessional. He just wanted to give the boys a warning that someone could stop at nothing to get there first. But they could see it in his eyes, and there was no use in trying to deny it. Everyone involved knew who the teams were now, and there were no big secrets about who all the players were.

"Boys, he is eaten up with this legend. It was a great big hobby for him for many years. Ya know, researching and just having fun with it. He would research something and then go around with metal detectors every time he had an idea where it could be. It has consumed his adult life and even cost him a marriage! But since you two have uncovered this document, it has lit a fire in him that you cannot believe. He is like a marathon runner with the finish line in sight… a second wind. There is evil in his eyes and nothing will stop him now. He… he thinks he is entitled to it. He really believes it is his gold! And I'm not just talking about pushing people around, Josh. I mean violence. I'm concerned for him and I'm concerned for you! His mental health is not right these days."

Josh and Eddie were nodding their heads, acknowledging what the Mayor was saying as they began consuming the fries. He looked at them once again with significant concern, using his hands while talking to make his point.

"I am doing what I can to dissolve our partnership in this matter without him really realizing it. I just want to float away from him. I just want to float away from this entire matter, but I know things about the sheriff that no one else knows, and it's going to be hard for me. Being on his team could bury me politically."

Billingsworth paused again, looking down and then up at the boys.

"Guys I'm just going to tell you, I have seen it in his eyes. I have heard it in his word. This gold has become his destiny and he may stop at nothing. Death was at the beginning of this gold mystery, and death could be at the end! He knows how to do it and he knows where to hide the bodies. I don't know how to tell you any more directly than that," the Mayor of Blue Creek said solemnly.

The boy's eyes widened as big as their French fry plates.

There's the revelation!

CHAPTER TWENTY-EIGHT

The bike ride home from Ryder's was quiet and slow. The boys had never thought this fun little summer-time adventure could turn morbidly cold. Could it really cost someone their life? Was all that talk from Billingsworth just to scare them away or to buy some time while he and Collins worked up their plan, or was he sincere? Josh read Billingsworth's eyes as sincere, but he was a politician… a professional truth bender.

Josh and Eddie wheeled their bikes into the garage and rested them on their kickstands. Josh grabbed the can of worms they had previously gathered and looked inside, shaking the can a little. They were all below the surface of the dirt now. He sat down on an empty five-gallon paint bucket and looked outside. Eddie selected two fishing poles from the rod holder on the wall.

"So what do you think, Josh," Eddie asked. "What's your opinion?"

Josh thought for a minute.

"Well, for me, I think we have to go on with it. I think we take what the Mayor said as a very strong precaution. I don't think we should quit, but I do think we should be very careful. We haven't come this far just to quit now."

"Okay, I'm right with you on that. But I think we have to watch out for both of them. Shoot, I think we have to grow eyes in the back of our heads and watch out for everyone!"

"It's true."

The boys made their way to the riverbank to take the V-bottom boat across the river to the sandbar.

Burl Otis brushed the rust off the last of his steel traps, lightly oiled it, and placed it back on the nail on the wall. Twenty-five traps cleaned, oiled and ready for the season. December couldn't arrive soon enough for him.

His trapping cabin was a small log structure, roughly 12 feet square, and was built on a very small shelf on the side of the hill right beside the stream that flowed from the mountain down the hill, through the old trestle and onto the sandbar. It was rustic, to say the least, with a sturdy hammock-style bed for spending a couple nights on. Around him were the tools needed for trapping: fur-stretching boards, knives of different sizes, traps and a small table that would go outside for "preparation" of the fur. In season he would trap muskrat, beaver, fox and mink. He did well enough to provide him with the basics that a mountain man needs to survive. About once or twice a year he would be seen after the season had ended and the furs were tanned, at the Blue Creek General Store, cashing in for his salary. This income, along with a very lucrative ginseng crop that he told nobody about, would easily carry him through the year, with money left over. He didn't use banks.

Burl finished straightening up the cabin and then, satisfied things were ready for him come December, locked up the cabin and started his walk down the stream, under the trestle to the sandbar where he would meet with Tiny and the boys.

From his back porch, Tiny Brooks looked out over the Elk River with fondness, just as he had done thousands of times in his lifetime. For now, it was a beautiful bright sunny morning with shafts of light shooting through the trees and onto the water, creating glimmering islands of light. He sat thinking about the gold and about Washington Brooks and the era in which he had lived and struggled and prospered. Tiny was sure that Washington Brooks was equally happy along the banks of the old river as he was. What's not to like here on the Elk River in summer?

He glanced at his watch as he finished a big glass of tea and then pulled his walking shoes on to go meet with the rest of the fellas to discuss the plan for locating the *Southern Jewel*.

John Hopes paced back and forth in his home office with his phone to his ear. On the walls were many plaques and awards for investigative journalism he had earned through the years. There were pictures of him standing beside esteemed colleagues, politicians, and sports figures of the past. A black and white of him and an Army buddy in Guam in 1945 at the Navy base where he served four years. In the corner were two 25-pound dumbbells with no dust on them. Hopes was still within a few pounds of his Navy weight and still quite energetic for his ripe old age.

John Hopes was listening to the caller on the other end.

He then spoke, "So what do you make of it? You think it was Collins who went back in there? And how could he have gotten in?" He paused and listened. "You have the tape from the door? You kept it?"

It was Mansfield, who went on excitedly about his suspicion of Collins reentering the library after they had gone home.

Mansfield said in an excited whisper, "I went back downstairs after Giselle had arrived to look around for anything else that didn't look right. I found the papers we copied in the folder still on the computer desk by the monitor. She was off to the side doing some work on book returns. All the copies were there but if he found them, then he could have made another copy and took it with him and that would be why the copier was left on! John, we deciphered that code and left it lying there for him! It was my fault. I was exhausted. But all he has to do now is go to the island and conduct his search!" Mansfield was nearly panicked.

Hopes processed all the information from Mansfield. "You don't have surveillance, do you?"

"John, this library can't even afford computerized cataloging, much less surveillance cameras. And Collins would know that!"

"Alright, we have to meet. We have to act fast, because if that crook Collins unwraps this deal first, he will leave the country with the gold. I have so much dirt on him through the years… you wouldn't believe what a crooked cop he is," Hopes said. "That kind of discovery with the recognition that goes along with it could do so much for our county and our towns here along the river. We need it!"

Mansfield said nothing in response to that. "Where do we meet?" He asked.

They agreed on a spot, and Elton asked Giselle to hold down the fort while he ran out for an hour or so.

As Josh Baker stepped out of the boat and onto the sandbar, his cell phone rang. Eddie looked at him and grinned with approval of the ring tone. Lynyrd Skynyrd. It was Giselle.

He said, "Hey, what going on?"

She began urgently as Josh tapped the speaker button, "Listen, Mansfield and his buddy John Hopes know everything! I found some papers this morning beside our downstairs computer. They took the copy of the yellow legal pad thing that you left here and deciphered it! It's all written here. They know where to go to look for the gold. There are a bunch of notes and... hang on, let me read it to you!"

"No, wait... Giselle, it's okay, we have it too. We have it all deciphered. The gold is on the island. In an island bank, right?"

Giselle calmed a little. "Yeah but what does it all mean?"

Josh went through their method of deciphering the document at Tiny Brooks' house and how they concluded what it meant. He told her about Billingsworth's warning to them and how time, now, was money, literally!

"Oh my gosh! Okay, Josh, listen! This is really important. Mansfield has bad hearing, so sometimes he talks louder than he needs to."

"Um... okay."

"Stay with me here. I heard him talking to his friend John Hopes, the old news reporter guy. I'm pretty sure he and Hopes are working this thing together and these papers are a result of their late-night investigation last night. From what I could hear, trouble came later."

"What do you mean?"

"Looks like they suspect Collins of breaking and entering sometime after they left, so he could see what they were up to."

"But why?"

She went on, "Again, from the pieces that I could hear, it seems that Collins stopped by long after closing to see why the lights were still on. I'm sure that Mansfield didn't give him any information, so it looks like he came back later to have a look for himself."

"Oh wow. Gutsy."

"Yeah, and if Collins found these papers too, and it looks like he did, he now has a fully deciphered treasure map to 162 pounds of Confederate gold. You can bet that he will be there to find it very soon!"

"So, Collins and Billingsworth have a copy, Mansfield and Hopes have a copy and we have a copy of a fully deciphered treasure map."

Giselle said, "May the best team win!"

"That's not funny!" Josh popped.

"Well, if you guys really want to find it, then you better get busy! What's the plan?"

"We're meeting with Tiny and Burl right now to make our plan for the island."

"Okay, keep me posted."

"Will do, thanks!"

"Bye."

Josh thought to himself that if he had not left that yellow copy of the document lying at the library that day, this weirdo Mansfield would not be a factor, and if he would have used better brains and put the original deerskin somewhere safer, he wouldn't have Collins and Billingsworth to worry about, either. Minor mistakes cause colossal problems sometimes. But it is what it is now, and they must hurry!

Tiny Brooks and the boys arrived onto the sandbar within five minutes of one another. Eddie had taken the poles out of the boat and had sat the can of worms on the rocks to give the appearance of fishing. To better give the appearance of fishing, Josh baited a line and flung it out into the middle of the river, resting it on the bottom with a pyramid sinker.

Tiny smiled, "That's a real good idea there." He pointed to the fishing poles. "If you're gonna be down here, ya might as well fish."

"That's what we figured, too!" Eddie agreed.

"Middle of the day, maybe nothing's happening, but ya never know."

Behind them was the tunnel through the trestle that let the stream flow out to the river and deposit rocks from the hills to the sandbar, giving river-folk a place to stand and fish for over a hundred years since the older wooden trestle stood there in the late 1800s.

The tunnel through the trestle was about fifty feet in length and daylight could be seen through it to the other side—normally. At this time, however, eclipsing the light through the tunnel, a big burly man stepped from rock to rock to make his way through, and onto the sandbar.

"Afternoon, gentlemen!" Burl said, staying close to the mouth of the tunnel and surveying the area for lookers.

The morning sun was giving way to a few noontime clouds just as forecasted by the local weatherman. Also forecast, was light rain in the afternoon. As the clouds passed they cast shadows onto the river and the sandbar, giving moments of relief from the direct summer sun. Plants and trees were in full bloom and it was the growing season for them. The hillsides were thick with brush and saplings. The river was a beautiful light green and flowed gently past the river rocks the four guys stood on.

"Afternoon, Mr. Otis," Josh said.

"Where's Brad?" Tiny asked, looking around.

"Not sure… he said he would be here. I kinda expected him early."

Eddie said, "Could be his dad has him doing something."

Josh looked out at his fishing line and flipped a couple of rocks over with the toe of his shoe. Burl noticed he was a bit edgy, "We need to move quickly. I don't think we can waste any time."

Burl said, "What's wrong, Josh? You look a little tense."

Josh and Eddie looked at each other as Eddie walked closer, and the boys recounted their morning so far. From collecting the worms to the flashing headlights and the nerve-wracking walk to the dark-windowed sedan. They told Burl and Tiny of the French fry lunch with Mayor Billingsworth and his peculiar warning about Collins.

The two older gentlemen listened carefully as Burl Otis stroked his full black and gray beard, and Tiny looked on in concentration.

Eddie said, "So we are thinking that we go on but we have to be very, very careful."

Tiny looked at Burl, both knowing neither wanted the worst to happen. They were just boys, young boys doing what every young boy dreamed of—having an adventure! It wasn't worth their lives. Not for a crazy kook like Collins. Their eyes said maybe they should just call this entire thing off and let the bad guys have it. But inside they knew that it was not the best thing to do. If those two men got that gold, it would never get back to where it belonged. Collins and Billingsworth would be long gone with it, or at least Collins would. The Mayor would manage a way to get his share, they reasoned. Maybe he would still hang around the area since he had family, but he would be high on the hog. Collins could maneuver his partner's share to him, filtering it through foreign banks and setting up a new account somewhere far away. No, they couldn't let that happen when they had an opportunity to prevent it. They had an obligation as citizens to do the right thing.

Burl looked down at the ground and then his eyes rolled up to Tiny and then over to the boys. "I think we can move on but we have to really watch our backs."

Tiny Brooks was nodding. "Yeah… we can take no chances with these guys. If Billingsworth came to you with that kind of warning, then maybe he is just as capable as Collins of doing the unthinkable. They could be two very crazy men focused on finding that gold. I would say they don't want to kill anyone for it. Especially kids. That's why they came to you with the warning. They want to scare you into quitting so it doesn't get to that, and they have to decide whether to do… the unthinkable. But I'm also saying they might be willing to do it."

Tiny's words were like ice and gave Josh the chills.

They all paused for a second as one of the fishing poles bounced one time. They all looked at each other and put their right hands in together and smiled a brave smile. They would move on but must train their eyes and ears to perceive anything abnormal in their surroundings. They were men and boys of the mountains and rivers. They would do well.

"Let's go get it!" Burl coached.

They made a plan to meet back at the sandbar at 9 o'clock that evening. The boys would have to tell their parents they were camping on the riverbank that night, which they did often and, since they disliked lying, they would pitch their tent and bring their gear. They would take Brad's raft to the island loaded with the gear they might need—shovels, picks, an axe and lanterns—and live out the adventure of a lifetime.

Brad Radcliffe's raft drifted around the river bend to the north and floated towards the four guys on the sandbar. He was a little late, but the guys would brief him on the plan and use the coolest vessel on the Elk River later that night!

The rod tip bounced hard this time and stayed down. *Fish on!*

Sheriff Collins sat studying his copy of the deciphered document while pouring over a survey map of the island that was on record at the Town Office. His reading glasses were low on his nose as he looked for the best location to tie up the county-owned johnboat in order to access the old tavern and to do a late-night search for gold. Daytime would not work. It had to be at night. In the daytime, parts of the island were used for outings and sporting events, but at night, it was deserted and Collins knew it. There were no caretakers.

Collins looked out the window as cars passed, and he wondered where the Mayor was. They had to make a plan. They needed a meeting point, a plan "B". But so far the mayor had not been at work that day, which wasn't unusual. He had things to do other places. He had meetings with other mayors in the county or business in Charleston with business owners or proprietors looking to locate their business somewhere up the river, and he was there to promote his little town for the sake of tax dollars. Billingsworth was a busy man—but not today.

By the end of the day, it frustrated Collins that the mayor was not answering texts or calls. Collins would make the plan by himself. He pulled his 9mm service pistol from its holster and snapped in a full clip. He then attached a suppressor to the end of the barrel. It would make no more noise than a pellet gun now.

Mayor Billingsworth stared out the upstairs window of the cupola of his Victorian home, which overlooked a two-acre backyard that sloped gently to the Elk River. Grass cleanly cut, trees and shrubbery expertly landscaped and mulched, this was prime property on the river. He could see his beautiful walnut tree, a golden delicious apple tree and a red delicious. Things were in good order.

With his elbow on the table, he nibbled on his thumbnail, deep in contemplation. He weighed his options back and forth. He watched the river flow past as it carried leaves and an occasional jumping fish downstream. He knew what he had to do, and he knew it had to happen tonight. He was certain that the other players involved would be on the move sometime during the night as well, and so must he. He stepped into his home office and looked at an aerial photo of Blue Creek and the surrounding area. Confidence filled him as his plan formed in his head.

He would now go gather the tools he needed for his mission and be ready.

1903

Edmond Mansfield

Edmond never worked in the dark, never on weekends, never in a crashing rainstorm, and never with anyone who wasn't a trained stonemason, but he would do all these on this night. It was the only day of the week that the rest of his regular crew would not be there, and he and his temporary partner must do this by themselves.

At 3:00 a.m. he chipped away at the only single slab of sandstone that would go into the entire project. This slab must be two feet tall, three feet wide and only six inches thick. The rest of the project would be limestone and much thicker—up to two feet thick! At only six inches thick, he could manage the block and tackle system with only one untrained helper, to set the stone in place.

Sandstone is soft and easy to chisel into shape. It could easily be broken apart, and Edmond could ruin the entire stone if he miscalculated a single swing of his chipping hammer. But this section must be sandstone! That's what the man paying him wants. And it must be finished and set in place by daybreak. His work also had to be cleverly disguised and hidden from his workers coming in tomorrow morning. Edmund Mansfield continued to do his job well as the other man carried the cargo and placed it inside the vault. They would both finish up right on time after a rainy night of robbery and death in May 1903.

CHAPTER TWENTY-NINE

The campfire popped and crackled and the firelight danced off the river as the boys set up their campsite on the riverbank just below Josh's house. Emily Baker looked out her upstairs window and saw her son setting up the tent and rolling out sleeping bags as Josh and Eddie had done so many times before. Burl and Tiny would be along soon, and one of the boys would row across the river to pick them up at the sandbar. Of course, Mrs. Baker didn't know about the extra guests in the campsite that night.

The fire was not big, just some kindling and a single log. It would not need to burn long that evening because they had an appointment with adventure. Their plan was to meet up at the campsite, load their tools onto the raft and pole their way quietly upriver to the south end of the island to a landing area where the church does their summer-time baptisms. Josh and Eddie were dunked there just three years ago. They knew it was shallow with a silt bottom, and there were trees where they could tie off the raft. They would take the information they had and the tools they loaded and go explore the island and, in particular, the old tavern. Everyone seemed to agree the tavern was the obvious place to look since they had decoded the document to say *In an Island Bank.*

The milk jug raft sat bobbing in the water along the edge of the river and with just a little more darkness and a little less campfire light they would begin putting the tools onboard to head upstream. Fog had lifted its way off the river and laid a low blanket of vapor along the banks. This would work in their favor to obscure them from houses along the river that night. But it would also add to the creepy factor.

With camp set up and the last of the purples and blues disappearing below the hills, the day was fading into black and the adrenalin was finding its way into the veins of the explorers. They sat on five-gallon buckets around the fire.

"It's a perfect night for this," Brad commented. "We have a half moon for a little light, but not too much." He looked at the night sky with Orion's belt becoming more visible and Venus sitting bright just above the ridgeline.

"We're not going to be able to see Burl and Tiny for the fog," Eddie said. "They should be along any time."

Burl had spent part of the day at Tiny's river house, and the two men had gotten to know each other pretty well. Tiny had served up his specialty all-you-can-eat catfish dinner and hushpuppies and they had enjoyed an evening of socializing and coffee-drinking on Tiny's front porch as they spun stories and memories about the river and mountain life that they both enjoyed so much. They had also decided it would be best for the safety of the boys for them to arm themselves that evening, but they would not tell the boys about that.

Josh shielded his eyes from the fire and looked across the river. He had heard a branch crack and figured it must be the two men working their way from the railroad tracks, down the path to the sandbar. He could see nothing. About thirty seconds later he heard a *Hooty-hoo, Hooty-hoo!*--a comical imitation of Barney Fife's poor impression of an owl. They could then hear the two men laughing in the darkness of the sandbar and the kids looked at each other, shaking their heads, wondering what those two had been into that evening.

Josh returned an equally bad *Hooty-hoo,* which in owl-talk would mean, *"I'll be right there."*

As Josh rowed the V-bottom across to the sandbar to pick up the two men, Brad and Eddie began loading the raft with their treasure-finding tools. The raft was ready by the time the three arrived back at the campsite in the boat. Josh threw Brad a line to tie off the boat, and the three guys stepped ashore and looked around.

"Tidy little campsite ya got here," Burl commented, impressed at the boys' knack for simplicity.

"Looking good, looking good," Tiny said, smiling and making his way to the top of the bank.

"We got everything we thought we would need and still save weight on the raft," Josh said. "Basic digging tools and a sledgehammer, just in case. A compass, a flashlight, and something to write with and write on."

"Looks good. I can't see us needing anything more than that. Just one lantern should be good. We can dim it way down going up the river and we shouldn't be seen." Burl paused and looked around at the three boys and Tiny. He took a deep breath and exhaled hard. "Well… everyone ready?"

They all looked at each other with the same amount of nervousness as excitement and Eddie said, "Let's do it!"

One at a time they made their way down the riverbank and stepped onto the raft, each one positioning himself to keep the raft level and stable as the others stepped on. Josh noticed the two men both had small backpacks but didn't ask about the contents. He figured waters and maybe a sandwich. They kept the packs on their backs and didn't lay them on the raft once onboard.

The lights went off for the night in the Baker house as Josh took point on the raft and dimmed the Coleman lantern down to a minimum for river travel. The fog had gotten thicker by the minute and visibility was down to about twenty feet. The boys could nearly navigate this trip with their eyes closed because they had been up the river to the island many times. They knew every log in the water and where all the big rocks were. They knew they just had to stay in the channel, the center of the river, and the trip should be uneventful.

Brad held the tiller as Tiny poled on one side, and Eddie poled on the other. Burl stood at the mast to keep his nearly three hundred pounds centered on the craft, and they were off! The wind was non-existent, so the sail would do no good. It was removed and stored on the back of the raft. They exchanged very few words. The only sounds were the bugs and frogs on the riverbanks and the river water gurgling and sloshing between the jugs underneath them.

Sheriff Collins banged around in his storage shed to find the things he was looking for. From the mess he threw a few items out on the ground and then climbed his way over his big mower and gas cans to step out and load the back of his personal pickup truck with enough tools to dig a canal.

It was getting well into the night and he figured the later the better. There would be less traffic, fewer people awake along the river, and fewer eyes to see what he was doing. Most folks were sound asleep as he drove north on Elk River Road, passing the wide spots that made up the small dots on the roadmaps. He arrived at the boat dock built just for the town of Blue Creek, where they kept the sixteen-foot aluminum flat-bottomed boat. Equipped with a 40-horse Mercury, it would skim along plenty fast in just eighteen inches of water if needed. It was used for official business only, in the event of flash flooding rescue, but mostly for citing boats along the river that were not properly licensed. It had paid for itself quickly for the latter.

Tonight, the taxpayers' boat would not be used for official business. He loaded his boat, started the motor and, as quietly as possible, started humming his way downriver to the island. He had a plan to first pass by the island and go check the licensing status on a certain homemade river raft and a certain V-bottom AlumiCraft. Even a homemade vessel had to be licensed and if he could tag it and lock it, or impound either vessel, then the boys would be without river transportation and he would be a leg up on his competition to recover 162 pounds of gold. He had no idea that the boys and the two men had gotten a two-hour head start on him that night.

He pushed away from the dock and passed under the bridge that crossed the river at Blue Creek, as a shadowed figure watched from above.

John Hopes drove a Buick Enclave SUV. In the back, he and Mansfield had placed a few things for digging and searching, but much less than the competition. They knew where they wanted to go—it was right there on the document. *In an Island Bank,* but they weren't sure what to expect when they got there or where to even start. Mansfield wasn't one hundred percent convinced it was even in the old tavern. Where could Clyde Franklin hide 162 pounds of gold in a wood structure with no one seeing him do it? They figured this would only be the first of many trips to the island, to gather information and eliminate possibilities. They were unaware of their competition's plans.

Hopes and Mansfield did not plan to use a boat to cross the river to get to the island tonight. In 1945 John Hopes had left the

Navy as a HT (Hull Tech). Those were the guys back in the day that would do all the locksmith duties aboard ship, along with many other responsibilities. Together with communication and journalistic skills, John was a pretty good lock picker.

They planned to park at the small parking lot along US Rt. 119 made just for the island, pick the padlock, and walk across the suspension bridge to the remains of the boarded-up and condemned Cross Roads Tavern.

"Land ho," Josh proclaimed softly as he saw the outline of the island landing starting to take shape in the fog directly in front of the raft, about one hundred feet. As they drew nearer, they saw an eerie scene. Large, and very old oak and maple trees had stood tall since the time of the tavern's heyday, like sentries guarding their post. The willows hung like ghosts, with the fog draping them not unlike the cold mist of an apparition. With their branches nearly touching the water, it was as if they were warding them off.

"Man, this place is freaky at night, especially with fog," Josh said. "I'll get the rope."

"We have to take the lantern, but we have to keep the light low," said Burl.

"Maybe even turn it off. We have a good moon," added Tiny. "The tavern is just right there, maybe fifty yards up the path. Hard to believe Washington Brooks worked at this place over a hundred years ago."

"Hard to believe it's still standing?" Brad said.

They poled the raft in as close as they could, and Josh jumped from the front with the rope in his hand and landed in about six inches of water. He walked the rope up to a big willow and tied a quick and simple knot. Josh spotted an old board lying by the shore and laid it from the shoreline to the raft as a gangplank.

"Thank ya buddy!" Eddie said. "Don't even have to get my feet wet."

All but Burl walked the plank, each carrying their share of equipment. Burl knew it would not support a sizeable man like himself. He stepped into the water, as had Josh. Burl and Josh then took the rope and pulled the raft over under the low-hanging branches of the willow tree so it wouldn't be seen in the unlikely event of a visitor.

All five of them, once ashore, paused at the beginning of the path that led up to the old tavern and looked at it. The moon stood behind it and cast a glow around the old structure that, indeed, was a bit eerie. Fog was moving now—rolling as it does when it gets heavier.

Brad said, "What are we looking for when we get up there?"

"Anything, clues. I guess we will know better when we get there, where we will start and what the plan is," Tiny said. "It's not going to be easy. That gold will not jump out and say, '*here I am*!' If it's here, it was hidden here in the early 1900s and stayed hidden all these years. This place operated as a hotel and casino long after the train robbery, and no one stumbled across it in all that time."

"Well, maybe we don't know that for sure. If someone did find it, they could have secretly hauled it out of here years ago, unloaded it somewhere, and that's it!" He paused and let that sink in. "It could still be a wild goose chase. It could have been found accidentally long ago without the use of the skin. We didn't really think about that." Burl paused again. "But this is what we've been working towards and waiting for. So let's get on up there and see," Burl finished.

No one spoke for a minute; they just took in everything that Burl had said. He could be right. The gold could be long gone.

Josh broke the silence, "Yeah, let's go."

They packed up their tools and hiked their way up the shallow bank towards the tavern. The walk was easy because there was no thick brush to speak of and the slope was gradual. They were there in less than a minute.

"I think it's still here," Josh said, as they neared the tavern.

Burl grinned and winked at him. "Me too!" he said.

The three-story wooden structure still stood proudly. Decade's old white paint clung to the exterior, lead paint no doubt, and the forest green shutters that were still around the windows hung loose and sideways. The tavern sat on a four-foot tall sandstone foundation, and each of the three levels had a porch that wrapped completely around it. It still looked sturdy from the outside for having been built so many years ago, but they would need to use caution when entering.

The steps that led from the ground to the first level had been removed, part of the process of condemning the tavern. Fog continued to roll along like a ghostly smoke from the old train and visibility was still bad.

"We have to get something to prop up there to climb to the porch," Tiny said, looking around.

Eddie pointed, "This place has a cellar in it. Maybe it has a way to the first level from the cellar,"

Tiny shrugged one shoulder. "It's an idea that's worth a look."

They needed to walk around to the back of the structure to get to the old door that went into the cellar. It was a thick wooden door that hadn't been opened in years. One could tell by the amount of earth that was lying along the bottom. It was hinged to swing outward and there must have been six inches of soil, vines and weeds growing there, preventing the door from being able to be opened.

"Not sure we can get that open," Brad commented, holding the lantern close to the door.

"Let me get a shovel in there. Might need the axe to cut the vines away," Burl said.

They hacked and dug out the bottom of the door and eventually got it cleared. If the hinges weren't rusted beyond movement, they should be able to open the door and enter the old cellar. There was no lock on the door and they didn't expect to see anything in the cellar except for, hopefully, a set of stairs that led up to the first level.

Being the biggest, Burl grabbed the old steel door handle and yanked it downward. There was corrosion inside the handle but it moved and that was encouraging. He then gave the door a hard pull. It creaked loudly and moved about an inch. Burl could smell the staleness of an old cellar rush out the small opening.

"Wow, it's tight," he said, getting better footing for a second pull.

Pound for pound, Brad was maybe the strongest one there.

He said, "Let me get my fingers in there with you and see if I can help."

Brad got down at the bottom of the door and put his feet up against the outside cellar wall and then put his fingers inside the crack that Burl had managed to make.

"Ya ready?" Burl asked.

"One, two, three!"

The two guys put their country muscles into their work and pulled hard. The door gave, but complained loudly, creaking and groaning all the way, but it was working. The door trembled with resistance but opened about a foot. Brad and Burl let go, both breathing a little harder.

"Let's get our shoulders on it now," Burl said.

They each put a foot inside the dark and dank cellar, hunkered down like lineman on a football team. Brad was low on the door and Burl was high. They shouldered the door and pushed again. They had much more energy this time and were able to heave the door nearly all the way open.

"Good job. We need it wide open to carry out 162 pounds of gold!" Josh smiled. The optimist.

Everyone laughed. Eddie grabbed the lantern and Josh pulled a MagLite from his belt. Eddie held the lantern high and slowly stepped inside the old forgotten basement as Josh beamed the flashlight around. Eddie turned up the lantern flame, and the room lit up.

There were gasps of amazement. It looked like a time capsule. The room was bigger than anyone thought it would be, and the floors were completely dry. Only the walls of the sandstone foundation were slightly damp. Three stone steps led down to the cellar that encompassed the entire foundation of the tavern. It was sectioned off into three separate rooms. The first room they entered was for storage of larger things, it appeared. There was an old wooden table, maybe eight feet long with thick spindle legs and about ten chairs stacked against the wall. The furniture was heavily covered with dust but in amazing condition for the number of years it had been down there and, sure enough, in the middle of the room, was a set of old stairs that led up to the first level of the tavern.

To the left was an incredible antique roulette table. The wheel was missing, but the wood defied its age and was a beautiful relic of the late 1800s.

"Look at this." Josh walked over to what looked like a workbench and on it stood two very early slot machines. They would have sat on top of a wooden pedestal or a table. Josh wiped the dust off the badge on the front and it read *Mills Pace 5 cent.*

"Gold mine of relics down here!" Tiny commented.

"Yeah, I'd say you're right," Burl said, shaking his head in disbelief.

There were wooden boxes labeled with their contents as well as tables, lamps and hall tree pieces for the rooms upstairs. There were dressers and old bed frames and headboards, all left behind and amazingly forgotten for all these years. It crossed Josh's mind that he sure hoped there was a big pile of gold somewhere in this place that had been forgotten, too.

"Okay. Where do we start and what are we looking for? Besides the obvious," Eddie asked.

"Why don't we clean house from the top down?" Burl Suggested. "Start at the top and work our way down. Don't leave a floor until it's completely searched."

"That works. Let's go up and see what we've got," Tiny said, nodding.

The cellar stairs were sturdy and ascending them was no problem. The door at the top was unlocked and opened normally as Josh led the way into what looked like a bedroom-sized storage room inside the center of the building. The group stepped into the room and looked through the doorway that led out. They continued on with Josh leading the way with the lantern, and behold, it brought them out right behind the old, original sixteen-foot bar of the Crossroads Tavern.

"Oh my, my, my," Tiny said in disbelief. He put both hands on the bar and stood there looking up and down it for a moment, smiling with amazement. "Washington Brooks… worked behind this very bar. He supported a family and put down roots with the money he earned right here." Everyone stood quietly, letting Tiny absorb the moment that was his. He continued speaking slowly and softly. "And guys, my great-grandfather stood right here wiping glasses and serving drinks as Clyde Franklin stood probably over there with your great-grandfather Burl, hammering out a plan to… umm…. liberate the government of their gold problem."

Everyone laughed at that one.

"Well, that's true. I like to say he *commandeered* it! It just sounds a little better than stole!" Burl said.

The quiet laughs continued.

The bar area itself was amazing for its age. It was a bigger room than they expected and had many pillars for support of the upper floors, but, other than the storage room they just came out of, it was a very open floor plan. There were still a couple tables and chairs in the place, along with glasses still under the bar. Mirrors hung on the walls that still were adorned with wallpaper. As they stepped across the floor, the wood boards creaked, but the entire tongue-and-groove floor was intact and seemed strong. Along the back wall was the stairwell that led up to the other floors. They made their way to the stairs.

Josh said, "I'm going to turn this lantern down a little so…"

"SHHHH!!!" Brad put up one finger. Everyone paused. "You hear that?"

They all turned up the senses in their ears, looking blankly at the walls and ceiling. In the near distance they all heard it, the unmistakable sound of a small boat engine making its way down the east side of the island. For the first time that evening, they all felt the trepidation of being caught trespassing on the island. Without words, they continued to listen for a few more seconds as the boat passed the island and faded out of earshot.

"Who in the world could that have been?" Eddie asked.

Tiny thought for a minute. "On the river, I hear boats occasionally going up and down at night. I think there are some guys who are running turtle hooks and trot lines… but… it's usually later at night and even into the early morning when I hear them." He thought for a second. "And that engine… that engine sounded bigger, deeper." It puzzled him.

"Well… it went past the island and on downriver, anyway," Burl said. "Might as well resume. We are still the only ones on the island." He looked around at everybody, searching for agreement.

They all recommenced breathing, looked at each other and refocused on the task at hand. They headed up the stairs, all the way to the third floor. There was a center hallway and two rooms on each side. They stepped down the wooden-floored hallway and opened the door to the first room on the right. There were the remains of a bed with a wrought iron headboard. No mattress, but a bedside table and a hall tree coat rack identical to the ones they had seen in the basement. The room was rectangular, a pretty good size, and had no closet. They all looked around and then at each other.

"There is no place to hide gold here unless it's in the walls or in the floors," Josh said.

"And Clyde Franklin would not do that. He could not rip up boards or rip away a wall, hide the gold in there and put it back together to make it unnoticeable," Eddie finished.

"Without being seen. I agree," Tiny said. "Of course, it's not out of the realm of possibility, but it is not that probable either."

They all nodded in agreement.

With the lantern on low, they continued down the hall and into the other rooms. Identical—leftover furniture and rectangular rooms. At the end of the hallway there was a washroom that would have been shared by all the guests on that floor. There was a little something different about the look and feel in there. There was an old four-footed bathtub still in place. In those days, someone would have had to haul hot water up three floors in order for their high-paying guests to have a nice bath in the evening after traveling upriver on the steamboat. Maybe Washington Brooks handled some of those chores, too.

The area behind the tub had some shelves made of wood and built into the wall. This wall stood out, even in the shadowy darkness, almost obvious, as if its abnormality was meant to be noticed by someone, eventually. The make-up of this wall looked like it was an afterthought. Tiny and Burl walked over and looked more carefully at the shelves, which might have held towels and soap. Tiny reached and lifted one of the shelves and it popped out easily. The wall behind the shelves was what interested him the most. Burl got down on one knee and tapped around on the wall which was made of three-inch wide tongue-and-groove material just like the flooring. It was painted to match, but still it was a little curious. It was worth checking out. Josh, Eddie, and Brad all came closer and watched as Burl and Tiny inspected the area. Tiny joined Burl in tapping the individual boards that made up the wall behind the shelves. Finally, about three feet off the floor, Tiny hit a board that rattled. It was loose. Everyone froze.

Tiny and Burl glanced at each other, and Tiny shrugged one shoulder.

Tiny said, "Well, I guess it's worth looking at, although it doesn't really make sense to hide gold on the top floor of a wood structure. What if it was found by a carpenter doing repairs, or what if the place burned down?" He studied the slats some more and jiggled the board again. There was a lot of movement to it.

Josh added, "The document said *sand is a vault*. This is not sand, and it's hardly a vault. I was figuring the basement will be the place to look."

Tiny said, "That's true, but it could be anywhere on this island. I think we have to search thoroughly… everywhere, and then move on."

"Well, let's check this out then," Burl suggested.

Tiny located the loose board again and gave it a couple of good taps. It rattled. He then tried to slide it left or right to see if there was any lateral play in it. He pushed right, and the board hit something solid. Tiny put both hands on it and pushed hard, but it would slide no farther to the right. He then tried to slide the board to the left. The loose board moved to the left about an inch and stopped, but not abruptly. Tiny turned and looked over his shoulder at the other four guys. There was anxiousness in the eyes of the three young boys. Burl looked on with cautious optimism. Tiny moved the board back to the right again and put both hands on it to get more force this time. With all of his arm and shoulder pressure that he could muster in the tight place, he slid the board to the left!

Wham! Whatever was holding it the first time let go, and the board slid a good twelve inches to the left as if on a track of some sort. Dust rolled out of the hole from the impact of the board hitting its stopping point.

"Holy cow," Eddie said, "that's intentional! That's supposed to do that!"

"It sure looks like it," Brad said from his position behind the others.

"You got the flashlight?" Tiny asked no one in particular as he looked into the hole.

Eddie handed the light up to Tiny. Tiny shined the light into the hole in the wall behind the shelves. He grinned.

"Well, my, my, my," he said, flashing his big smile.

CHAPTER THIRTY

The hole was no bigger than it looked from the outside—about three inches by twelve inches. And this mini-vault had been constructed for a purpose, but not to hide gold.

Tiny reached in and carefully grabbed something that was rolled up and tied with a piece of leather string. He cautiously pulled it through the hole for all to see. Brad took the lantern and hung it up high so they could all see a little better.

When the light hit it, Josh and Eddie gasped.

"That's it! It looks just like the document we found in the red can!" Eddie exclaimed.

"It sure does. Maybe another copy! But it's smaller, smaller for sure," Josh said.

Tiny carefully laid the skin on the floor and untied the leather string. The lantern light danced across the piece of deer hide as Tiny slowly and carefully unrolled it, and letters and numbers began to reveal themselves.

"This one is in much better condition than the one we found. The other one had lots of stuff that you couldn't read at all. This is easy," Eddie said.

"Well, it's been here all this time. Dry and warm. Not rolling around in floods and rain like the red can did," Tiny said. "Put the light on it."

The deer hide was rolled out flat, and everyone looked on. In clear legible text was a message. Not a treasure map with an "X" on it, but a message that read:

Key from the door 6 O, 2 D, 8 O, 1 D

They all paused.

"That's it? That's all that's on this thing?" Josh asked. "What is that supposed to mean?"

Burl read it aloud, "6 O... I think that's an *O* and not a zero because all the numbers are followed by a letter."

"That's right," Tiny agreed.

"So, it's 6 O, 2 D, 8 O and 1 D," Burl read.

"It's a code that we have to figure out. It could be telling us right where to look, but we have to figure this, too. This entire treasure hunt is written in riddles and code. It wasn't meant to be easy, that's for sure," Tiny said.

Burl added, "I can't understand why Clyde Franklin did all this. Why not pass this fortune on to your kids or just live the high-life after the heist? He went to great pains to hide it and make it hard to find."

Tiny thought for a second and said, "Well, if you think about it, how are you going to hand down stolen money to your family? How can you suddenly start living like money is no object right in front of your own wife and kids? They are going to have questions." Tiny was smiling as he was talking.

He was right. If you truly wanted no one to know about what you had done, then that money is of no value to you.

Tiny added, "And it's about pride and respect. At the end of the day, you don't want your kids to think you are a thief—a criminal."

"That's all true," Burl agreed.

Josh stopped them. "Well. What does this mean? Let's put our heads together."

Brad Radcliffe's ears perked up again. "You guys hear that? A car door."

Everyone straightened up to listen. Brad had the keenest hearing Josh and Eddie had ever witnessed in a person.

A second door shut. Everyone heard that one. A little shiver of fear ran up Josh's back.

"It's a quiet night. Sound carries well. It could be over in Blue Creek at the store. They have the apartments above there. Maybe someone is getting home late," Eddie jabbered nervously.

There was a lengthy pause. Everyone listened.

"Well, anyway, we know there's no car on the island!" Brad said with a half chuckle.

Burl and Tiny just listened, making sure they heard nothing else. They all turned their focus back to the deer hide.

Tiny spoke as he was looking at it, "I think we have to look at this as the final piece of the puzzle. We have to look at this like it's telling us where to go."

Josh said, "Right. So, before we get to the numbers, before we try to figure that mess out, it says *Key from the door.*"

"Right, that's right. It doesn't say key *to* the door, it says key *from* the door," Eddie said.

"So we are not looking for a key to open a door, we are looking for steps or measurements from an actual door. Key *from* the door would be telling us where to go from a certain doorway," Burl said.

"But what door? How are we supposed to know what door to start from?" Eddie asked.

They all looked at Tiny. He was grinning. Once again, he had figured something out. He was thinking back to the original document and the code that they had already deciphered and how it would fit with this one.

"What?" Josh said anxiously with his pleading hands out. He couldn't wait to hear.

He said, "Sand is a vault, gentleman. The gold is hidden in a vault. A vault that is near a doorway and was built by a guy who had access to this island. A guy who had the tools and the knowledge and maybe even a couple helpers who could keep their mouths shut for a couple gold coins as promised. That stone mason team camped on this very island while they built a series of trestles along this stretch of river. The foundation of this entire structure sits on sandstone, and they were here every night."

Burl Otis knew what Tiny was getting at. The gold was nowhere in the wood structure of this old inn. That would be way too risky and conspicuous. That would be too easy for someone to stumble across.

"We need to go down three floors," Burl said.

Tiny smiled in agreement, nodding his head.

"Let's go!" Eddie exclaimed.

They dimmed their lantern, exited the old washroom, and headed down the hall and then down the stairs. They walked without haste past the old historic bar and back into the little storage room behind it. Single file, they descended the steps back down into the time capsule of a basement they had forced their way into. At this point Josh turned the lantern back to full flame to get a good look around the room. They were all thinking the same thing again.

"There are three doors in here. Which door is it, and then what do we do?" Josh said.

Burl thought out loud, "We have three doorways, all framed out with sandstone. One goes outside, one goes into this room, and one goes into that room. The two doors that go into the rooms are along a wall that divides this main room in half. So, personally, I don't see a vault being in that wall anywhere near that door. Unless the vault is down... like in the floor."

Tiny said, "And that wouldn't be smart because water could get to it. The water table for this island has to be shallow. Probably if you dig four or five feet down, there is water. Even if you built a vault of stone, water will wash into the vault. Not that it will hurt the gold, but it just doesn't seem likely."

Brad concluded, "So it's got to be the main door that comes in over there."

Everyone shrugged in agreement as they looked across the room at the main doorway.

Tiny laid the deer hide with the code on it on the long table with the spindle legs. "Bring that lantern closer, Josh," he said. They all gathered around the table. "Okay, now... the numbers are just numbers, but the letters represent something. And it's just *O* and *D*. Give me your ideas, young people. What could they represent?" he said, smiling at the boys.

They started rattling off ideas, "Order and Deliver, Open and Door, Out and..."

Tiny and Burl also had their minds at work, but silently. Looking at the door and then the letters and numbers.

Josh said, "Over and Done."

Burls eyebrows pulled down hard as if to reveal discovery. "Josh, that's it! Over is right."

Tiny picked up on Burl's thoughts. "Over and Down! It's Over and Down!"

"Over and Down!" Burl confirmed his breakthrough.

"We are supposed to count stones! Edmond Mansfield was a stonemason. Of course, we are supposed to think like masons," Eddie said.

The team stepped towards the doorway that Burl and Brad had worked so hard to enter. Tiny was holding the code and Josh had the lantern. Eddie now had the flashlight. They looked at the stones that surrounded the door and then walked over to one of the doorways to the interior rooms of the basement. All the doorways were constructed the same way.

"According to the code, we start at the door and go 6 over, 2 down…" Tiny looked confused as he was speaking. "But the thing is, where do we start? Which stone do we start with? There are fifteen stones that make up the perimeter of that doorway. Seven up each side and then a long header stone that runs across the top."

They all turned towards the center of the room and talked in a circle like a football huddle with their backs to the entryway door.

Burl said, "Yeah, we could count from each stone and it will take us to a different final stone every time. There is something about this that we're not seeing. These foundation stones are only about a foot tall by two feet long. How could there be a vault behind any one of these?"

Eddie suggested, "Let's just take the small hammer and tap on them and listen for hollow sounds…."

"You're wasting your time!" A firm voice said, coming from the doorway.

The shock took every breath in the room as they jumped with alarm.

Two men stood in the doorway, silhouettes in the heavy fog that rolled behind them. Both men wore light trench coats and hats. The lantern couldn't catch their faces, but after the tremors of fear had shaken their way out of Josh and Eddie's bodies, they both knew the voice.

Mansfield!

Josh walked closer to the doorway, and the lantern light moved with him. As the light worked its way across the room and up the coats of Mansfield and his unknown partner, the gentlemen stepped into the basement.

Mansfield said, "You kids have done magnificent work. And very fast, too. There are people who have been trying to get to this point for years, myself included."

There was a lengthy pause as Mansfield waited for a response. The five guys were looking around at each other, sizing up Mansfield and his partner. They didn't know whether to start kicking butts or to hear him out. Mansfield was kind of a jerk, but that was just his personality. That was the way he was.

Josh spoke up, "Yeah… and we know who else."

"I know you do, Josh. And the other team is not nearly as friendly as we are."

"We know that too," Josh said. "Who is your friend?" he asked, slightly disrespectfully.

Elton Mansfield smiled, and he turned an upward palm to his friend. "Gentleman, this is my good friend John Hopes. Navy veteran, newspaperman, and investigative reporter."

Mr. Hopes spoke up. "And retired from all of it," he said with a grin, touching his hat. He lightened the mood a little with his pleasant demeanor. They could immediately tell that he was a much friendlier person than Mansfield.

Burl looked at Josh and Eddie.

"You're the reporter who bought the old Bible that belonged to Clyde Franklin!" Josh exclaimed.

John Hopes walked over to Josh. He was happy to give him the story. "Right you are, young man. In 1958, I walked into a small bookstore. You know, I am always looking for rare books and even first editions. I was looking around and just happened to see this very old-looking King James Version, and I just thought it was a nice piece—something that would look good on the fireplace mantle at home, more for decoration than reading. I had my reading Bible, of course. So I bought it and walked out. When I got to the car, I put it on the seat and drove off. It was a nice warm day, so I had the windows down. The wind started fluttering the pages around and something caught my attention, a piece of paper."

"The note about the red can and the document." Josh assumed.

Hopes nodded his head slowly. "Clyde Franklin's note that told about something very important on this river. Of course, with that note being discovered, he was a guilty man, but he was long dead so it mattered none."

"True." Josh nodded his head. "Then you wrote an article about it."

"Yeah, big mistake, as it turns out. That article sent a lot of people exploring for gold over the years. We never thought the old can would ever turn up, though. Never in a million years. Not after the flood carried it away from his porch on Blue Creek. Terrible flash flood, that was."

Burl, Tiny, Eddie, and Brad were listening intently, still not sure of what to make of the situation. There was a moment of silence and then informal introductions were made for all those who did not know each other. There was some handshaking, and the atmosphere began to feel a little less edgy after everyone knew everyone. Josh couldn't wait to ask, "Mr. Mansfield, why do you say we are wasting our time?"

Mansfield grinned confidently. He had the same look in his eye that Tiny got when he knew something that everyone else didn't.

Tiny had rolled up the deer hide and was now leaning against the big table with it securely in his hand, just listening.

"Well, the first document, the one you left a copy of in my library, indicated there was something here, another clue, *in an island bank*." Mansfield smiled at Tiny, looking at the deer hide in his hand. "Looks like you found it."

"We did," Tiny responded.

"And that's just what I figured. I figured there *was* another clue here and not the gold itself because the reference to the island was *key to the vault*. You understand, it didn't say *Gold in the vault*. It said the *key to the vault, in an island bank*. And that could have meant an actual key or the final clue. And from what I overheard you guys say, you *have* the key. You have the directions to the vault once you find the right location. But what I have is the location… and it's not here."

"The gold is not on the island?!" Burl said.

Elton Mansfield slowly shook his head.

"But how do you know?" Josh asked. "We were so sure."

"Let me ask you something; does your clue make any sense in this basement?" Mansfield asked.

"Kinda doesn't," Tiny responded. He paused and then said, "So what do you have? What information do you have that tells you the gold is somewhere else?"

Mansfield paused. His mouth opened, but no words came out at first. Then he spoke. "My great grandfather's dying words. Handed down from generation to generation. His last words to his wife were; 'Gold…. E-21.'"

"Gold E-21. What does that mean?" Brad asked.

"No one ever knew. No one ever knew until last night." He turned to Josh and Eddie. "Do you guys remember that little drawing at the bottom of the page on the first document?"

"Yeah. We drew it line for line but never figured it out. There were parts that were faded from getting wet or age or whatever."

"I studied that last night, looking real carefully at it and I had to use some imagination, but the more I looked at it the more I wondered and it soon became clear. I knew it was important or it wouldn't be there. I added just three lines to it, where it was faded, and it jumped off the page and struck me as clear as day."

"What? What is it?" Josh pleaded excitedly.

Mansfield looked at all the men in the room with concern. He let out a deep breath. "You see, if I tell you, then *you* will have the location and the key to finding the gold and I will still only have the location. So let's face it—we have to come together. We must become an alliance to find this gold, to solve this mystery. You have what I need and I have what you need." He stared at each of them in turn.

There was an interminable pause in the old basement. Stone cold quiet. They all, once again, heard the unmistakable sound of the small boat engine going back upriver. Turtle hooks must be all set. No one paid it too much attention.

Everyone knew he was right. The only answer was to form one team to locate the gold. Josh looked at Eddie and nodded his head and then looked around at Tiny and Burl, who gave the go ahead with a swish of his hand.

"Why not… it's not ours to keep anyway, right?" said Brad.

"Let's shake on it gentleman," John Hopes said. "It's the way I like to do business!" He smiled.

CHAPTER THIRTY-ONE

Emily Baker rolled over and looked at the bedside clock. She always slept a little lighter when Josh was camping. 12:25 it read. There was a half-moon that night that lit the bedroom a little more than she liked for sleeping, so she got up and closed the blinds a little more. As she did so, she looked out the window with sleepy eyes toward the riverbank where Josh and Eddie were probably telling ghost stories.

She could see that the sky was clear and the moon was high, but a blanket of fog lay along the river and rolled up on to the riverbank where they were camped. The fire was out and there was no light at the campsite other than what the moon provided but what she could see, terrified her. She gasped hard and immediately woke up Mr. Baker.

Giselle sat at her computer desk at home with her newly purchased pile of college textbooks beside her. She was excited to start school and was flipping through the first chapters of her new books, eager to get a head start.

Her cell phone ringer was turned off, but as she sat there killing time until she was sleepy, her phone vibrated, and "Bakers" illuminated on her screen. At this time of the night this was unusual, and she was immediately concerned. She took the call.

"Gather around, gentleman." Elton Mansfield reached into the inside pocket of his light trench coat and pulled out a yellow piece of legal pad paper. Josh smirked. He unfolded it and spread it out flat on the large table as Burl grabbed the lantern and sat it down beside it.

"Now boys, you say you copied this line for line from the deer hide, correct?"

"Sure did. We traced it and looked at it again and again to make sure everything was there. There were some smudge marks that… you couldn't tell where they went. Just smeared ink, but yeah, all the lines are on there," Josh responded.

"Okay, look here." Elton Mansfield took a pen from his pocket and pointed it towards the drawing. "Look what happens when I add a line here, here and then a curved line here."

"Woah!" the five guys said, nearly in unison. They all knew exactly what the drawing was immediately.

Mansfield continued, "Now… do you guys think those three lines are too much of a stretch? I mean, you could add lines to any part of this drawing, but the empty spaces that were there, to me, were just begging to be filled in and when I did, this is what popped out at me."

Nodding, Josh said, "That's exactly where the smudge marks were on the original."

Burl Otis was shaking his head in disbelief, and said, "I think you nailed it. I think we have the location. It's got to be it!"

Tiny looked on in disbelief, beaming. "Can you believe it? After all these years, it's right there. Right there! And not a quarter mile from where the holdup took place!" He paused for a second. "Ya see? Now that makes sense!"

Seven men stood around a table with a lantern dimly lighting a century old basement stocked with supplies from a time gone by. They were captivated by what they were looking at. Although small, it was a perfectly illustrated drawing of what had been an area of recreation for so many people and for so many years. Many adolescent Brooks boys had grabbed its stones and skipped them across the river to see if they could hit the banks on the other side. Goodness, Tiny Brooks even had a picture of his great grandfather fishing there. Josh and Eddie would row and even swim across the river from Josh's house sometimes, to play or fish there. The *old sand bar and the stone train trestle*!

The sandbar had been a starting point for many of Josh and Eddie's camping adventures when they would head into the hills of Blue Creek for a night or two. They had caught many fish standing on those rocks in front of that trestle. They had run through the tunnel many times, jumping from rock to rock to keep from getting their feet wet in the creek that ran through it. Could it really be? Could that gold really be in a vault constructed in that trestle over a hundred years ago?

Burl continued to shake his head and smile. He had set traps near that tunnel, had taken refuge from hard summer rain showers in there and had never considered in a million years that it was anything but a limestone train trestle built to carry the C&O coal trains out of the hills of Kanawha County. He glanced over at Tiny.

Tiny recollected how, as a boy, he had many, many times walked those tracks down to the trestle with a cane pole in his hand to see if he could catch lunch for his family. And many times he did! He would walk back home at the end of the day with his big trademark smile and a stringer of catfish. This old sand bar, as simple as it was, had provided a lot of enjoyment for many people through the years.

And now for everyone in that old basement, that sandbar and trestle took on a whole new element of excitement. Adventure, like never before for any of them, waited downstream just a half mile.

Elton spoke solemnly, "You see, my great grandfather helped construct these train trestles along this river all the way from the Clay County-line to Charleston. There were a lot of crews, but he was a foreman on the crew that was camped here on the island. He and his men would frequent this tavern. Times were very hard back then and a man would sometimes do things he wouldn't normally do to earn money to provide for his family. Three months later, after striking a deal with Clyde Franklin, Edmond Mansfield was shot and killed by Franklin… for knowing too much. When he lay dying, he muttered Franklin's name. That's how we know it was Franklin, although it could never be proven. Then he took his last breath and then said, 'Gold- E21'."

Everyone knew that story.

"So he built the trestle that holds the gold! Trestle E-21, and the vault that's in it. And I know from research that Trestle E-21 is that exact trestle just downriver. They were marked. The trestle numbers were chiseled into the top of the arch."

"I never noticed that," said Eddie.

"We will look, but we need to get on down there… tonight. I know Collins will be hot on the trail," Hopes suggested.

"Mansfield asked, "How can we get there?"

Brad Radcliffe smiled his biggest! Burl wasn't so sure.

The newly formed team gathered all their equipment from the basement and exited through the door through which they had entered earlier. They pulled the door closed as best they could and headed over to the wide path that lead to the where the raft was concealed and securely tied under a willow tree. The fog was incredibly dense, but straight up you could see the moon well. A beautiful summer half-moon that helped to light the path from above.

From about a hundred yards away Brad's keen ears detected movement. His head spun around to the north side of the island from where the disturbance had come, and he scanned the trees. It could have been anything—a deer, a muskrat, a bobcat, or even a bear. Brad put his hands around his eyes to block the lantern light and stared into the darkness. He saw nothing, but definitely heard a branch crack. No one said anything, but all stood motionless for a few more seconds. Brad shrugged one shoulder. They were leaving anyway.

Brad and Josh walked over to the willow tree, untied the vessel and pulled it over where they could lay the plank across to board it. Brad made a mental note to get a permanent plank that he could keep on the raft for this purpose.

John Hopes and Elton Mansfield looked at the craft, both in amazement and apprehension.

"Will it hold us all?" Mansfield asked with concern.

Tiny responded, "We had all five of us on it and it only set down in the water about four inches. I think she has room for two more." He smiled as he passed equipment to Eddie on board.

After studying the craft, Hopes looked forward to the adventure. He had been quite the fun-seeker as a kid, too.

Downriver would be easy, just a matter of keeping it between the banks and dodging the rocks. The current would do the work for them. With Josh's sharp eyes on the bow and Brad at the tiller, they pushed off from the island. John Hopes smiled and even laughed a little. He was a kid again.

They drifted effortlessly and, without incident, floated within a few yards of the sandbar as Brad was setting up his approach. Josh took a glance to the right, where their campsite was set up, and knew immediately that something didn't look right. Even with the fog and low light he could see that their tent was down and their V-bottom AlumiCraft boat was gone! They had been raided!

"Brad! Steer us over there!" Josh said in a screaming whisper.

"What in the world?!" Eddie followed up. "What happened? Where's the boat?"

In a few seconds they bumped the bank with the raft and Josh jumped off to go survey the campsite. He looked around in disbelief. The tent was cut up with a sharp knife and was lying flat on the ground. The rope securing their boat had been cut, sending it downriver to who knows where. Their sleeping bags and gear had been searched and ransacked.

"This is unbelievable," Josh said. "Who would do this and what were they looking for?"

Eddie looked around. His thoughts went right to what Mayor Billingsworth had told them about Collins. *He would stop at nothing. He knows where to hide the bodies.*

"Collins," Eddie said.

"The boat we heard," said Tiny, from the raft.

A chill ran up the spines of every man there. It must be true. Collins really could be mentally capable of taking lives to acquire this gold. The knife cuts in the tent were disturbing. Collins would know that with the kids camping and not in their campsite, they would likely be on the trail of the gold… tonight. This would make

Collins even more desperate and take him to a new level of insanity.

Josh had a piece of the tent fabric in his hand and then tossed it onto the ground as he glanced up to his house. A light appeared to be on but towards the front of the house and not the back. Josh thought this was unusual but gave it no more thought. "Well, what's done here is done. We may as well get across the river and get our gold," he said with a slight look of concern on his face.

Burl and Tiny looked at each other, both holding their backpacks and thinking alike. They would keep their packs close to them for the rest of the night. They prayed the unthinkable wouldn't have to happen, but if it did, they would be ready. Eyes and ears must be sharp from here on out.

Josh and Eddie stepped back onto the raft, and John Hopes grabbed the long pole and gave a shove to move them away from the riverbank. He poled them straight across the river about two hundred feet to the sandbar and, as he did that, all of them stood silently on the raft contemplating the campsite.

All seven of them knew that they had to put what they had just seen behind them and move on quickly but cautiously to the task at hand. It was disturbing, and they were pretty sure the boat engine noise they had heard earlier was that of Collins running up and down the river. But how did he know the kids would camp that night? Or did he simply come to cut the boat loose so they would have one less means of river transportation and just got lucky to find an empty campsite to tear apart and inflict some fear into the young boys? If so, it had worked, to a point. But it wouldn't stop them. Not tonight. Because apparently, somewhere on their sandbar, encased in the stone trestle, was a big pile of gold. About three million dollar's worth, and they all intended to find it.

The milk-jug raft drifted to a stop in about six inches of water and about four feet from the dry sand bar. John Hopes placed the long pole in its storage position and the guys began jumping off the raft and onto the rocks while handing digging tools from ship to shore. Brad tied off his raft to a large old log that lay across the bar and stood proud, once again, of what his river-craft could do.

The fog was still dense and rolling along the river as they approached the one o'clock hour of the morning. The moon radiated its light through the water droplets of the fog and gave the old tunnel of the trestle an eerie look. Thick vines hung down either side of the trestle, looking like the dreadlocks.

Elton Mansfield spoke up softly, "Well gentleman, we are at the location. Can we see the final clue and see if we can finally make history?" he grinned.

Tiny pulled the deer hide from his backpack and the men came to huddle around it. Hopes held the lantern which was showing signs of running out of fuel. Tiny held one side of the deer hide and Mansfield held the other and they all tried to make sense of what it said in relation to the sandbar and the train trestle with its tunnel.

"We need to verify the trestle number. We have to be sure," John Hopes reminded them.

They all looked up at the arch of the tunnel where the trestle number was supposed to be. They saw nothing. Josh pulled the flashlight from his pocket and beamed it upward to the top of the tunnel entry—the highest point of the tunnel entrance. The rocks were beautifully arched overhead, expertly cut and laid into place, but the number could not be seen because of the ferns, vines and other vegetation that draped the tunnel entrance. John Hopes made a mental note of something while biting his cheek.

Eddie looked around on the sandbar. "Josh, help me find a long skinny tree for a pole." Josh didn't know why, but he helped his friend look for something long and skinny lying on the sandbar. They shined the flashlight around. Brad jumped on the raft, grabbed the pole for propelling his vessel upstream and jumped back to the sandbar. "Is this long enough?"

"Oh yeah, maybe so," Eddie said. He then walked over to the tunnel entrance and held the pole high in the air, up to the ferns and vegetation that covered the highest stone in the arch. Everyone followed. Eddie began working the pole up and down to remove the plants, dirt, vines and all other leafy things that blocked the one stone that they needed to see. He worked hard at it for a couple of minutes and by then, he was covered with the dirt and sand and plants that had fallen on him. He stopped when it felt all clear to him and they all backed up for a better view. Josh beamed the powerful flashlight up at the top stone once again, and there it was. Deeply engraved into the limestone was the letter E and then the number 21. Trestle E-21.

They were at the right spot!

There were smiles all around on the sandbar, and Josh clicked off the flashlight. No need to draw any more attention than necessary, even at one o'clock in the morning. Only the dimming lamplight provided illumination as they directed their attention back to the final clue, the deer-hide document recovered from the upstairs washroom of the Crossroads Tavern.

Key from the door 6 O, 2 D, 8 O, 1 D

Tiny then explained to Hopes and Mansfield what they believed the code represented—an over-and-down series of counting blocks to get to the vault. Hopes and Mansfield agreed that it could be very likely, and at least was a good start. The question was, once again, just as in the old basement, where do they begin counting?

Burl mentioned, "You know what puzzles me about this is on the first deer hide, it said *Sand is a Vault*. This trestle is limestone. Solid, heavy limestone. So what could that mean?"

Mansfield looked up at the trestle and thought a minute. "That's a good point. Maybe it's referring to the sand of the surrounding hills, or of the sandbar." He shrugged.

Burl stroked his beard while thinking about that. "Could be."

Josh said, "The real question is, where do we start? There must be two hundred stones in this trestle. It's the same problem as before."

As they were all looking and walking closer to the entrance of the tunnel, Eddie noticed that John Hopes had his head cocked a little and was in thought about something while looking up at the engraving above the tunnel entrance. Eventually he had everyone's attention as he smiled. Now it was his turn. Now John Hopes knew something about the trestle that everyone else didn't know, even Mansfield.

"What is it, John? What do you know?" Elton pleaded.

John walked over to the mouth of the dark tunnel. The creek water ran steadily off of the hill and down through the tunnel and now across Hope's feet, but he didn't care. He had something figured out and could now be just minutes from 162 pounds of gold being rediscovered after over a hundred years. He looked back at the others and pointed up at the engraving. "There," he said, "that stone right there with the engraving. That's where we start. It's called the 'keystone'. Look!"

He walked back over to the deer hide that Tiny was again holding. "It says *Key from the door*. It means start with the keystone. The keystone above the door or mouth of the tunnel! I guarantee it! That's the rock we need to start with, and if we follow that pattern, we will find the vault."

Mansfield got excited. He knew that. He knew the top rock in the arch was the keystone. It had been for centuries. How could he not have thought of that? Look at the pictures of ancient Greece. Arches! Keystones! Start with the *key* above the door!

"Tiny, bring that hide over here!" Mansfield said excitedly.

They all ran to the mouth of the tunnel.

His steps were calculated and slow as he beamed his government-issued flashlight through the door of the old cellar. *This door should not be so easy to open. Footprints. Lots of footprints on the dusty old floor. Too many for just two kids. Who were all these people?* They had already been here for sure and now were gone.

He stepped further into the basement and meandered with his flashlight pointed at the floor. Over by the long wooden table he spotted huge prints of a work boot of a sizeable man. "Otis," he said to himself. He considered the stairs and checked the upper floors to see if there was anything disturbed. He prowled his way through the old tavern, checking every room and broom closet. He walked out of the last room on the upper floor completely sure that there was nothing to see and then noticed the old washroom at the end of the hallway. Leaving no stone unturned, he flashed his light into the room, poked his head into the doorway and looked towards the big bathtub that was still there.

Everything looked to be in order until he did a double-take with his flashlight at something lying on the floor. It was a board about as long as his forearm. This was curious. He beamed his light around the floor for missing boards but couldn't find a hole anywhere in the bathroom. He shined his light up the walls to the ceiling, thinking maybe a ceiling board had fallen—nothing.

He then zipped his light around the room at the walls and that's when he noticed a gap in the wall over behind the bathtub, in the shelving area. He stepped over to get a closer look. Sheriff

Collins' mouth hung open in amazement as he looked at the hole, the secret mini-vault built into the shelving. He nodded his head slowly in disgust. He once again spoke to himself, "They found something else… and again, before me!"

He looked around at nothing in particular, forming his next move. Two kids and an old mountain hermit would not defeat him. His eyes changed from crazy to insane as he ran out of the old Crossroads Tavern and down to his county-owned skiff. The muddy footprints on the downriver side of the island said that they had tied up there and were now gone, most likely back downriver.

He would go downriver too… drifting with no lights and no engine. He would not see the shadowed figure standing on the north bank of the Elk River.

CHAPTER THIRTY-TWO

Josh Baker set the dimming lantern on the rocks of the sandbar and turned the small pump shaft to unlock it. He then gave the lantern about twenty-five good pumps to bring the fuel pressure back up and brighten the light. It worked, and he hoped that they would have enough fuel to finish their work that night. He set it down close to the entrance of the tunnel.

Excitement filled every man on the bar as they gathered around the coded deer hide.

Mansfield said, "Okay, from the keystone... Josh put the flashlight on it... From the keystone, *six over*."

"Which way, right or left?" Josh asked.

There was silence for a second as Mansfield looked back at the deer hide and then Tiny said, "Let's go left first."

"Okay to the left, Josh, *six over*," Eddie coached.

The beam of light hit six stones and then the code called for *two down*. "One, two," they all counted as Josh beamed every stone.

"Now *eight over*," Mansfield called out. Once again, they all counted and, with the eight stones, they were now about fifteen feet *inside* the dark tunnel. Everyone repositioned themselves so all could see the final stone as Elton Mansfield took a deep breath and called out, "*One down.*"

Josh Baker also took a deep breath and crept the beam of the flashlight straight down one stone. Everyone shuffled to get a better look. This stone, like all the others, was about three feet wide by two feet tall. They all studied it for a moment, and Josh brought the flashlight closer.

John Hopes suggested, "Are there any markings on it? Could be very small, even. Anything at all?"

There was nothing extraordinary about this particular stone. It was just like all the rest of the stones on that wall—limestone, fairly smooth, nicely cut, with a small amount of moss growing on it. Hearts thumped so hard in that tunnel that it almost sounded like jungle drums. Josh's heart was beating so fast that he could hear it in his ears! Eddie too.

John Hopes said, "Pass me a small hammer." He wanted to try something. Brad ran out of the tunnel, splashing in the small creek, and grabbed a small rock hammer. It had a chisel on one side and a blunt square head on the other side. He handed it to Hopes.

Hopes took the hammer and looked over the stone. He drew the hammer back about eight inches and began tapping the center of the stone and then moved to the outside perimeter of the same stone and did the same. No change in sound. Solid rock. He then moved over two stones and did the same test. It sounded just the same. Solid rock. Everyone was watching in earnest excitement.

His eyebrows drew down in thought. The dim flicker of the lantern light undulated off the stone walls of the interior of the tunnel and danced in every eye that was looking on. Bullfrogs and crickets sang their songs along the muddy banks of the river, undisturbed by the treasure hunters who had invaded their night.

Hopes spoke while shaking his head a little, "It doesn't sound right, it just sounds solid like all the rest."

Burl Otis was biting his lower lip in thought. "How about we count to the right? Start all over and count to the right side and see where that puts us."

Everyone murmured their approval, and feet started shuffling, stepping from rock to rock.

Elton Mansfield stated the obvious, "Wait, wait, hold on. We don't have to go back outside. This structure is symmetrical. The final stone will be right over there, directly across the tunnel from this stone that we just counted to. Josh, bring the light."

Again, Josh Baker negotiated a couple of rocks and hit his flashlight on the tunnel wall. "Which one would it be?"

Elton located the previous stone and then looked across the small creek that ran through the tunnel to the opposite wall. His arm came up and his finger pointed. "It would be right… THERE!"

Josh followed the librarian's finger and hit the light on the stone directly across the tunnel where he was pointing.

"OK, now," Hopes said, stepping across the small creek. "Look at this! This one looks different. Look at how much moss is on this one compared to the others. Maybe because it's hollow?" He shrugged.

"Oh my gosh! This could be it then!" Josh could not contain his excitement.

Eddie repositioned himself for a closer look. They had worked hard for this moment and he wasn't about to have a bad view of it.

Josh, Eddie and their new buddy Brad had been totally engrossed in this adventure for the better part of two weeks. It had captured their spirit, ignited a passion and motivated these teenagers to get out of bed early in the morning to go chase their next lead or find their next clue and now they had done it! They had persevered and now it was the big moment, the moment that a century of Otis' and Brooks' and Franklins', and the Mansfield family, had dreamed of. And it was their discovery! *They* had found the Red Can and from then it had been a whirlwind.

Josh Baker looked at John Hopes. Josh held his hand out for the hammer and John knew what he wanted to do and, yes, it was the right thing. Hopes handed the small chipping hammer to Josh, and Eddie moved in even closer. Josh took the hammer, drew it back about eight inches as Hopes had done, and began tapping the center of the big stone. *Boom, Boom, Boom!* Definitely different. They all looked at each other, smiling, and Josh did it again. He banged on the center of the stone and then moved over to the next stone and hit it just the same way. The hammer bounced off the next stone and the sound was flat. Josh went back to the mossy stone. *Boom, boom, boom!* It sounded like a bass drum compared to the other stones.

Tiny Brooks moved close and rubbed the moss with his hand. He rubbed it hard so it would come off. He removed about a one-foot square of the green moss and took the flashlight from Eddie, who had been holding it while Josh banged the stones. Tiny Brooks put the light up to the rock and studied it. He turned and smiled that big Tiny Brooks smile!

"What?" Eddie asked. "What is it?"

"Sand is a vault!" Tiny said. "Sand is a vault!" He was laughing with triumph. "This stone and only this stone is sandstone, and it's holding more moisture and growing more moss just like Mr. Hopes said! It was meant to be broken apart at some point. It was meant to be easy to remove!"

"It was probably meant to be easy to spot, too, if you knew what you were looking for," Burl Otis added, chuckling a little. "I have been through this tunnel many, many times and never noticed it."

"Yeah, you and many other people!" Tiny said, still smiling.

Brad stepped up and set the sledgehammer on a rock in the middle of the small stream. Everyone looked at one another. Who would do the honors?

The big stone sat two layers up from the bottom. The bottom of the stone was at a height of about four feet, and the top was at about the six-foot mark. Looks were exchanged and, by the process of elimination, without words. All eyes went to Josh and Eddie.

Josh gave that little sideways grin of his and put one hand on the twelve-pound sledgehammer and then the other. He looked at his best friend. They would never have a better moment of friendship and adventure together in their lives. This was their finest hour!

Josh lifted the sledge, drew it behind his shoulders and eyeballed the spot he wanted to hit—smack dab in the middle of the big stone! He twisted his shoulders and brought forth all his might in his first swing. *Boom!* A nice wedge of sandstone dropped from the wall. He drew his hammer back again and *Boom!* Another slice fell and shattered.

"Your turn, buddy." Josh handed the sledgehammer to Eddie. He, too, drew back hard and gave a mighty swing. *Boom!* Every swing of the big hammer brought wedges of the sandstone down. Eddie took two more swings. A nice dent was forming, but neither boy had made a hole.

Eddie said, "Step up, Burl, It's your turn!"

"Alrighty!" he accepted cheerfully.

Burl took the hammer in his hands and positioned his feet firmly on two solid rocks. He stood tall and didn't have to reach up as the boys did. He could swing level and inflict maximum damage on the stone. He drew the hammer back and took a Babe Ruth swing at it. *Whaammm!* A massive section of the stone crumbled and fell to the tunnel floor.

"Oh my gosh!" Josh said, laughing. "Not only does he have an arm like a left fielder, he can hit, too!" He and Eddie laughed, as did the others. It was nervous laughter. They couldn't wait to see inside!

Burl repositioned his feet again. Everyone took a step back because Burl's swing had made sandstone debris fly everywhere.

He reared back and heaved another swing at the stone and *Whaaam!* Another enormous piece of sandstone fell to the floor of the tunnel. He kicked it out of the way and then offered the hammer to anyone else who might want to try, but everyone agreed that he was the guy to do it. He looked at them and accepted the job.

Again, he positioned his feet firmly on two solid rocks and drew the sledgehammer back across his right shoulder. With everything he had and a loud growl, he brought the hammer around with all the force of a wrecking ball. To the boys it almost seemed in slow motion and the past few days flashed in their eyes—all the hard work, the research, the new friends, a raft ride, a mountain lion, the island—everything came down to this point. Was it here?

Whaaaam! A hole! They had finally made a hole! This *was* the vault of the Southern Jewel! This stone was only about six inches thick as opposed to two feet thick like the others. And the way Edmond Mansfield had laid it in there, it was not load bearing. It could be taken out and not upset the structural integrity of the trestle.

The hole was small, about a three-inch jagged circle, but it was a hole. Cheers erupted in the tunnel with smiles all around!

"Flashlight!" Burl said excitedly. "Hand me the flashlight!"

Josh handed him the flashlight, and all fell silent again. Burl put it up to the hole and shined it around inside the sandstone vault. Josh noticed that even the frogs and crickets outside had gotten quiet. That was kind of strange, but it was probably from all the sledgehammer impacts. Brad noticed it, too, and turned to look outside, but then looked back at Burl and moved closer to the vault.

"What's in there?" Josh asked with excitement. "What do you see?"

Burl pulled the flashlight down and looked down at the tunnel floor with a look of disappointment. He paused a second and Josh's and Eddie's stomachs fluttered. He then looked up and a broad smile spread across his face and his eyes lit up like a Christmas tree. "Fellas, someone mark the time and the date because we have just made history! It is our lucky day!" he announced. "Brad, no offense, but we're gonna need a bigger boat"!

Cheers and high-fives were shared. Even some tears. It was the culmination of a century of search and infatuation of many, many people and Josh, Eddie, Brad, Burl, Tiny, Elton and John had done it. They had teamed up, combined their resources and their knowledge of the event, and had prospered! They had found the 162 pounds of Confederate gold that had been cleverly robbed from a train by two desperate men in 1903. This generation could now right the wrongs of the past and return the gold to where it belonged. No one would be rich; it wasn't theirs to keep, but a century-old crime was solved.

The congratulations continued until Eddie said with exuberance, "Burl, knock the rest of it out of there! We wanna see it!"

Burl handed the flashlight back to Josh and began whamming on the stone again. Over and over without a break.

With the breach in the stone, the rest of it began falling out much more easily and Burl moved pieces out of his way with his hands and his boots. *Wham, Wham, Wham!* A cloud of dust was all around the hole, which was opened now to about a two-foot square. Burl laid the hammer down and began fanning the dust.

The six other men moved up closer in a semi-circle. As Burl Otis fanned the dust away, a form began to appear—a mound about two feet tall. Everyone was captured in the moment. Mouths hung open and eyes strained to see. Josh brought the light up high and shined it through the thinning dust cloud and onto the mound. Covering the mound was an old cloth, an oiled canvas-type material. The oil had preserved it from deterioration all these years, and it had continued to do its job of lying on top of whatever it was covering.

"Look how big the chamber is!" Tiny exclaimed. "I wasn't expecting it to be so big!"

"Goodness," Burl agreed. "It's like a small room in there! It goes back and up too!"

As the dust settled, they saw the vastness of the vault. The entry was just the size of one stone, two feet by three feet, but after one entered, the vault grew into a chamber about six feet by eight feet! It was amazing to see!

Burl looked back at Elton Mansfield. "Your great-grandfather did a nice job!" he said, smiling.

"He should have stuck to stonework!" Elton replied. "We don't make good criminals." He smiled, and everyone laughed.

Josh stepped up to the entry of the vault and looked at the cloth that covered the mound just inside the opening, a couple of feet. He looked at Eddie, and his friend stepped forward, too, and each boy reached in and pinched at the cloth with a thumb and forefinger.

"Moment of truth," Eddie said, looking at his buddy. "One, two, three!"

Simultaneously, they gave the old canvas a jerk. Dust jumped off of the cloth and the boys pulled their heads around to keep it out of their eyes. Slowly they turned their focus back to the mound that stood inside the entryway. Josh pulled the flashlight up and hit it directly on the pile.

"OH MY GOSH!!!" He shouted. "Look at it! Look at it! It's here, Eddie! We found it!!!" Josh was now beside himself. He began jumping up and down and high-fiving everyone once again. The excitement was contagious. All seven of the guys were looking on in amazement and disbelief. Right in front of them was a beautifully stacked and sorted mound of gold bars and coins — very old Spanish coins they would later learn were called *Escudos*, left there just the way Clyde Franklin had put them.

The oilcloth that had covered it had done its job very well. The bars and coins were in remarkable condition. It was unmistakably gold, still clean and shiny.

Josh and Eddie both reached in and grabbed a gold bar, both in awe of what was in their hands, what had been right there, literally, in their backyard. The weight of it was amazing for its size, and they both realized that they were experiencing a moment in their lives that boys only dreamed about—adventure and gold!

The team of seven all stood around the entryway to the vault, now as close as possible so that all could see inside.

Tiny said, "Brad, why don't you grab that lantern on the sandbar and we can set it inside the vault and take a good look!"

"Yeah," Brad said, turning to get the lantern immediately.

He returned quickly and Tiny took the lantern and placed it inside the entryway and over to the right a little so the light wouldn't hit them in their eyes but project well back into the chamber. What Tiny saw then jarred him. "Oh, my… Oh my goodness!" He said.

"What? What is it? Mansfield asked."

Tiny moved out of the way to collect himself, and the others stretched their necks to see what he had seen.

"Oh Gosh!" Josh said, with a look of nausea.

Eddie groaned, and Brad turned away as well.

Against the back wall of the vault that held the gold, were the skeletal remains of a large human. There was no flesh, just the dusty, tattered remnants of some of the clothing that had been worn on his last day, draped the skeleton.

Burl Otis looked in and knew instantly whose remains they were looking at. He was somber but expressionless as he looked at the bones of his great-grandfather. The body was shoved back into the corner in a fetal position with the skull facing toward vault opening. There was a large hole in the skull's forehead, which was most certainly a gunshot entry point. In front of the skeleton was a leather holster and belt that held what looked to be an old Colt revolver called a *Peacemaker* back in the day. Standing up and off to the left of Art Otis' remains was an old railroad lantern with its red and green lenses in beautiful condition. It was stamped C&O on the front.

Burl studied the remains a bit, looking in and contemplating the size of his great-grandfather and how he had gotten himself into a situation like this. *What made him do it?* He was a self-reliant mountain man. His kids were grown and gone, and money was not something that he valued or needed. The reason may never be known. He then stepped away from the vault.

"I'm very sorry," Tiny consoled quietly. "Nobody expected that…"

"No, No, No," Burl said. "It's OK."

John Hopes patted him on his huge shoulder, offering comfort, as did the others, and Burl nodded his head and smiled an appreciative smile back at them.

Burl said, "Well guys, we got it! Let's get it out of here!" He clapped and rubbed his hands together, ready to work.

Mansfield spoke up, "Wait, we have to contact some authorities, I guess. I don't think we can just march out of here with this gold like this. This could even be considered a crime scene, and I'm sure they will document everything with photos and such."

Everyone agreed this was true and three cell phones popped out of pockets quickly. Mansfield, Hopes and Josh looked at each other, confused.

"Who do we call?" Josh laughed.

At that moment, a shadow moved across the sandbar.

"Drop the phones! Drop them now!" A calm but firm voice ordered from outside the tunnel.

All heads spun towards the sandbar and that jolt of shock once again ran through the bodies of the seven guys who were standing beside three million dollars in gold. A tall figure stood at the entrance to the tunnel. He was silhouetted by the back porch light of the Baker home across the river which was now turned on. Behind him on the far riverbank were trees and bushes making, it even harder to discern his features. The voice was an obvious disguise, but the tone was familiar to Josh and Eddie. Burl thought he knew it, too.

"I sure appreciate the hard work that you guys have saved me," the voice said, "but now I must ask you to step away from it. I will ask you one more time to put your phones on the rocks."

Everyone froze for the moment, except Josh. "Why should we?!" He barked.

The unmistakable report of a gunshot through a silencer was Josh Baker's answer. He jumped and slipped off the rock that he was standing on and landed, one foot in the stream that ran through the tunnel. Tiny grabbed him to help him back up. The bullet had gone safely into the riverbank. A warning shot.

"Are you okay, boy?" He whispered with concern.

"I'm fine." Josh said, regaining his composure and staring out at the shooter.

Tiny was ticked and frightened at the same time. "Who's out there?"

Another shot. "I'll do the talking here. Is that clear?"

No one answered him, but all three guys placed their phones on the rocks in front of them inside the tunnel. Josh noticed that his phone screen was lit up, so he placed it face down on the stone. When he jumped from the first gunshot he had inadvertently hit the call button and dialed a number. Emily Baker had tried to call him four times since looking out her bedroom window and seeing the disturbed campsite. Josh's sound was turned off, and now he was returning her call… without knowing it.

"When I was a young boy my mother told me of the story of the train robbery and how my great-grandfather had masterminded the holdup. He was a clever man, smarter than most people in his day and was able to outsmart people to get it done. From stealing the lantern and dynamite from C&O, to tricking your stupid great-grandfather into building this vault for a couple of coins, Mansfield. And Art Otis was his scapegoat, the fall guy."

His vocal disguise was getting lazy, but by this time there was no mistaking who stood in front of them at the end of the tunnel, shrouded in back-light and fog. Sheriff Collins had gone off the deep end. It was too late now. He would pay dearly for his obsession… if they ever caught him.

"Do you know why Art Otis did it? Do you know how my great-grandfather talked him into it, Burl?"

Silence.

"He promised him gold."

Burl Otis was now agitated. "He didn't want gold, especially stolen gold. He worked for every dime he made."

"Yes, that he did," Collins agreed calmly.

"Clyde Franklin pulled off *old school blackmail* on Art Otis. He promised Art gold if he helped him, which was only fair, but he also promised to reveal the whereabouts of that nice little three acres of ginseng that has been in your family forever, to anyone who wanted it."

"That's a lie! Art Otis would have just put a bullet in his head for saying that!"

"He *was* angry at first, furious. But Clyde Franklin was a good talker. He started describing the plan to Art Otis, and your great-grandfather became very intrigued by it. His family, all his boys, would never have to worry about money, ever! That homestead up there would never fall to taxes, as many were back then."

"It was a good plan up to the point where Clyde murdered my great-grandfather," Burl said.

Collins smiled and stepped a little closer to the group inside the tunnel. The lamplight reflected out of the vault and onto his face. Everyone knew there was a silencer on the gun that was pointed at them and knew that the situation was grim.

He smiled with malevolence. "There's no honor among thieves, gentlemen."

"So what's your plan, Collins? What do you want?" Mansfield asked.

Tiny had his backpack on his back and was fully aware of how its contents could be beneficial, but had no idea how to use it without taking a bullet himself. He had to wait. Burl, too, had the same dilemma. No way could he go for the gun in his pack.

Collins paused, then said solemnly, "Well gentlemen… sadly for you, I can have no witnesses. *Dead men tell no tales!*" He smiled, showing no hesitancy.

John Hopes spoke up, pleading. "Collins, these three are just boys. You can't do this. You are a lawman. You *know* the odds of getting caught are high. All this gold can't help you before a judge."

"Oh yes, I know the odds. The odds are terrible unless you have a plan. But cleverness runs in my family and just as my great grandfather, Clyde Franklin, made a good plan and got away with it, so have I." He took a break and contemplated his plan. "You've heard of Costa Rica, gentlemen? Beautiful beaches, great food and immunity from deportation if you know the right officials, *los federales,* and if you have the right form of payment. Gold is universally accepted, you know. I have a source, an old friend who will process it and make a sweet little deposit into a new foreign account that's all set up. He will take a small commission, of course." He grinned again. "So what's stopping me? I have no family left. I'm divorced, my only son is somewhere in California, a punk who never calls or comes home. The warm sun will do me good." He paused again. "Let's get this over with, gentlemen. I have a boat to load."

Burl Otis had a thought. It was desperation, but it's all they had left. He was standing by the opening to the vault. About three feet inside the vault was the *Peacemaker* which he hoped had at least one unspent bullet left in it. The cartridge would be over a hundred years old. He had a clear shot, if Hopes would shift just a little to the left. His move would have to be swift and smooth. He remembered that the grip to the gun was facing out, which was perfect. He just had to get Hopes out of the way.

The grimness of the situation was now on every face. They all knew that Collins had lost his mind. They knew his intentions were serious. He would take the life of everyone in that tunnel and, within an hour, be on his way out of town, state and country, never to return. They knew also that he would never get away with it. They would capture him before he reached the state line. But that couldn't save them. There would be seven more lives lost to this gold, including three young boys.

Josh's attention was then diverted down to his phone. The screen was face down but he could tell it was lit and he was sure he heard the buzzing of a voice from the small speaker. Could it be? He needed to give some information to whoever was on the other end of the line. Fast!

Josh thought quickly.

"What happened to you, Collins?" He asked loudly. "You used to be a good guy in this town. You used to look out for people in Blue Creek and now look—here we are standing on the sandbar in front of the trestle right behind my house and you have a gun pointed at us. You want to kill us and take the gold? You will never get away with it." Message delivered.

Eddie looked at Josh as if he were crazy. *What was that?*

Burl saw Hopes swaying just a little to shift his feet to a different rock. There was room now. There was about four feet between Hopes and Mansfield, and Otis was an expert shot. Just ask the cougar.

Collins lifted his weapon up and took aim at Mansfield, who was standing to the left inside the tunnel.

At that second, Burl Otis made his move. Swift as a cat he threw himself toward the opening of the vault, his arm reaching inside and making a perfect grab on the pistol grip. Out of the holster it came, and in a continuous motion he whirred around with the Colt and snapped his aim toward Collins. Collins' eyes caught Otis, and he reacted.

CLICK! The *Peacemaker* failed to fire.

Burl saw the orange flame first and then felt the excruciating pain just below his right shoulder.

"NOOOO!" Josh screamed!

Burl went down to his knees in the creek, holding his upper chest.

The silencer on Collins' gun added to the bleakness of the situation. No one could hear the violence beyond the tunnel. The guys began to run, including Burl Otis, who was grabbing the boys while holding his chest in a desperate attempt to shield them so they would have a chance to live. But there was nowhere to go except out the other end of the tunnel, and all Collins had to do was point and shoot. He would get them all!

"You're next, boy!" Collins swung the service pistol toward young Josh Baker.

BOOM!!! BOOM!!!

"*JOSH*!!!" Emily Baker screamed in horror from across the river. She was now standing on the boat dock that belonged to the Bakers, along with Mr. Baker, Giselle O'Connor and the Debords.

"MOM!" He called back from the tunnel.

The thunder of a .38 caliber handgun echoed through the tunnel and up and down the river in the early morning hours. They were all shocked at the sound. It didn't make sense. What happened to the silencer and who was down?! The guys pivoted to look back. They saw Sheriff Collins' right arm drop to his side, and his service pistol fell to the river rocks of the sandbar. Collins swayed once and then fell to his side. Many sirens could be heard in the distance. Police cars were roaring down Elk River Road to get to the scene. Emily Baker had made the call.

Josh looked back at Burl, who was grimacing from the gunshot wound. The *Peacemaker* lay on the rocks where it had fallen when he was shot. The enormous gun was not the source of the two shots that had been fired. They looked towards the entrance of the tunnel, as yet another shadow passed across it. A much larger shadow.

Mayor Billingsworth stepped over Collins as he lay unconscious and then beamed his light into the tunnel. "Who's hurt! How many?" he called out desperately in a huge booming voice.

They couldn't believe it. Mayor Billingsworth! Josh and Eddie had been sure that he was still in cahoots with Collins.

"Just one! Mr. Otis is hurt bad!" John Hopes said.

It was hard to follow what happened next.

Tiny Brooks looked around at everyone. He grabbed the lantern from the vault and held it out into the tunnel and then knelt at Burl Otis' side. Josh and Eddie gathered around.

"We need help!!! We need an ambulance!" Eddie shouted, near tears, towards the tunnel exit.

"JOSH!! Josh answer me*!!"* Emily Baker shouted again!

"EDDIE!!!" called Mr. Debord!

Burl gave them a reassuring, albeit grimacing smile. "Go let them know you're okay, boys. I'll be fine. I'll be fine."

With that, the two friends ran out to the sandbar to show their parents they were OK. They had to jump over a motionless Sheriff Collins to do it. Sirens screamed down both sides of the river now as Emily Baker had directed them towards the opposite side where the trestle was. Emergency vehicles were arriving, and two officers came running through the Bakers' lawn with a small boat to access the sandbar on the other side to secure the scene.

Brad Radcliffe said, "I'm going to run up to the dirt road down the tracks and bring in the paramedics." Brad knew the area well and could get them in quickly.

Elton Mansfield, John Hopes, and Tiny Brooks were now around a badly wounded Burl Otis.

Tiny looked him in the eye. "What made you go for that old Colt in there? You knew it wouldn't fire." Tiny said, grinning. "I'm surprised the trigger even pulled after all these years."

Burl looked at him and started to speak, but then stopped. Tiny knew exactly why. First, it was a long shot. There was a ninety-nine percent chance that that gun was not going to fire, but it was worth a try.

"You wanted to take the first bullet. You wanted to create a diversion away from these three young boys. You wanted them to at least have a chance to run because you and I both knew Collins was sincere. Collins was going to execute these kids right there in the tunnel, along with us." He looked at Otis and the big man could not deny it.

"They're just kids," Burl said. "You would have done the same if you were the one by the gun," he said.

Tiny smiled at him. "You're a brave man, Burl Otis."

"Pretty tough for a couple old river rocks, ain't we?" he replied with a painful grin.

They both shared a laugh as responders began to arrive.

CHAPTER THIRTY-THREE

Within minutes that area of the Elk River and the train trestle with the tunnel was lit up like a baseball field. Police, FBI, reporters, and medical teams covered the entire area from Josh's backyard and campsite, across the river, to the sandbar and even up to the island. There were 12 boats total that were now being used to transport investigators, police personnel, crime scene photographers and various government officials. As it turned out, this was most certainly a crime scene. They were taking pictures and asking a lot of questions of Josh, Eddie, Tiny, Brad, John and Elton. A *lot* of questions! Everyone was completely amazed with the vault and all that gold that was piled in there. Most of the first responders had never heard of the legend and were amazed as the legend was explained to them. Armed security was called in to remove the gold, and the Medical Examiner was called in to remove the skeletal remains of Arthur Otis.

Giselle O'Connor was waiting her turn to talk to the boys and finally got her chance after many police, FBI, news crews, and Mr. and Mrs. Baker swarmed them.

Josh and Eddie walked toward her, all with smiles of friendship. "Could be that you guys are going to be quite famous, ya know," she said, hugging them both. "I'm so glad you're okay."

"Your name was mentioned too, lady! You are in on this!" Josh said, happy to see her.

"They're going to be talking to you, don't worry!" Eddie followed up.

"My Gosh, we were so scared over here. I was crying so hard with your mom when we heard the two big gun shots! We just knew it was bad."

"How did you get here? How did you know?" Josh asked.

"My phone rang, and it was your house number. And this was late, too. So I got it and it was your mom. She was scared to death, saying you guys had camped out down here below the house and she had looked out to check on you and the campsite was all torn up and the tent looked slashed. She wanted to know if I knew anything about what we were up to because she knew that we had met and were hanging out some. I had to be honest, so told her I knew that you guys were going to the island to poke around and she was kind of okay with that but was scared about the cuts in the tent and the campsite being all torn up."

"I can imagine," Josh said.

"Yeah, your mom was pretty hysterical," she said. "So we got in the car and drove to the island just to look across the bridge. There was an SUV there, but we couldn't see any lights or movement, so we went back to the house, to the back porch. We were talking, and she was trying to call you the whole time, but I guess your ringer was off."

"We had to be quiet so we didn't draw attention, so I turned it off, and that SUV was John Hopes'."

"So, we were on the back porch and thought we could hear voices now and then and you can't imagine the relief that your mom started feeling. She was sure that were you coming off the hill or something, over behind the tunnel."

"That was probably when we were in the tunnel and getting close to the vault. We got a little excited."

Giselle continued, "And we started seeing lights flickering around and then heard pounding."

"Busting out the vault." The boys looked at each other, smiling.

"Your mom said, '*What in the world are they doing?*'"

"I started getting excited then because I knew you guys may have found something… something big. That's when I had to tell her everything. I started telling her the story, the entire story, which took time, and in the meantime, we were listening to the pounding and watching the lights change in the tunnel. As I was telling her all of this, she was staring across the river in disbelief… and your dad too! But your dad was a little more impressed than your mom. Anyway, your mom's phone rang, and it was from you. She was listening. And then I saw fear in your mom's eyes— extreme fear. She ended the call and then called 911 and told them what was going on and to get here as fast as they could. So, we started running down towards the river to the dock and then we heard the two big, loud gun shots… that's when your mom screamed and so did I! Your dad ran to the river but the boat was gone, the V-bottom. He was looking for a neighbor's boat to get across the river, but it was so dark…"

"Yeah, I have never been so terrified in my life. I really thought we were all dead." Eddie said. "But those were the *good* shots that you guys heard. Those were the ones that saved our lives. The gun shots before that were the ones that…" He paused and looked at Josh. Eddie didn't have to finish. Giselle hugged them both. These new friends had a tight bond already.

Mr. and Mrs. Baker had walked up to hear the recounting of the story as well as Mr. and Mrs. Debord. They were all extremely grateful to have their children unharmed and back with them that night. They would also have some questions for the boys at a later time.

Tiny and Brad did their share of explaining things to law enforcement officials that early morning and of course, everyone's story matched up perfectly so there was no reason for the police to take anyone into custody. The only bad guy had been taken down by the mayor and quickly rushed to Charleston Area Medical Centers' Memorial Hospital. Collins died twice on the way, but they were able to get him back both times. He had a very weak pulse as he arrived at the hospital and had lost a lot of blood. Doctors were not optimistic.

By then it was close to five o'clock in the morning and it was pretty certain that no one would get any more sleep that night. Across the yard Mayor Billingsworth was doing multiple interviews, as by this time the TV crews had arrived with their vans and broadcast dishes. Mayor Billingsworth was a good man who loved his hometown there on the Elk River. He had been tempted in one of the greatest ways a human can be tempted and had refused to let the lure of money overtake his dedication to this little town, this little map-dot of a town that he was proud to represent. He had stood up and saved the lives of seven men that night, and he was rewarded for it in a big way by the State of West Virginia. His courage would pay big dividends for him in his future political career, but he was just happy and relieved to have seven of his townspeople alive and well on that night.

They took Burl Otis to the Charleston General Hospital Emergency Room, where doctors extracted a nine-millimeter bullet that was lodged just above his right lung. They said if it had entered just a half inch lower he would have been dead in minutes. He walked out of the hospital the next morning and by that afternoon he was on Josh's back porch, drinking iced tea and getting to know the Baker and Debord family a little better. They insisted that he stay with them until he recovered some and they saw to it that he went back for his one-week follow-up appointment.

It took a while for things to get back to normal in the small town of Blue Creek. Tourists came from all over the state and many surrounding states to try to get a glimpse of the locations of the island, the vault, Tater Holler and the Elk River. The Baker and Debord family had people nervously knocking on their doors for weeks wanting to meet the kids, and they did their best to accommodate the curious. Some wanted autographs, some wanted pictures, and some just wanted to say hello and shake hands. It got overwhelming, but things settled down soon enough.

The recovery of the Southern Jewel was, by far, the most historic discovery event ever to occur in the state of West Virginia. Years from now, Josh Baker and Eddie Debord, as well as Brad and Giselle, will be able to sit their grandchildren on their laps and tell them what really happened. For these four kids, in the greatest summer of their life, they rediscovered the *Legend of the Southern Jewel*—162 pounds of Confederate gold stolen from a coal train in the year 1903.

THE END

EPILOGUE

The next few days were a blur of activity. The news of the rediscovery of the gold went viral on social media in a matter of hours. There were interviews by local TV and radio and as the news spread, travel plans had to be made. New York for the Today Show, Los Angeles for the Tonight Show, and other shows in between. In the months to follow, Josh and Eddie would be on the Weather Channel, Discovery Channel, History Channel and The Learning Channel and also made a couple magazine covers.

The State of West Virginia benefited by all the publicity that was generated and worked with the Federal government to make good on the reward, even far surpassing what everyone expected.

For Josh, Eddie, and Giselle; full ride, four-year scholarships to any West Virginia university they wanted to attend. This included dorm, books, and transportation expenses. Upon graduation, there was a tidy little present for them that would be deposited into their bank accounts. For all their hard work, they would each receive the value of one five-pound gold bar that they had helped to recover. Somewhere in the range of $100,000 each—depending on market value at the time.

They awarded Brad something a little different but equally cool. Brad Radcliffe was awarded a full scholarship to MMI, Marine Mechanics Institute in Orlando, Florida. It was recognized that he had a love of the water and a knack for engineering marine craft. It was his ticket to a positive future and he could not have been happier. He, too, would receive the value of a five-pound hunk of gold upon graduation.

Brad's raft was put on a six-month display at the Avampato Museum in Charleston along with the original deer-hide document that was expertly made by Clyde Franklin, with a little story on how much they both played a part in the discovery of the *Southern Jewel*. It was a huge attraction and when the six months were up, Brad eagerly returned the raft to where it belonged—Brads Landing, Elk River, West Virginia. The deer hide became a permanent display at the museum.

Brad's father underwent treatment for alcohol abuse, paid by the state. It was a long road, but eventually he became the father and husband that his family needed. John Radcliffe would start his own landscaping business and eventually was awarded government contracts for all the state-owned buildings in the Charleston area. Billingsworth pushed that through for him.

The state of West Virginia sent Tiny Brooks on a weeklong, all expense paid Mississippi river-boat cruise. When he returned, he had a brand new twelve by thirty-six foot boat dock sitting at the river's edge below his house. It replaced the eight by ten-foot sagging dock that he had used for the past 30 years. It had served him well, but Josh had made the recommendation for the gift for Tiny, and the state had come through. Also, there was a sixteen-foot Carolina Skiff tied up to the new dock, with a 65 HP Evinrude outboard engine for buzzing up and down the river. The construction crew that built his dock also did some reinforcing work on Tiny's house and a fresh coat of paint. Tiny smiled for three days when he got home.

Burl Otis recovered fully and returned to his home on the mountain, *Tater Holler Homestead*, and graciously refused any reward for his part in the adventure. The State respected his request however refused to accept any further property tax to be paid from this property... ever! Also, before trapping season started, he came home one evening to find a brand new John Deere hunting quad fully equipped with racks and rifle holders. The state also cut an improved road off his mountain for personal use to go down to Hickory Holler Gas and Go to fuel up his new toy free of charge. Burl had never driven anything in his life but had a real good time learning with Josh, Eddie and Brad, and he soon mastered it. Burl also made a special place in his gun cabinet for a very old Colt Peacemaker.

Elton Mansfield, like Burl Otis, wanted no personal reward for his part of the discovery. He asked that any reward that the State of West Virginia felt like they wanted to give him to be directed to his baby, the library. The State delivered. They awarded him a generous grant for upgrades. He went fully computerized with bar-coded automated check-in and check-out. He kept his card catalogue for sentimental reasons (it became non-functional furniture) but added fifteen new user-friendly iMacs for members to use to locate books within the newly expanded library. They built an addition on to the original building that nearly doubled its square footage. All new tables and chairs and a kids' corner with a wooden train set fit into the budget, as well as a coffee center close by for moms and dads. All microfiche was now on a huge hard drive in a cooled computer room, and all those old tapes and cabinets were a thing of the past.

John Hopes came out of retirement and wrote an award-winning front-page story about the legend past and present and a full firsthand perspective of how it unfolded from the time the boys found the old red milk can to the climax of the event on the sandbar in front of the train trestle. He would go on to write a full non-fiction story about the legend and would finally be inducted into the U.S. Journalists Hall of Fame for all his works, past and present.

Sheriff Ronald Collins would recover from his two gunshots to his upper torso but would lose the function of one lung. After recovery, he would stand trial for the attempted murder of Burl Otis while his attorneys would contend he was acting in self-defense since Burl drew on him first with the old *Peacemaker*. The piece of tape that was saved from the library break-in matched with Collins right thumb and made him guilty of breaking and entering into a public building.

Mayor Billingsworth would visit Collins in the hospital, feeling remorseful for what he had to do to his longtime friend and co-worker. Billingsworth had done all he could that dark, foggy night to not make his shots fatal but to only disarm Collins. Collins was sentenced to ten years in prison.

Just a year later, Mayor Billingsworth was offered the running-mate position of Lieutenant Governor in the general election alongside John MacMurray. MacMurray knew Billingsworths' popularity would propel him to the win, and he was right. They won in a landslide victory over the incumbent Governor, and the town of Blue Creek celebrated big! The team began their journey to do exceptional things for the State of West Virginia in a common sense, non-political, bi-partisan manner and demonstrated a fresh way to lead a democratic society. Washington would take notice of it too.

Billingsworth returned to his home on the river often and would visit with the boys and stroll around the neighborhoods of his town to shake hands and spend time with the people that helped him get his start in politics. He was truly appreciative.

The remains of Arthur B. Otis were re-interred at the old Otis cemetery back in the hills of the *Tater Holler Homestead,* and a small private service was held. His grave can be seen alongside all the previous Otis family deceased… if you can find it.

The Bakers' old V-bottom boat was recovered and towed back upstream to the Baker boat dock. It had drifted downstream as far as the shoals and gotten hung up on the rocks far to the right of Brad and Tiny's buoys. Josh was glad to have it back, and so was his dad. Emily Baker was glad to have a beautiful rhododendron adorning her garden area in her front yard.

The four kids' lives were changed forever that summer. What was nearly a horrific ending to an adventure of a lifetime had ended up as a silver platter to an exciting future. The world was now at their fingertips and they would never forget one minute of the past two weeks for as long as they lived. The best thing for them is that all of this had come about by doing what they love and following their heart every day of their young lives. Their passion, as kids, was simply to fish the cool shady banks of the Elk River and to hike and camp the beautiful hills that were just outside their doors, and for that, they were rewarded and happy right there at home in *Wild Wonderful, West Virginia*!

The adventure continues in "What Lies in the Hills"!

I sincerely hope you enjoyed

"River Rocks"

If you feel inclined, please go back to Amazon and leave a quick review! It helps other book lovers find good stories!

Want more? THE ADVENTURE CONTINUES!!

Book 2 in the series is also available at Amazon.com and is titled **"What Lies in the Hills."** It is a fast-paced adventure/mystery with the same cast of characters, and some new ones as well! Two years later, Josh and Eddie are the first responders to a crashed airplane...that went down in 1953!

Book 3 in the series is titled **"What Lies in the Sea."** It is a road trip / treasure hunt adventure also featuring Josh, Eddie, Giselle and some new friends you will love! You won't want to miss this one!

And there are more! You can find all my books on Amazon.com simply by entering S*teve Kittner* in the search box.

If you would like to join my "Readers Community" and get early news on future books, please email me at the address below!

steve.kittner@yahoo.com

Like us on Facebook at: Steve Kittner Books

Next, continue the adventure with "What Lies in the Hills."

Made in the USA
Columbia, SC
02 April 2021